Joe Pete

Ian McCulloch

Cree language translations/tranliterations are adapted from: Turner, Daisy. (1974) *Moose Factory Cree*. Cobalt, Ontario, Canada: Highway Book Shop.

Library and Archives Canada Cataloguing in Publication

Title: Joe Pete / Ian McCulloch.
Names: McCulloch, Ian, author.
Identifiers: Canadiana (print) 20230474152 | Canadiana (ebook) 20230474284 | ISBN 9781988989723
  (softcover) | ISBN 9781988989730 (EPUB)
Classification: LCC PS8575.C83 J64 2023 | DDC C813/.54—dc23

Printed and Bound in Canada on 100% Recycled Paper
Cover Artwork: Candace Twance
Cover Design: Heather Campbell
Author Illustrator: Jack Smallboy

Published by:
Latitude 46 Publishing
info@latitude46publishing.com
Latitude46publishing.com

We acknowledge the generous support of the Ontario Arts Council.

ONTARIO ARTS COUNCIL
CONSEIL DES ARTS DE L'ONTARIO
an Ontario government agency
un organisme du gouvernement de l'Ontario

For Matthew, Elena and Bobbie-Ann. And for the Ancestors.

Joe Pete

a novel

Ian McCulloch

Joe Pete's Family Tree

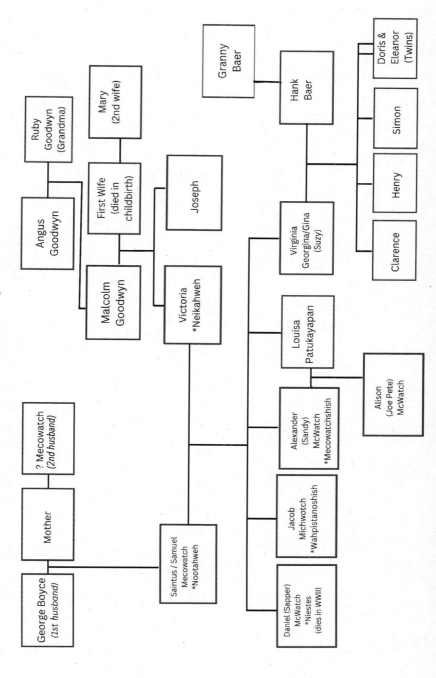

For Dad, who left this final gift for all of us.
Thank you/Chi-miigwetch for everything.

We loved you. We still love you. And we think about you and miss you every day; but we can take solace in the fact that you will live on, forever, immortalized in the stories and poems you have written, and this book that has come to life even after you have passed on, across the river.

This is in memory of the man who taught me to listen, but also to question; who taught me to give generously, for the act of doing so. This is a book that was written by a father who was always there for his children, and a husband who loved his wife dearly.

It was an honour to know his laughter, unconditional love, wisdom, and warmth. His spirit lives in this book. We are proud and grateful to be able to share his memory with you.

Matthew, Elena, and Bobbie-Ann McCulloch
August 2022

Some Fragments Shored

An Intimate Introduction

I/

I was driving through Oshawa, home of your brother and sister, fearing this, my dear friend. I have been looking out through trees, from rocks, beaches where we have landed canoes or have taken our children swimming. I am now beside a fire on that island where we first camped. Water boils in your old pot with the wooden handle. Vigils...

I know you would take much pleasure in knowing this is killing me.

-

Now this book! A miracle. I remember you talking, reading passages late into the night, your frustration with this novel (within novels within novels...various titles...King Philip's War), its exfoliations, shape shifting narrative purposes, directions, a sense, because of other works, of a problematic audience, so many named faces in forms moving over an all too human deep. I am so grateful for this search and rescue. I think of Frank Polson's painting, The Spirit Canoe...How we need the presence and strength of others in community to make or to heal. Or to have balsam or an artefact to offer. This book takes one's breath away. As you said of editing Dorothy Coffman's collection, this represents a faithfulness to life. A covenant, as Heaney puts it, with the unpublished. Or treaty.

—

'We are reduced to what we can carry,' you wrote in that canoe poem. To carry the tumpline's weight tugging down with life, memory, like your marvelous character, Nanny. Or that bundle your grandmother, you imagine, leaving on shore:

> And when she looks back
> there is a bundle forgotten on the rocky beach
> a package that was meant for me. (Louisa)

I walked part of that trail beside the Oxtongue, a month after you left, not all the way to that lake whose name is imaged for our country and hockey team we have tried to love, that same trail we hiked with our sons well over twenty years ago. Like Mecowatchshish, his lifetime's preparation to go to war, it's as if your whole life and inheritance has been meant for this novel's arriving in this moment. Not merely in the book's making. I believe this world – this country – is finally ready. Readiness is all. The rest need not be silence.

II/

Poetry, says Seamus Heaney, involves a dining with the dead. Out of this feast with ancestors issues this humbling, inspired poetry from another space. In essence, this is spiritual autobiography; in its lyric, raw worthiness, its making sense of life through family, memory, the graced weight of motherhood, it reminds of Camus' *The First Man*, also posthumous. Its restles s, driving hunger for association, destination, value in relationship, identity, again concerned with a mother's presence, the sense of seasons, brings to mind Virginia Woolf's *To the Lighthouse*.

Whereas *Childforever* proffered an almost journalistic one person point of view, *Joe Pete* aspires to a rich, complex narrative with a deeply poetic dignity of utterance. It establishes a compelling, intriguing ambience conveyed by shifting perspectives, contexts, nuances. Implications...natural, cultural, historical, sociopolitical, and always personal. How you loved, Ian, poetic fiction (Proulx... your reading Cormac McCarthy's passage about the stars by flashlight in the tent at Big Thunder). In *Joe Pete*, even through the title character's names, both pun and metaphor, the language is charged with music, sparks and valences. Your narrative logic and structure, as Ken Stange contended about your sensibility, concerns itself with persons. At heart, it is elegiac and in its present, unspoken witnessing one gets an implicit sense of the mystical, always on the precipice, like Hank, of tragedy's human river.

Consequently, you have conjured fragments into a story attentive to all that is momentous: nature's hard, rich beauty in its elemental danger and wonder; with Joe Pete and loved ones, others who have passed on life, stories rich in a conditional, conditioning past; each a profound receiving of ancestral grace, wonder, and echoing legacy. Yet all this is explored under the pressure of misfortune, illness, cruelty, racism, injustice, and trauma inherent in the mystery of life itself. There is resilience...*Never give up*. All this finds a place and focus in these selfsame 'fragments,' 'objects of ritual': 'mementos'...'talismans'...'remains,' from a tool in Poppa Sam's shed to a dog's collar. Or Joe Pete's father's axehead. Incarnate, resonant... As Beckett would write of another remembered past, 'things as symbols of themselves.' The river. Various fires...

III/

Ian, this day has come. With the courage and creative joy, the searing challenge in testimony, demand for responsibility and a dream of hope, alive now in this new, renewing gift to whomever, whatever we might become, we are blessed with this marvelous fact, this renaissance in Indigenous literature. In spite of and because of ourselves, while all of us can carry through this dark wood, this torch of story and song offered by artists from ancient nations to, as Jesse Wente suggests, a very young country, *Joe Pete* will take its rightful place. It will make its own fire beside your heroes (Wagamese, Maracle, Thomas King and especially your favourite, Tomson Highway). This novel offers much, much to those with ears to hear as Sandy hears, hearts to attend to the same memorable and fierce compassion and thirst for justice, like Scout Finch, in Joe Pete. With gratitude towards and compassion for the ancestors' stories, *Joe Pete* makes its own contribution in guiding us towards a 'Canada of light.' In the presence of all our crimes and shadows, of reclamation, redress. Perhaps the eventual wisdom, in truth, in reconciliation (at least with some...), nation to nation, of reverence, friendship. Out of these shared fragments, my friend, you leave us, your readers, with this artefact grounded, shining in your own remembering, imagining presence, something to strengthen us, a wholeness in witness, vision. How blessed we are to have this story to carry with us. *Micwek*. You have shared Mecowatchshish's spirit as he declares by Neikahweh's grave with the same courage, my friend: "I've come here to tell you, all these years later that now I understand and appreciate what you taught me. I want you to know I still carry the stories of you and my brothers with me."

Denis Stokes, Pine Lake
2022

Prologue:

Stories

"Tell me the story," the little girl says and although she offers an encouraging smile a deep river of sadness flows through her eyes. "You know, the one about Daddy and the bread."

"What story?" her mother asks. She's weary and only wants rest. The memories her daughter is seeking are too cumbersome a burden for her. "There's lots of stories about me and..." there is a moment of hesitation because his name is on the tip of her tongue and she must not let it slip out "...your Daddy."

Mecowatchshish is there already and he wants to hear this story as well. He exists now in these stories, in recollected moments of the past. These fragments of remembered love. He should be somewhere else but he is there among the familiar shadows, waiting to hear.

"You know," the girl chides. She wants something that will ease her sorrow for a while. A soothing evoking of the past to hold against her wounded heart and erase the echo of the sombre hymns and the prayers that to her are only surrender. "The burnt bread..."

The mother sighs. "Not again. Pick another story. Something

else. How about I tell you about your Auntie Gina? Her most guarded secret. Georgina always hated her name. If you called her Georgie when she a was kid she got real mad. Once, right in the schoolyard, Indian School not your school, she knocked out Donnie Fletcher's two front teeth and he was a grade ahead of her. Those teeth were already loose but she smacked them right out of his head. He used to always sing Georgie Porgie in this loud croaky voice like a big frog, only he'd sing 'Kissed the boys and made them DIE.' She got in big trouble teacher dragged her up the stairs into the school by one arm, 'You can't behave like little savages here,' she said. But nobody called her Georgie after that." She leaned in close, whispering conspiratorially, "You know how sometimes we call her Suzy. She doesn't like that either anymore... but it's a funny story. She got the letters S and U...well like most of a U...burned right onto..." She throws her hand over her mouth, popping her eyes wide dramatically. "No. Can't say that. What am I doing? That's not a story for ahwahshishuk. 'Specially her own son."

The boy looks up and she pantomimes buttoning her lip as though he is already in on the joke. It is a ruse meant to draw him to her side, but she begins to relish the idea of revealing her sister-in-law's past wickedness. There may even be a bit of spite in it, though this is directed more at the dour man that is her nephew's father. The boy blushes and looks away and she does not pursue it any further. In reality, it is a confidence she has been saving to share with her daughter when she is older and capable of a more adult understanding. An amusement they could delight in together, as women. It is only her desperation in the moment, her desire to avoid confronting their recent loss. Not on such a night, with so much grief in her heart, the world gnashing its teeth outside the door while she struggles from one minute to the next. She wants to be strong for her daughter and it is dangerous to think of past happiness when all that is waiting is an empty and comfortless bed. When she looks at her daughter's face she is forced to bite off an insincere chuckle and cough against the back of her hand, swallowing the diversion whole.

It is the deepest part of winter, dark and cold and a blizzard howls against the cabin and rattles the warped windows. The wood stove pops and cracks and throws waves of heat against them but still they can feel the wind on their backs. Mecowatchshish rides the turbulent air, high above, amongst swirling wind-driven snow looking down on what was once his home. He soars higher to take it all in. The landscape, the town that sits between the two frozen rivers. The hills and valleys, the forests and lakes where he hunted and fished. The seasons change as he rises, years turning backwards, the scenery below flickering through shades of green to brilliant reds, yellows, oranges, then to grey and bone white. Day. Night. Day. Shadow and light. Up and up until he can see from James Bay to the Wolf's Head of Superior all the land that is in his blood. Then down like the wind through the nebulous past, gathering the years he has known as he goes. He comes from out of the west, passing the spectres of the recent dead as he travels till he is following the trail of his last journey towards home. Over the frozen river he moves catching up to a night, not so long past and sees his own footprints in the snow, sees where they end abruptly at a ragged fracture in the ice. The chill of the cold water lances through him and he is suddenly heavy with the sorrow of those he loved. He fights now to make it through the last stage dragging himself towards the cabin through the swirling storm resisting the pull to turn back.

He is there, inside, filling the warm space. He is the vessel out of which flows all of the memories now swirling around them. The three, a woman, a girl about ten and a boy who is older by almost two years, sit huddled in the thin light of a pair of coal oil lanterns, drinking sweet tea with evaporated milk.

The boy sits listening quietly, trying to be unobtrusive because he feels a little as if he is intruding, sensitive to the ineffable sorrow that has infiltrated the bond between mother and daughter. He has his own sadness over the loss of his uncle, but its grip is not as relentless and each day it slips a little farther from him. He welcomes this duty that makes him feel needed and is glad to have something to offer. From time to time he gets up and tip-toes over to throw another chunk of hardwood on one of the fires. Occasionally, both the cook stove and the squat little heater need replenishing and he tries to choose wisely each time. Something to suit the present need, to keep them comfortable and yet leave enough to burn through the long, turbulent night to come. He feels a wet chill along his spine, under his shirt where melting snow has trickled down inside his collar. Only a short time ago he braved the driving wind and struggled through growing drifts to bring in a last armload of wood to stack against the wall. He knows it will take a lot to keep them warm through the night and he has some doubts, but he is also proud to be there, occupying the place of a man. There is no way of knowing it will be the biggest storm of the past decade or that in the morning he will have to crawl out the back bedroom window and fight through the immense drifts to shovel away snow which has packed so high against the door that it can't be opened.

"We were just married," the woman begins, acquiescing as she shivers involuntarily with a sudden need to tell the story. Gazing into the liquid brown eyes of her daughter she sees the shadow of her lost husband, "and we came to live here. Your father built this place after the war. Times were not so hard. Not like now. There was no depression then. He built here, away from town, close to the river to be near his father and so he could get out to the trap line. Besides, after he came home from the war, he was very shy around people. Because of the deafness. He worked in the mill for a while but he got tired being inside all the time. Too hot. Too many people. He wanted to be in the bush but that was not easy for him anymore either."

Her voice is flat, without emotion. She will tell the story for her girl but she will not relive it. She pauses for a sip of tea then looks around the room peering into the dark corners. Her eyes come to rest on the boy. "Simon go look under that tea towel and you'll see half a bannock there. Bring it over, please."

He leaps up to retrieve the bread and is embarrassed by the noise of his chair scraping on the rough wooden floor, betraying how fervently he was hoping to be asked this.

"And bring that other plate there while you're up." He turns back to the counter and doesn't notice his aunt wink to her daughter. People have been bringing food since the accident. She knows that he faces stiff competition at the supper table from his older brothers.

"It still has some of the baked whitefish your mother sent. Might as well finish that up; I can't get any more in the icebox. And the jam too. That's good blueberry jam Mrs. Ricci gave me. I say it's good but I can't taste it. Can't taste anything since..."

Simon places the thick plate with the fish and the bannock on the table and tears away a chunk. He holds it out to the girl, "Here you go, Joe Pete."

He immediately regrets his mistake in using the nickname and when their eyes meet the girl drops her head to hide the nervous smile spreading across her lips. He feels the disapproving glare of her mother burning into the back of his head and passes the plate without looking up. The woman tears off a corner of the flat loaf and places it by her teacup, her smoldering eyes locked on the boy the whole time. Then she shoves the plate back towards him.

"You didn't take a piece, Simon."

It is a cool invitation which the boy takes as a hopeful sign of clemency. He begins to breathe again waiting for what might come next. She takes the knife and chops the fish into three roughly even pieces and then uses the blade to saw open her bannock. She slips a morsel of soft white flesh into her mouth and then holds the plate out for the children and they chew the oily offering together in silence. This has been her manner of dining since her husband disappeared. Bites and mouthfuls taken here and there, standing near the stove, going out the door, sitting with Gina in her parlour drinking tea. They have lived on the gifts left by friends and relatives. She hardly ever sits to have a meal. She cannot stay in her place at the table sitting with her daughter; food catches in her throat as her eyes are drawn to the empty chair. The absent place setting.

She sighs heavily. "Can't taste anymore. Can't even smell it."

She pulls the preserve jar in close and coats it with jam. "But the sun still comes up doesn't it." She does not lift it to her mouth and instead she passes it to the boy.

"Good bannock but not as good as my bannock, eh Simon?" Cold emphasis and a pause singling him out. "I could always make good bannock. Sometimes we lived on bannock in the bush when I was a kid. Bannock and boiled fish bones. But when I was first married I wasn't so good at baking. I never liked it much at St. Bart's when I had to help in the kitchen. I was like you, Alison. I liked to be outside." There is an even more obvious emphasis on her daughter's given name.

What was it, she asks herself, with her daughter and names? She pauses to study her trying to determine what it was that had made the name she had picked for her baby girl so unsuitable. It had come from her own childhood, her days at Residential School when she heard the older girls talking about the book the teacher sometimes read aloud to them. A book about a little girl in a might be. She understood this but it was a fragile and tangential comprehension. Like the smoke rings her grandfather playfully blew into the flickering light of the candles. They could not be grasped or held. When you reached for them they disintegrated, melting into drifting, sinuous tendrils.

Sometimes the door might rattle struck by a violent gust or a spark would explode and ping vehemently around inside the stove. Okemah would pause to rub his stubbled chin or stroke his moustache before nodding and correcting himself over a point in his story before carrying on. A name or location or a subtle shift in chronology. It would make the hairs on the nape of her neck lift and sometimes she might shiver in that way that invariably prompted the old man to ask teasingly, "Somebody step on your grave?"

It was an aphorism that Joe Pete never understood and unnerved her in the way that it shifted Time; future affecting present, evoking her own death and relegating her to memory before she had really even lived. It caused her to wonder if her grandfather's reminiscences were flying back into the past, like the bright explosive embers sometimes propelled out of the open stove door, to tingle along the spines of those long dead. It often frightened her, that immediacy waiting there in the shifting light of the simple kitchen, her grandfather's face with its deep furrows and thick moustache floating in front of her. She knew he was part of the legacy of the people who had risen out of this place, the lakes and rivers and the forested landscape from where they were to Lake Superior, north to James Bay and beyond. She could feel its magic and immanence in her bones as she sat listening to the old man, who was lost himself in the telling. She could sense the great span of time that fed his knowledge, actually see it there in the sinew and stark knuckles and calloused contours of his hands.

Her mother seemed to be reading her thoughts. "And no lip-flapping tonight. Straight to bed."

Alison sighed. "I'll be okay here," she mumbled, rocking

unsteadily on her heels a bit and pulling the blanket more tightly around her.

Louisa fed the biggest log she could find into the fire. "I hope that will last till I get back. You go up and gather your school clothes together and then skedaddle to your grandfather's. I don't want you missing any more school."

Poppa Sam was standing out on his porch, a glowing lantern casting light under a sky that had surrendered all its stars, even as his drowsy granddaughter was given a little push towards The House. Louisa was not surprised to see the waiting beacon. Somehow her father-in-law seemed to always know what was going on in his little domain no matter the hour. He had been their guardian whenever Sandy was away and he had taken on the role with more resolve since the accident. She waved, despite knowing he could not see to where she stood in darkness, watching her sleepy daughter's progress a moment. Then headed off with single-minded purpose along the path that led to town and the fruitful Mrs. Turkula.

Joe Pete stumbled across the short, familiar distance and into the weak circle of light clutching the bundle that held her school clothes against her chest.

"Wahchay, Noo sei sim," he said when she started up his porch steps.

"Wachay, Okemah," she answered.

It pleased him when she used this term of respect rather than calling him Poppa Sam. When she wanted to tease him, and thought she could get away with it, she conjured his official name, Saintus Mecowatch. Sometimes he regretted that he had given in to her insistent curiosity and revealed it after he'd let slip that Samuel was not really his name while she was helping him learn cursive writing to improve his signature. He wryly referred to the moniker it down by himself. Twenty feet up a branch broke unexpectedly and he pitched off on the steep side with a short exclamation of surprise as if the old birch had tricked him. He plummeted like a goose killed on the wing, slamming down through a brittle tangle of half-rotted logs and landing hard on his back across the point of a gnawed stump projecting out of the snow. Samuel hurried to where he had seen his son fall and even though the echo of something splintering stuck in his ear as he fought his way through the intertwined brush and detritus he was half-expecting to find him sitting among the broken branches laughing and ready to do it again. But the boy was still, half-hidden by debris, his torso arched over the decaying trunk as blood dripped onto the ground below. He scrambled to him fighting the saplings that pulled at him and whipped against his face and looked down at Wahpistanoshish.

His face was scratched and his eyes closed, filaments of snow melted on his ashen cheeks and a small stick was caught in his hair like a bony finger. He seemed to be having difficulty getting a breath but his father had seen him with the wind knocked out of him before. Samuel used his teeth to pull the beaded moosehide mitts from his hands and worked his fingers tentatively under the boy. He found where the blood seeped from a deep gash in the boy's side but was relieved that he had not been impaled on the pointed remnant which had been softened by decay.

He lifted him clear of the snarl of roots and branches, dismayed by how tightly his son's small hands clutched his arm and his sharp inhalation through clenched teeth. Despite the pain, the boy did not cry out. He carried him carefully up the bank and laid him on top of his parka in the snow then removed his own coat and covered his son. His eyes fluttered open. "My legs, Nootahweh. I can't..." he struggled for air,"...they're sleeping. My legs are sleeping." He sounded almost apologetic.

"Rest a bit, Wahpistanoshish," he wiped the melted water from the boy's face with gentle strokes and tried to push away the choking fear closing his throat. He could not look at his son's legs, crossed awkwardly above the ankles, the pant legs looking strangely flat, the angles unnatural. He remembered a hunter from his boyhood, whose gun misfired, the powder damp, and was trampled by a charging Bull Moose. Spine shattered, he was left sprawled like a child's doll cast aside on the cold, frozen ground, refusing to be moved and sang his Death song under a grey restless sky late in the Moon of Setting Nets. With each star in the darkening twilight, his voice grew fainter, as if another bit of him had burned away, until he was silent and the darkness was pierced with uncountable pinpoints of distant flame and the wolves took up his song.

"Daniel!" He looked for his first-born as his voice echoed through the stark woods grown silent and dim. "Daniel! Hurry, your brother is hurt!"

They left their secluded world in the woods and with Wahpistanoshish strapped onto the big toboggan travelled six days to the Revillon Frères Trading Post, west across the Moose River thinking they would not be as well-known there. The last time his brother had visited them he reported hearing rumours of efforts being made to find Indian people who were hiding their children from the school.

They laid him on beaver pelts and covered him with muskrat because it was said that these would draw away pain. Samuel walked ahead carrying his pack on his back, harnessed to the toboggan while his wife Victoria followed, bearing Little Virginia in a tikanagan, though the girl had almost outgrown it. His wife made no complaint and did not question where they were going even though it was her fear that had first compelled them to leave their friends and relatives and live alone in the woods. Neither did she speak of the terror she felt now over the condition of her middle son, though at night lying exhausted in the tent Samuel could hear her whispering Psalm 23 till sleep overcame her.

Daniel pulled a small sled he had made for himself that very autumn with instruction from his father. It carried their blankets and the rolled tent and other supplies. Alexander trudged steadily behind most of the day, except for starting out each morning when he did his best to run along beside his brother and keep him company. They went slowly, as long as there was light, eating only pemmican, the girl still breastfeeding. When they saw Alexander growing tired and falling behind, then Samuel would carry the tent up across the top of the pack on his shoulders and Daniel would pull his brother on the small toboggan for a while. The first two days he sobbed quietly over his weakness, arms crossed over his face to hide the tears as he was tugged along between the tall, silent trees.

By sunset Samuel would be far ahead and, finding a suitable spot, would take his axe and cut poles to set up the tent and start a fire for tea. Wahpistanoshish would do his best to entertain his little sister lying flat on his back singing and telling stories while she straddled him. When their mother arrived she would take him inside and clean him and put fresh moss around him as she had done when he was a baby and she would do the same for Virginia and this was hard for the boy to bear.

When they arrived at the Trading Post he was already wheezing and beginning to cough. The Factor found a small room in the Servant's barracks for them with a bed for the boy. A man serving as physician examined him and tended to the wound on his side but could not fix the connection to the boy's legs and could only make him comfortable. He tried to offer some consolation before he left, saying the boy was young and maybe by spring he might heal, but they could tell by the pity in his eyes that it was false hope. Saintus was grateful for all the kindness and after the first week started hunting with two half-breed brothers who made their living providing game for the fur-traders.

All the time he was away he could think only of his son and because he was afraid that the boy might already be on the three-day road, he refrained from speaking his name even in prayer. It was said that a spirit could be distracted hearing the distress of those being left behind and lose their way to the western door. It was not easy for him to do this. His son's name was there, perpetually on his lips and in his thoughts. He wanted to speak it, to hear the sound of it in the world. He wanted to offer it as a plea, call it out to the grey, impassive sky so that the Creator might hear the love he had for his boy and make him whole and let him live. He carried in his medicine bag, among the small relics that reminded him of his family, a tooth that had fallen from Wahpistanoshish's mouth a few years before. His son had toddled over to him as Samuel was preparing to leave on a hunting trip and without a word placed it like an offering in his father's hand. He had carried it with him ever since, a memento of love and inevitable change, and now he put it in his mouth, a smooth shard of fear. It seemed like a dream now, those years of struggle and love as they built their nest away from the demanding world and their family grew. He kept his lips closed tightly around it so that it would not fall from his mouth and said nothing at all to anyone. The hunters understood his silence and left him alone and only talked in whispers between themselves. At night he kept his own fire and sat a little apart from the brothers to spare them feeling so restrained and because he was afraid of them. Afraid they might speak kindly or try to offer some hope and he knew that then, sitting by the flames under the stark, waning moon, his broken heart would crumble and he would not be able to go on. When they got back to the post, he discovered that his boy had indeed died. The second night away and hearing the news from men he hardly knew, it was like a blow to his stomach and he gasped and swallowed the slick tooth. The last of his boy gone.

There had been no priest but the Catholic factor had come and asked for the boy's Christian name and offered a final prayer over the boy's body. He had been buried as Jacob Michwotch in a shallow grave hacked out of the frozen earth, the name carved into a rough plank. Though neither one of them spoke of it, both Samuel and his wife chose to believe that their son had forgotten his baptismal name and that Wahpistanoshish had not hesitated in his journey to be with his ancestors in the West. The next morning, even before the sun was over the horizon, they departed and stopping by the shallow forlorn grave Samuel bent and slid his hunting knife from his belt and left it among the frozen clods. Then, without another farewell to anyone, they began their numb journey to return to their waskahekun, even though now it seemed like an indistinct location, as if it could not exist there in forest without all of them to live in it. Little snow had fallen in the frigid days they had been away and they followed their own packed trail. The sled that had borne Wahpistanoshish was now almost empty, Alexander refusing to ride on it, and it seemed to Samuel to float above the ground as they made their way through the mute and brooding trees.

Chapter Two:

The House

Louisa had been busy all week with her duties at the Turkula's looking after the new baby and helping throughout the day until stumbling home and lurching through the door long after dark. Joe Pete fried some eggs for their supper and they had gone to bed early unable to resist the cold and the dark and the clamour of the impertinent wind banging things around. After the brief respite of temperate days, it seemed all that remained was surrender, as though their time in the sun, instead of rejuvenating them, had evaporated the last of their resolve.

Joe Pete awoke in her small room to find it was frigid and she knew the stove had not been tended through the night. She pulled the quilt up over her head trying to ignore her full bladder and her mother's loud grumbling as she piled kindling to get it going. In a fit of determination, unable to ignore her mother or the need to pee she kicked off the covers, her legs bicycling out into the bracing air as she flung herself from bed to dress as quickly as she could. She shivered in the cold embrace of her clothes, dreading the walk to the outhouse. When she got downstairs her mother was standing in front of the woodstove, her winter coat thrown over her shoulders, looking stern, a length of what she called biscuit wood gripped in her hands, mostly alder that burned hot and fast to heat the stove.

"I wish once in a while you would help keep this going at night," she said and shook the branch at her.

Joe Pete was surprised by the rebuke and she stopped short, deeply stung and surprised to find herself on the verge of crying. She tried to look after herself and always did her chores without being asked. Looking after the stove after bedtime had never been one of her responsibilities. Get your sleep she had always been told. Be rested for school.

Her mother shrugged. "Oh it's my own fault. I've been so beat. Last night I slept like the...like a log." She swung open the fire door and tossed in the wood. "It's goin' now. Won't take long. I'm getting old before my time." She held out her arms, the coat slipping off into a heap around her ankles and the sad look she gave Joe Pete cut through her. "Come here and warm me up." They held each other, Louisa pulling her daughter in tight, squeezing and Joe Pete could not hold back her tears. "I know." Her mother said. "I know. It's not your fault."

After a brief embrace Joe Pete slipped into her boots and went out for more firewood with a quick detour to the outhouse. Louisa worked at stoking the fire, keeping the door propped open a crack to provide a steady rush of air that made the flames roar, and feeding in fuel till it could take no more. She moved the big kettle over the heat so that the metal pinged and the cake of ice inside began to crack and hiss. Joe Pete placed an armload from the woodshed near the stove then went out again and packed a pot with snow to melt so they could make oatmeal. Their water supply was running low and what there was lay frozen solid at the bottom of two big ten-gallon riveted milk cans that they kept behind the stove. Poppa Sam would come later to collect them and haul them on his sled to be refilled in town at his son-in-law's, and Gordon would help haul the heavy load back. They did not drink from the Big River because they were downstream from the rail yard where a steady slick of diesel and creosote oozed from a drainage ditch that emptied into its waters. They lit a lantern to add to the warmth and chase out the gloom. Joe Pete noticed her mother repeatedly staring out through the small window over the wash basin at the dull grey sky hunkered down over them. There was nothing else to see and looking at the sombre expression on her mother's face she could feel another day begin to revolve around what was absent.

"Tell me about the big house on Railway Street, about...about how Uncle Hank's dog got out at the party and chased everybody." She said it out of impulse, a little worried that it would provoke a sharp reproach from her mother. Her temper had grown lightning quick, her mood spiraling around a kind of impasse that circled constantly back into bitterness and grief. As though any happiness could only be pulled from the past, in brief interludes that always seemed to drag with it an equal measure of despair.

"That crazy dog. What is it with you and old stories?" She pulled out a chair and sat, her hands clasping each other, elbows resting on the table. "How I miss that house."

"Mostly I miss my room at the top of the big stairs...," Joe Pete felt the shift and knew her mother was with her sliding into reminiscence. "...and how Goliath would be lying on the landing with his bushy tail twitching back and forth when Daddy carried me up to bed on his shoulders. Remember how horrible he looked after the fire?"

"Poor Goliath. He was a real hunter, always leaving a bird or a little dead mouse at the door for us." She paused, for a second a clear vision of the stairway appearing in her mind. All intact, the polished steps, the dark wood banister, the big cat lolling on the braided rug that lay on the landing. Then, in an instant, gone to ash like a struck match.

"You were born in that house. My miracle child. You took so

long to come to us. Nurse Myrtle delivered you. She was a wonderful woman and she helped a lot of people in this town God bless her. She was the one who taught me about babies. That was before she went to live with her son in Sudbury." There was no way to tell her daughter how she had tried for so long to have children or of the devastating miscarriages. These were not burdens for a child. Not the kind of thing to be discussed with a ten-year-old girl.

Joe Pete did not see the look of longing her mother gave her. She had closed her eyes to conjure their old home in her own mind but found it impossible to imagine a single clear picture. What she saw was more fragmentary. Bits and pieces tied to particular events. A hazy black and white picture of her parents standing proudly side by side in front of their new home. The same thing already happened now when she was determined to remember her father's face and it frightened her. She wanted something animate and real but got only flickering images that changed the moment she tried to focus. Different expressions, changing backgrounds. His stubbled chin, the crooked front tooth, the way his eyes would shine when he told a funny story.

She thought it had been a beautiful house, two full stories with a big veranda that went around the front and along the south side and a summer kitchen in the back and lots of windows. A little too close to the tracks so that the trains would make the whole place shake in modest earthquakes that would set all the china and pots and pans dancing and chattering on their high shelves. At night she could hear the trains shunting in the yards, the powerful sighing of released steam, the heavy rumble of the cars being hooked together and the melancholy whistle of a locomotive pulling away into the distance. It was strange and frightening to listen to them in the dark, their authority and mystery pulsing through the night to shake her in her bed. In the daylight when she heard one rumbling past, the dishes clacking in their places, she would run out into the yard, the screen door slamming behind her, to wave madly to the man in the caboose. Sometimes she walked the tracks to her cousin's house and imagined she might look up one day to find the house still standing, untouched by flame.

"Anyway," her mother began, "Uncle Hank, he loves to read you know. He's read all kinds of books. His favourite book was *The Call of the Wild*. He was always talking about Jack London and the trail of ninety-eight and White Fang and the Yukon. Then, when he saw this puppy that was supposed to be part wolf part dog, he had to have it. You could tell from the size of its paws it was going to be a monster and it was. A great shaggy monster with a square head that looked carved out of oak and these spooky light blue eyes. Buck he called it, like the dog in the book. Buck never seemed to like other people and the more people moved around and got excited the more upset Buck would get. But Hank just had to bring him everywhere. I guess it made him feel like his hero, Jack London. He was more of a farm boy really. He came here after the war. Didn't even know if your daddy was alive and Daddy didn't know if Hank was alive. And they saw each other and it was like long lost brothers. They spent every day together for a while, your father and Uncle Hank..." She paused to consider if there was some way to explain The War and how men can be wounded in many different ways but decided it was best not to try. "...then Hank met Auntie Gina and you know," She leaned in close to her daughter, raised her eyebrows, "they fell in l-o-v-e. And he ended up staying and trapping with Daddy and one thing led to another." She raised one arm off the table, turning her hand slightly in a gesture of "there you go."

Then she pushed away from the table, swiping a few crumbs off into her hand and went to the stove to shake the big kettle.

"I need some tea."

She lifted the pothole lid, deposited the few dry bits into the flames and looked in the fire chamber but there was no more room for wood. She turned and stood with her back to the stove, a wistful look on her face.

"He was different then, your uncle Hank. Happy to be here, easy going. Devil-may-care we used to say. Not angry. Not bitter. Not when I got to know him. He came alive up here I think. I remember we went up onto the west ridge one time, to the look out over Sawbill Bay, your Daddy and me and Hank and Auntie Gina. There's a place down on the cliff that seems scooped right out of the rock, where you can sit and there's a flat stone on either side for your arms." She lowered her voice to a whisper. "People call it Satan's Armchair. I never liked it. Never liked that name, it always gave me chills. You can see way out over the valley and lakes in the distance. And he was sitting there in the armchair like a king and we were lying at the edge looking over and I just wanted to get going when he said, 'Look at those trees. God I love those trees.' And I almost laughed because I'd never heard anyone say they loved trees like that before. But the way he said it I looked out too, at all the green and the way they swayed in the breeze and I saw that place different. And then, I loved the trees too."

"He was hurt in the war too wasn't he? He only sees out of one eye."

"He and your daddy were in the same crew and they got wounded at the same time. They thought Hank was dead and they were taking him to be buried. It was Monk Little that pulled him off the wagon and saved his life. When he came here he was coming to see Monk and then he found out Daddy was alive." She shook her head mirthfully.

"Daddy never talked about the war much? About how he got wounded?" There were questions Joe Pete had never asked. She had expected that one day, when he thought she was ready for such things, he would tell her.

"He never liked to talk about it. Once he told me a bit about how he was buried by in that shell burst. I know he and Uncle Hank were the only ones who lived."

"His friends all died?"

"I don't know if you would say they were all friends. But they were soldiers together and I think that's something special for men. I know not everybody liked him at first. Didn't like Indians and some even spit on the ground whenever he walked past. They didn't think much of being sent some skinny redskin? But he showed them. He could carry and he could shoot. He could even outshoot me." She winked.

"The thing he talked about most from those days was how surprising it was to find so many people in the world. He was just a kid from the bush, you know. Not much older than your cousin Clarence. But he lied about his age. You learn in school about other places, other countries, big cities, but to come from here and see such things...more people than you could imagine, all living their lives. All alive in the world together. He used to say it was a wonder. And then..."

She turned back to the kettle which was starting to boil. She could not tell her daughter about the killing or the nightmares filled with terror and the dead. So many dead.

"He used to like to tell about the time in England, waiting to go over..." She poured the boiling water from the kettle into the little brown teapot. "...and they were billeted on this big place. I don't remember the name now some kind of estate they called it. It had some forest and big fields and I know he liked it. Anyway, he said all they were fed was what they claimed was lamb stew. The meat was tough as leather and tasteless and the farm boys all agreed it was most likely goat. So he finds some wire and goes out at night where he saw there was a bit of bush and sets snares and pretty soon he's catching nice plump rabbits to eat. Then one day he hears a familiar click, remember he could still hear, and then he turns around to find an Englishman with a shotgun pointed right at him. The man takes the rabbits from him and says," she cleared her throat and sat up very straight to invoke her best imitation of what she thought was a proper English accent, "'Lad, I don't know where yer from but his Lordship don't take kindly to poachers on his land. Now clear off.' And that was it for rabbits. Your daddy almost got shot before he could even get to the war."

The heat from the stove was beginning to radiate throughout the cabin chasing out the gathered chill of the night before. Louisa sat back and put her feet up on a short stool resting in front of the stove. Joe Pete saw that she was wearing a pair of over-sized heavy wool socks that had been her father's.

"Weren't we talking about the old house? Remember how hard we worked to salvage this old stove."

Joe Pete had helped scour the carbon and ash off the cast iron, black up to her elbows, working to bring some part of the old life with them.

"And Buck? You asked about that stupid mutt Buck. How he got loose at my birthday party and cleared the decks." Louisa stood to slowly stretch, "I don't think too much is going to get done this morning."

She went to the shelf near the door that held the pipe and tobacco. Joe Pete knew that sometimes, sitting by the stove alone at night, her mother would pack a little tobacco in the bowl and light it, the stem held tenderly between her lips. She reached up and took down her husband's pocket watch which also rested there when not in use, opened it to check that it was running, then brought it back to the table with her and wound it fully. Joe Pete reached across the table and picked up the heavy round time piece, held it cupped between her hands against one ear to hear the steady strong beat.

Louisa watched the smoke drift in the rising air above the stove. She thought of the first summer in that house, early June and it was Sandy's birthday. She sighed, took another short draw from the pipe, and began to tell the story. They had just moved in, didn't have much furniture and the whole front of the house was one big room they loved to call The Parlour. Her eyes moistened recalling how they loved that word, the idea of it. She tilted her head back and took in the rough timber ceiling above her head. They had moved aside their second-hand furniture and rolled up the old Persian rug that had come with the place to make room for people to dance even though Sandy never would. Hank and Gina were there to help and shifting things around like that had driven Buck around the bend for some reason. He yapped and jumped and skidded around on the polished wood floor until Hank took him and locked him in an empty bedroom upstairs.

She recalled the warm evening and how it seemed to fill spontaneously with music and laughter, the sheen on every dancer's face and the dampness that made her dress cling. There was even some chagrin over the twinge of jealousy she felt when Gina, with baby Clarence less than a year old rocking sleepily in her arms, whispered that she was in a family way again.

It was a wonderful party. Jack Doolan, fiddling like nobody's business, which he doesn't do much anymore because of the arthritis in his fingers, and Charlie McClellan playing his guitar with five strings after one broke on the very first song. Hank flipped over the wash tub and beat on it like a drum. The windows were wide open, they didn't even have screens in then and you had to put up with the occasional mosquito that made it through the cigarette haze. Beer and bootleg gin and all that laughing and yelling and pounding feet on the floorboards. The whole house jumping and packed with people all having a good time. Then couples began sneaking off to spoon in the upstairs rooms and somebody released the frenzied Buck by mistake and suddenly there was mayhem. Yelling and cursing and the big mutt barking and nipping, running here and there, Hank roaring "Heel! Heel!" at the top of his lung as if that stubborn mongrel ever listened and Gina's right shoe tumbling through the air and clipping the dog on the side of his gargantuan head. People were jammed in the doorway pointing and bellowing, the most fearful scrambling to avoid Buck, while most of the men simply turned away, holding their drinks close to their chest and trying to maintain some dignity. Eddie Ryan attempted to be the hero and grabbed the dog's scruff only to get a nasty bite that gashed open his forearm, the sight of blood increasing the air of panic. People went for the doors and open windows and it must have been something to see from the street, the old house spitting bodies out of every available opening. Katie Chapise, mortally afraid of all dogs since childhood, flew out the window, party dress and all to land nimbly on her feet like an acrobat. It was all there in a flash in her mind's eye, floating like the fragrant pipe smoke around her head. It was a humorous incident in retrospect but it was the beginning of the end for Buck who only a few weeks later bit a boy who was chasing a hoop down the street. Hank had taken his rifle and led the dog on a leash out into the woods. Only Hank came back.

It was a whim of the wind and an errant spark that brought them back to live in the small cabin on the reserve. It had been Sandy and Louisa's first house and then, with plans for a big family and after they had saved enough to move into town, they had used it as a kind of cottage when the summer nights were sweltering and close. Down near the river they could swim and there was a better chance of a breeze at night. Away from the other houses, in the quiet, with all the windows out and protected by the screens, they were soothed by the sounds of the water.

Then on a hot July day, two years previous, after two weeks without rain and as Joe Pete and her mother were busy hauling water from the river to their garden, they heard the urgent whistle from the C. P. R. shop and looked to see a column of black smoke rising up over the town. Louisa dropped her bucket as if she knew immediately and Joe Pete had started to chuckle watching the water slosh over her mother's boots. Louisa began to hurry along the trail out to the road that led into town one hand shading her eyes trying to judge the precise location of the fire. A sick feeling settled in her stomach when she saw Gina's boy Clarence running towards them, breathless, a look of terror on his face. Even Joe Pete knew in that moment it must be their house.

The boy never said anything, only stood gasping, and before he could even point to the building pillar of smoke Louisa was running. Joe Pete let go of her pail and screamed for her mother to wait and she too began racing towards town. She was surprised at how swift her mother was, how quickly she was left behind. She was wearing a pair of hand-me-down rubbers from Simon that were two sizes too big. She stopped to kick them off then began to run barefoot. She became frightened and angry as her feet pounded against the well-worn path. "Wait," she cried out. "Wait." But her mother was too far ahead, too filled with apprehension to do anything but run. Clarence took her small hand in his and set off towing her behind. She grew livid and would not have it. She stopped, jerking her hand free and crossed her arms, locking her hands away and stomping her foot petulantly. Clarence turned, took a few steps back, and reached for her elbow but she twisted away. Her lips were set tightly and she glared at him and when he seemed about to raise his hand to slap her she lifted her chin to dare him. The whistle blew from town, a long and insistent wail that echoed out over the river and he waved at her dismissively and raced off after his aunt.

Louisa arrived, breathless, sobbing with the harrowing frustration of the long run to town, certain there would be nothing left. Several women from town had met her at the end of the street and Gina was there. Her sister-in-law made a weak attempt to hold her back but Louisa pushed by. She took her hand though and they walked together up the street. Louisa teetered slightly to one side for a moment, exhausted, her legs trembling from the exertion and Gina gently pulled her back and put one arm around her waist. The house was fully engulfed and the street was frantic with activity.

"It was the train," someone shouted in her face, though she could never remember who because all her attention was riveted on her burning home. Smoke billowed from the upper windows and flames could be seen leaping above the roof in the back. Sparks from the steel wheels had set the dry weeds along the tracks on fire and the breeze had pushed it swiftly into the tall grass of the yard and before anyone realized what was happening flame swept like a wave up against the back of the house.

Sandy had been in town, just up the block helping Hank who was putting new steps on his porch and now he was standing in the street, soot-covered, his face black and his hands burned. Some of their furniture and odds and ends were pulled out into the street. Hank was sitting in an armchair that had a large hole charred in it, smoke still drifting out from something smoldering inside. He was bent over coughing and hacking and spitting a thick sludge out onto the ground between his feet. The fire truck was there and the volunteers were working frantically to contain the blaze and keep it from spreading. Louisa collapsed on the dirt street next to her husband, Joe Pete who had hurled herself after her cousin the moment he left ran up crying inconsolably, chest heaving in short gasping sobs and fell beside her. Sandy knelt and put his arms around the two of them ignoring the pain of his burned hands.

Almost as soon as the flames were out Hank started rallying the townspeople to help his brother-in-law, but it wasn't to be. The house had been built in the early year when the tracks first came through and when they went to see about permits it was discovered that it actually stood on railroad property. They didn't legally own the land and couldn't even if they had been able to afford it and so they could not rebuild.

Joe Pete always found this part of the story difficult to understand and wanted to argue the point as though it might somehow change what had happened.

"Why not?" she would ask. "Why couldn't we just rebuild it?

The house was there before. Why couldn't they just let us have our house again?"

"That's just the way it is, Alison. Times had changed and once the truth of it was realized we couldn't go back. It's the way the law works."

"What about the man who sold it to you?"

"Mr. Stewart? He was long gone. Someone told me he'd gone back to Scotland, but no one could really say. It didn't matter. Nothing could be done." Louisa's tone became more impatient. It was painful and embarrassing to remember how they had put their trust in a kindly old man who had been cheated.

"But the people wanted to help."

"They did help. We lived with Poppa Sam for a time and fixed this place up. We added a big room on the back for your daddy and me and put the loft in for you. People were generous and it was already the hard times. We were just lucky to have a place to go. Now get up to your room and get dressed."

It was said with more irritation than she intended but she wanted to avoid re-telling the part about Goliath, their cat. No one could say for sure how the big Persian had come to be in the house. He must have slipped in the day before which had been Sunday when they went to church and had a big lunch at home, but no one could remember seeing him. He was often gone for days, especially when they stayed down at the cabin. He loved to hunt in the woods. One of the men helping salvage the day after the fire found him down in the root cellar, under a section of floor that had collapsed, and he carried him out into the yard and set him down among the debris and ruined artefacts of their old life.

"This their cat," he had asked, and someone touched Sandy's shoulder and pointed to the forlorn heap on the blackened ground. He went over and looked. There lay Goliath his thick fur singed away, scorched and blind, his eyes sealed shut, his proud tail naked and broken.

The man retrieved a shovel and offered to put the cat out of its misery.

Sandy had waved him off and knelt to cradle the cat in his bandaged hands. "No," he said and it was the only time he spoke that day.

The cat lived, nursed gently back to health, but he was never the same. Scarred and slowed down by ruined tendons and injuries and dulled senses he still refused to compromise. They tried to keep him inside the house, force him to join them in their new life on Indian Arm, into a kind of early retirement. He wouldn't have it and slipped out the door or an open window every chance he got. One day he didn't come home and all though everyone knew that probably a fox or an owl or some other more feral cat had been his end. For a long time after when Sandy stepped out onto the porch in the morning, she would see him look down expectantly and knew he was hoping to see the still grey form of a dead mouse.

Chapter Three:

Mecowatchshish in Hiding

Mecowatchshish knew the wind and the four directions. He knew the trees and the water and the sky. He knew the sun and all the faces of the moon. In his life there was Nootahweh, his father, Neikahweh, his mother, Neistes, the first born, and Wahpistanoshish the middle brother and the necessary work that gave them their place in the circle of things. There were the animals and the seasons and the practices that connected them to the world. There was the pure elemental pleasure of being alive.

This joy was everywhere for Mecowatchshish. It filled his heart every morning when he opened his eyes. He saw it in the smile of his mother and in the eyes of his father. He felt Peseim giving it to him when it warmed his skin and when it rippled radiantly across a summer lake. He heard it when the rain fell on the roof of their simple home and dripped from the green leaves of the trees. It sang in the voices of the birds in the morning when he woke and called out in the bold chanting of spring frogs as he drifted into sleep. It fell around him when snow floated out of the silent night sky in huge, delicate flakes. It was the joy that came from belonging in the world so completely and it had been in his life from the beginning.

His parents had known a different way of living but had left it behind years before Mecowatchshish journeyed down from the stars and entered the world. Even before Wahpistanoshish had been born. They were where they were because when Neikahweh first came to realize that her second child was on the way a terrible fear had begun to grow in her heart, a dark dread that altered her perspective of the world. It was a vague uncertainty that filled her with relentless anxiety and distrust and the need to find a place of safety. She began trying to convince Mecowatchshish's father they should leave Moose Factory and go live deep in the woods. Live the way their ancestors had lived. Nootahweh had not been completely surprised by this. There were things about living in the village neither of them liked. Trapping had become more difficult because there were fewer pelts to be had every year. In the south, trains were moving the furs to market and many of the old posts along the river, some that had been there as long as anyone could remember, had been abandoned. Each season his debt to the company grew. There seemed to be more and more sickness and people had started to leave, working their way up the big rivers to greener pastures.

By the time Neistes had begun walking, the urgency of Mecowatchshish's mother could not be ignored. It didn't help that her Aunt Maria and her cousin David, who was Maria's oldest, fled back into the north with their families. They told stories about the new Residential schools their children had been forced to attend, taken from their families to live far away. Maria told her that in these wicked places the Indian children were forbidden to speak their own language or practice their own traditions and were taught that the very way their people lived was backward and evil. The children came home with frightening tales of cruel treatment and humiliation, of beatings and worse. She cried when she told how her grandson, David's boy Elijah, had never come home, had become sick and died far from the comfort of his own family without any ceremonies. It was weeks before they even learned the news. There were ominous rumours of worse things done, stories of pain people could not bring themselves to relate and when she said this her own daughter Daisy, who was not that much younger than Neikahweh herself, also began to weep.

She divulged these things breathlessly to her husband, fear squeezing the air from her lungs as she pleaded with him to take them away now before it was too late. He was aware she carried a secret pain that had left her with more than just the physical aches that sometimes caused her to moan at night and walk with an awkward stiffness the next morning. He knew the stories that were told of what had happened to her brother, things she would not reveal. He knew there was nothing more important to her than being a good mother and protecting her children. She could not even bear short separations from their son without being overwhelmed by a pervasive alarm that something terrible would happen and she would not be there to protect him. He knew that it would kill her to have her boy taken away, but it was hard for him to believe such things even though he knew it was mostly the Waymeisteikoshoowuks world now. No one he had ever spoken to, not any Elder, not even his great grandparents had been able to remember a time before the White Man's influence. They had always been a part of his life and, even as it was with his wife, he carried some part of them in his own blood. Far from home on those cold winter nights they liked to have their Indian women, their Country Wives. And hadn't they always been fair to him? Treated him well? Weren't they all Christians?

Looking at his young pregnant wife and their child, asleep together on their soft bed of furs, he could not ignore the terrible urgency that plagued her and he too felt infected by fear and trepidation. He stared at the boy's tousled hair and his small brown hand curled against his mother's face and the thought of his son taken from them, taken from their way of life filled him with apprehension. Wasn't there already enough to be afraid of in the world? Didn't living already ask enough? He had witnessed the deaths of two sisters and a brother, claimed by sickness when they were still children, his brother only a baby. Every family knew this pain. There were entire villages deserted and left to be reclaimed by the forest because so many had died. He had endured hard winters when people starved and hunger grew into a cold evil and the Witiko walked among them in the forest despite every Christian prayer. When they began to hear rumours that such a school was to be built in Moose Factory, they decided it was time to go.

They left quietly that summer, only a few days after Wahpistanoshish had been baptized. Nootahweh's older brother and his cousin and his cousin's young family, went with them. They travelled the Moose River to the Missinaibi journeying to a place on the very southern edge of what had always been a part of their family's traditional hunting and trapping grounds. It had been harvested out years before, but they hoped now that no one had been poaching on it and that there had been enough time for it to be replenished. Enough game for them to live. Nootahweh believed in his heart that this self-imposed exile would not last long, that this foolish policy was unnecessary and could not be maintained. Things would settle down and his wife's resolve would weaken and she would see that learning was a good thing and there was much that white people could teach them. The two peoples needed each other and after all, what was to be gained in a fruitless effort to make Indians stop being Indians?

Mecowatchshish loved their little waskahekun. He had been born in the second difficult winter of their self-imposed seclusion and except for a swift journey to Moose Factory the following summer to have him baptized (Neikahweh could give up many things but not the merciful protection of The Lord), the simple log structure was all he had ever known in his short life. They had drawn ever closer to the earth, to the plants and animals, to the entire world around them and after a few seasons had come to be content in their new lives. After the first two winters Nootahweh's cousin and family found they missed having more people around and had gone back north to Fort Albany where his wife had family and his older brother had gone south seeking a wife of his own.

He could not imagine any other kind of house. In summer he would help Neikahweh and his brother Wahpistanoshish set up the big tent, which was cooler for sleeping. He knew then that soon the cousins would return with their own tents and stay for part of the summer. Neistes was old enough now to help their father with hunting and fishing. They had a little cast iron stove inside the waskahekun to keep them warm and his first job was to help his mother gather boughs to lay for a floor. He was envious watching his brothers, who got to scamper about on the low roof, replacing what had been blown about by the wind. His parents worked hard providing for their little family, but he and his brothers loved to explore and they didn't mind Nootahweh and Neikahweh being so busy. Sometimes he wondered why his father made no effort to clear the path out to the portage trail and why he went through so much trouble to move the canoe off into the woods and hide it. It was a game he played to only glance at the place where it lay hidden whenever he went to the river with his mother to bring back water in two large buckets she carried on a pole across her shoulders. If you were someone who knew where to look, there was a distinctive black spot near a seam on the bottom of the birch bark canoe and at a certain angle it seemed to be a big, ebony eye peering back. Everything, he knew, had a Manitou, a spirit and this was the spirit of cheman, the canoe sharing its secret with him.

He loved to go to the river, not just to share a furtive glance with cheman in its hiding place, but because of the river itself. It always called out its awesome power as he approached. Long before he could see it, even at the cabin, when it was quiet, and the wind and the muttering trees didn't steal its voice, it could be heard. He would follow behind his father and feel it grow even inside his own body, in his owns bones with each step towards it. Then they would step out of the woods on to the rocks and look down on the white tongue of the river as it poured over a ledge, writhed and frothed in its passage and went roaring through a narrow canyon, flowing north.

One night, as they laid in the darkness on the fresh fragrant bed of spruce boughs he had helped his mother gather, he felt a loneliness growing inside of him and he asked, Why don't we ever travel with our cousins?

It was quiet, only the sound of breathing, though he sensed his parents were awake. Finally his mother said, Someday we will.

Nootahweh sighed and shifted onto his side and there was something unspoken in the midnight calm that frightened Mecowatchshish.

One late December, when the cousins had come to visit and bring supplies like flour and sugar and tea, one of the older girls who had not been there before teased Mecowatchshish with a story about St. Nicholas. Perhaps she meant nothing by it, though he found her to be sullen and aloof and did not like the way her hair had been cropped so short. Maybe she was envious that his parents cared for him and his brothers enough to hide them and live alone away from the reach of the government.

She brought him long striped candy sticks and told him the story of the Baby Chee-Sus. Chee-Sus, she said, was born in a place where they kept the animals even though he was the Son of God and to remember his birth they celebrate Christmas. Mecowatchshish had heard this story before from his mother but then the girl told him about the reindeer and the flying sleigh and presents. She told him how St. Nicholas could turn to smoke and come down your chimney, even if your chimney was only a stovepipe. When he was in your house he would turn back into a man. A Whiteman with a big white beard and long white hair and huge black boots. Then some of the meanness that had been dealt to her at the school came out and she leaned in close and whispered, You must believe in Chee-Sus. You must believe the baby Christ was your saviour and had died for you or St. Nicholas, who was his servant, would not leave any presents. There were no gifts for bad little heathens who didn't believe. Instead, St. Nicholas will scoop you up and put you in the sack and take you away far to the north, far beyond where even the Ushke mayow lived and it is always winter.

It didn't make any sense to him. There had never been presents before, why should it be any different now? He tried not to think of the giant Waymeisteikoshoow and the dead baby. Where they were now, he told himself, even St. Nicholas couldn't find them. Then that night as he lay in the darkness huddled under the blankets and furs, squeezed snugly between his brothers, he heard his cousin's soft murmurings as she talked to Chee-Sus, first in English and then in Cree. Maybe, he worried, Chee-Sus would tell his saint where they were.

The visitors had left the next day and he'd wanted to forget about the whole thing but his mother liked being reminded of the story of Baby Chee-Sus, born in Bethlehem and honoured with many gifts. There were evil men who wanted to hurt Chee-Sus, who were jealous of the great power he would have. He wondered if Chee-Sus too had gone to hide in the bush and sometimes he liked to imagine that his mother had travelled to this place on the back of a donkey with him nestled in her belly. He imagined his father leading them through the bush on a narrow trail. He pretended the little donkey, which he had been told was like a small moose, was afraid of wolves and so had changed itself into cheman and hidden by the trail once they had arrived.

His mother would rub her stomach when she told the story of Mary and Joseph and he could see it held a special meaning for her, but he couldn't put away his fear of Saint Nicholas who could come like smoke into their lodge. Then Neikahweh said to him one day, Mecowatchshish, do you know what day it is tomorrow? Tomorrow is Muk osh a kesh i kaw. The day of the baby Chee-Sus. When she said it, she cupped her own belly, which he had noticed growing bigger as the weeks passed. She never spoke of St. Nicholas but only the baby and the story of the stable and the gifts that had been brought for him. She had been raised as a Christian, gone to church every Sunday in those early years. When they had first come to live in this place, she too had prayed every night before bed. When Mecowatchshish had been born, they had even risked returning to have him baptized just as his siblings had been. She did not feel it right for some of her children to have the protection of God and the Church of England and not all. She had been reassured by news from her husband's cousin that there was now a new minister and he would not recognize them and scold her for not coming to service.

As the seasons had passed and they became more and more comfortable, the Church and the life they had known seemed farther away and less important. She and her husband began to remember more of the stories told by Elders and to make connections in a way they never had before. She wished now she had listened more closely, had better appreciated what there was to learn, though she could tell there were gaps even in the knowledge of her grandparents. Things which had been lost or forsaken. Still, being reminded of Christmas she remembered hearing a poem about the jolly old elf being read aloud once during a celebration at the post. She remembered all the candles and the decorated tree and much singing and it softened her fears a little so that she felt a twinge of nostalgia for this former life.

A sound woke Mecowatchshish that night and he was afraid. He lay there very still next to his mother and tried to listen between the breathing of his parents for any sound in the darkness. He wasn't sure if he had really heard it or if the noise had come from his dreams. He remembered something about a big toboggan and flying deer. He looked towards the little cast iron stove but it cast no glow. Everyone slept warm together under the furs and blankets and the fire had gone out. His father would kindle it again in the morning with the help of Neistes while he and Wahpistanoshish huddled against their mother under the pleasant weight of the covers. It was quiet, not even the wind moved. He didn't want St. Nicholas to come, he didn't want any gifts. He only wanted to be left alone with his family together in their home.

He slipped away from the heat of his mother's body, moving slowly like a hunter, the way his father had shown him to stalk rabbits. He found Neistes's coat first and pulled it on, though it hung to his knees. His moccasins, like everyone's, had been placed near the stove early in the evening and he couldn't creep over his parents to retrieve them, so he went on bare feet across the cold ground. He found what he wanted near the door and slipped out into the moonlit night.

He woke the next morning with his mother shaking him and calling out to his brothers. Come on Awashishuk. There's something wrong with the stove.

Smoke was pouring out of every gap in the firebox and filling the one room lodge quickly. His father was kneeling in front of the heater poking at the inside of it with a stick, one hand covering his eyes against the stinging smoke belching out into his face. His mother was coughing and pulling at him and his brother. He could see his older brother at the bearskin doorway, holding it open. His eyes were stinging and his mother shooed them out gathering up garments as she went. They ducked out under Neistes's arm into the frigid morning air.

Something must be wrong with the chimney, his father said as he stumbled out rubbing his eyes and gasping for air. His mother, standing barefoot in the snow, was quickly pulling Mecowatchshish's clothes onto him, jerking him back and forth, lifting his legs and pulling his arms as she dressed him against the bitter cold.

Where's the bucket woman? I couldn't find the bucket. Do you know where it is? I'll pull the fire out of the stove.

It's inside. Near the door where we always leave it.

No! I looked it wasn't there. Where did you leave it?

Then they noticed Mecowatchshish was crying and pointing up towards the roof. When they looked, they saw the bucket. Upside down and sitting directly on top of the stove pipe.

Chapter Four:

Kah Kah Ge Ow

"It's a messenger," she said.

It was Saturday morning and Joe Pete and Simon were out checking snares they had set for rabbits. Simon had stayed over the night before, as he did on occasion, helping with chores and sleeping on the chesterfield. He felt very close to his cousin even though she was a girl and he was almost two years older and he preferred the quiet of the cabin to his own noisy, hectic house. Aunt Louisa let him stay up late reading as long as he kept the fire stoked in the heater and was careful with the candle.

The cousins had fed themselves bread and blueberry jam before slipping out the door at first light, crossing the trestle and heading northwest along the river and skirting the south-eastern edge of the Park. Technically they were poaching but they had not had much luck on the Arm of late and who would care about a few rabbits anyway. They needed an early start because they hoped to make the matinee at the Regency Theatre, desperate not to miss Chapter Eight of *Tarzan the Fearless*, "The Creeping Terror." First, they would have to sell what they caught in their traps to Mrs. Beck for her boarding house meals. More often than most of the diners preferred, she liked to serve a dish she called hasenpfeffer. Now, with the effects of the Depression insinuating deeper into the north, it had become even more of a mainstay on the menu. It was a secret between the less than fastidious Widow Beck and the two of them that she was not averse to buying the occasional squirrel or weasel for her rabbit stew as long as they arrived already skinned.

During the first part of the long winter months, they had relied on raiding their grandfather's cache of salted whitefish which they sold to the visiting Orientals, as everyone in town called them. These were a small cadre of engineers and train men from Japan, who had crossed the ocean and travelled out from the west coast in the summer of 1932 to gather practical experience and information concerning building and maintaining a railroad in the severe northern woods. A Japanese cook and housekeeper had accompanied them from Vancouver, and Whitey Douglas, who worked in the rail yard, had told them she would buy any fish they had. She would cautiously open the door just enough to inspect the offering and judge its size. After accepting the proffered fish, she would press payment into Joe Pete's palm. There was no negotiation but she would sometimes pause a few seconds to look into the girl's small brown face as she placed the money in her hand. After a few transactions, Joe Pete grew comfortable enough to peer back and be captivated by the perfect jet-black sculpture of the woman's hair, and unfamiliar fragrances wafted out. When their eyes met there seemed to be a kind of homesickness in the woman's gaze, something more like melancholy, as though she was reminded of someone or something. As the door slowly closed on the last wisps of aromatic steam, Joe Pete had often struggled to comprehend the immense distance that stretched between where she stood clutching the warm coins and the west coast and then tried to imagine the expanse of the Pacific separating that shoreline and Japan.

The cousins had felt entitled to a share of the catch having helped that autumn with the hard work of setting the nets, hauling them in, and preserving the fish. For a time, Poppa Sam tolerated these withdrawals. Then one afternoon when they went to pilfer one of the large, salted fish, they found an old padlock on the crooked door to the back shed. They understood this meant that by his accounting they had been paid in full. He preferred to avoid direct confrontation and neither of them had ever been subject to a harsh word or rebuke from their grandfather.

This meant either ice-fishing or supplying rabbits for Mrs. Beck, though both proved much less reliable than the ready store of whitefish. A fresh fish, even a skinny pike, brought better payment but they couldn't always manage their time around this and many people had turned to rabbit and other small game to fill out their food supply, so there was a lot of competition. More than once their snares had been poached.

Now that the season had brought days of wildly fluctuating weather, such endeavors had become even less predictable. For the most part temperatures had been mild and everything pointed to an early spring. The days, preceding the present cold snap, had been above freezing and the previous weekend there had even been an episode of heavy rain. The snow was beaten flat and went from a firm crust in the morning to wet and slushy by afternoon, though still deep in the bush. This was not good for travelling and some of the babiche on Joe Pete's old snowshoes had softened and come loose and needed repair. They tried to travel in the early evening and morning when the crust was firm though still challenging. They were only going to trespass into the Park this one time out of desperation because their snares set close to town were catching nothing.

"A message! A message from who?" Simon asked, peering at her over the top of his glasses.

"From..." She left the rest unsaid, and he could tell from the furtive look she gave him that she didn't think he would understand.

"It's Kah Kah Ge Ow," Joe Pete said.

They were a couple of miles from town, trudging along the trail that followed the north bank of the big river when she spotted it. She was always the first to see things. Only the night before, as he struggled to fall asleep under the quilt on the chesterfield, the old smell of the fire rising from deep in the upholstery, he had determined to be the hawkeye of the trip. He had tossed and turned worrying about what would happen if his father found out they were catching rabbits in the game preserve. Why did he allow her to talk him into these situations? It had made him angry, and he determined that this time he would be the one to shush her and point and she would be left squinting and bobbing her head to locate his discovery. Instead, he had drifted drowsily into a daydream, mixing an episode from *The Hardy Boys*, *The Mystery of Cabin Island*, and the anticipated *Tarzan* serial. The book had been a birthday gift from his father from the week before and he was already halfway through a second reading. He was imagining himself about to swing down out of a sturdy maple, sure and muscular as Buster Crabbe, onto the head of a pirate when his face abruptly ploughed into his cousin's canvas backpack.

She stopped short, her finger thrust towards a silhouette among the trees. Simon peered sheepishly and spotted a wavering shadow through the underbrush, dark wings fluttering weakly against the snow. A small trap had been set in hopes of catching a mink or a marten and the raven had blundered into it trying to snatch the bait, the jaws snapping shut on the bird's legs. One limb had been completely severed, though still pinched in the steel jaws, and the other was mangled but still attached well enough to hold the bird in place.

It began to flop and struggle frantically at their approach, the big black wings beating against the drifts creating contoured designs with vigorous brush strokes. Simon was reminded of how sometimes on cold nights, grouse burrowed down under the snow to lie hidden just under the surface. Occasionally an owl might hear or somehow sense them and a similar pattern would be left on the snow, decorated with feathers, where the taloned hunter ripped the unfortunate bird from its sheltered place in the middle of the night.

"You think it was Baldhead?" Simon asked, puzzled by how she could know it was a Cachagee responsible for the trap. They were second cousins and Baldhead, who was a couple of years older, seemed the most likely suspect. His name was actually James but everyone knew him as Baldhead because when he was in Grade Three the teachers at the Indian School had shaved his head with a straight razor after a second infestation of head lice during a persistent outbreak. Simon smiled remembering how he came home with his toque pulled down to his eyebrows, covering his exposed cranium. It didn't take long for the kids in town to figure out that he was trying to hide something and soon a small mob was pursuing him determined to pull off the hat. Laughter bounced from one cluster of people to another as older boys chased him down the laneways, street to street, James ran clutching the toque with both hands and pulling it down over his ears. He was slight and he darted in and out of knots of bystanders like a rabbit weaving through the brush hunted by howling dogs. Girls pointed and boys stood, hands in pockets, yelling encouragement to those that chased him. No one interfered at first, it was too entertaining to watch little James as he desperately eluded them dodging and ducking through the scattered throng of shouting spectators leaping over low picket fences and across yards. Then a hand flicked out as he went past and the woollen hat came off to reveal his naked scalp glistening and steaming in the cool fall air after his frantic efforts. BALDHEAD! A dozen children chanted at once. BALDHEAD! Everyone joined in and because of the fun in remembering that wild pursuit the name stuck for the rest of his life.

"Kah Kah Ge Ow," she repeated slowly. "Raven."

"Oh," he said nodding. Joe Pete had been picking up some Cree from Poppa Sam. It was something that Simon's father strictly forbade. Hank Baer was a stalky, taciturn man and although he loved his Cree wife and his brown-skinned children, as his family grew he had begun to increasingly demand she forgo her "Indian ways." For some reason his intolerance had become even more unyielding after the birth of Simon's twin sisters. It struck Simon at that moment that he had never before thought of his cousin's name as being more than a collection of syllables, as something that actually held meaning.

The raven was desperate to escape, willing to sacrifice its legs to regain the open winter sky, but the steel jaws held it tight. Joe Pete worked her way around behind the bird as it swivelled its head trying to keep an eye on the two threats before it. Positioning herself to best avoid the dark, ominous beak, she pounced and the raven squawked.

"Open the trap," she yelled as she wrestled the huge black bird to keep it still. "Hurry up."

The boy dove in without thinking, reaching underneath to part the metal jaws, while the raven pecked at his thick moose hide mitts. He acted without question and it only took a second for Joe Pete to pull the bird free of the trap, one leg dangling forlornly while the other was left on the snow like a broken twig. There was some blood but not as much as they had expected. The bird twisted free and tumbled out of the girl's arms, one wing striking Simon's head with surprising force as it fluttered past. He leapt up and his left mitt was pulled from his hand, the narrow end of the thumb snagged in the closed trap.

"I'll do it," he offered, rubbing his bare hand which had been bruised by the beak and looking around for a stick big enough to serve his purpose. All that was needed to end its misery was one solid knock to the bird's brittle skull. He had seen his brothers dispatch numerous snakes, fish, mammals, and birds with whatever blunt instrument they found lying at hand. It wasn't always mercy, but it wasn't always out of cruelty either and he knew that more often than not it was the necessary thing. His brothers would have acted without hesitation and Clarence, the bolder of the two, would probably have wrung its neck by now with his bare hands, blinking against the smoke from a neatly rolled cigarette burning in one corner of his mouth. He felt the chill air on his fist as his fingers closed reflexively. There was something wicked in the look of the bird's obsidian, bead-like eye and curving beak that gave him second thoughts. It seemed unable to move, tilted awkwardly to one side in the snow, mouth open, panting like a spent dog as it watched them intently.

"Do what?" Joe Pete was honestly puzzled.

"You know," he said. "Kill it. Bash its head in." He wanted to sound sure and tough, assert his elder male status, but even in his ears it rang false. "It's only suffering, Joe Pete," he added reasonably.

She gave him a sudden forceful shove and he tumbled back in the snow. "If I wanted to kill it, Simon, I could have done it while it was in the trap."

The raven's deep inscrutable eye stayed fixed on them, though it turned its head periodically as if seeking a better perspective. Simon looked from its thin tongue down to the pinched stump of its missing leg and the twisted wreckage of the other.

"You can't fix this Joe Pete. That can't be healed." He pointed at the miserable little appendage dangling uselessly under the bird.

A sudden gust peppered their faces with snow crystals and yellow tamarack needles forcing them to turn away. The maimed corvid found some strength and struggled to escape, wings rowing futilely across the packed snow, trying to catch the wind. Joe Pete recovered to deftly scoop it up and hug it tightly to her, whispering 'Kah Kah Ge Ow' soothingly over and over again, trying to let the bird know she meant it no harm. Simon knew what his father would say, even if he wasn't a Game Warden. He would be furious at their folly in trying to save this raven. He saw animals in very practical terms. He had been raised on a farm and when he came north had made a living as a hunter and trapper. Still, he was not a man to abide needless suffering and recognized that a quick death was an act of compassion.

"Maybe we could splint it or build a special cage. Give it a wooden one like Peg Leg."

"Joe Pete. Where would we get the stuff for that? It couldn't even sit on a perch." He looked at the bird held in her arms as he spoke. "You know better. You know what's best." He could see the resentment in her narrowed eyes, her body tensing.

"It's not best. There's nothing better about it." It exploded out of her. The raven cawed loudly and struggled in her arms and for a split second they seemed like one thing. She took a deep breath and Simon could see in her posture that she wanted to let him have it, but it was wearisome keeping the raven subdued. All she managed was a long shriek of exasperation and even as her frustration reverberated among the trees the look on her face changed. He knew immediately, his shoulders drooping, with a sick kind of certainty what she was scheming to throw at him.

"What about Patch?" she asked, though it was more recrimination than question.

Patch, the small white mongrel that had been her father's dog, a homely runt nobody wanted who he had saved from the drowning sack. Patch had been there when her father went through the ice and been the last living thing to see him before he disappeared. Then not long after, Patch came down with the distemper that had already killed a few dogs in town. At first they had thought the lethargy and vomiting were from something he'd eaten. But he steadily grew worse, drooling, a thick yellowy discharge running from his nose, twitching while his jaw worked compulsively in what Louisa called the chewing fits. She had seen it before and she knew it would not end well. Patch lay in his small house and did not come out and it could not be denied.

Hank was away on patrol as Game Warden and Poppa Sam was working his son's trap line for the winter trying to make some money for the family. He would not be back for a few days, so Louisa had turned to her oldest nephew Clarence to put Patch out of his misery. Joe Pete did not trust her cousin though and his callous way with animals and was distraught over this prospect. She did not want her father's faithful companion to suffer any more than was necessary. When she made this known to Simon he had volunteered thinking it would ease her worries and at the same time prove to his father that he could do the manly thing.

They had gently loaded the dog onto the toboggan that Patch had pulled himself onto so many times and set off to a secluded point back on the Arm with the .22 slung over the boy's shoulder. When it had come time to do it though, Simon could not pull the trigger. He sighted down the barrel but his muscles would not work and he began to shake and waver. Joe Pete had suddenly snatched the rifle out of his hands and fired the killing shot.

They stood for a stunned moment, the echo crackling through the cold air, looking down on the forlorn form of Patch in the snow. There had been a brief, spasmodic rigor, paws flexing like a dog running in his dreams, and then the sighing absolute release that signalled death. Simon looked at his cousin but she only gazed down at the dog, her face blank and expressionless. There were no tears. On the way back, pulling the empty sled, she had said, "Tell them you did it." He was not sure if she was protecting him, knowing his father would be displeased at the truth or if she was feeling some kind of shame. Either way, it had become their secret.

The raven croaked out another complaint writhing in her grasp, one jet-black wing slipping free to flail up and graze her face. She dropped the bird surprised by the strength and vehemence of the blow. It flopped down in a heap unable to stand, its wings beating against the snow in a pathetic attempt at flight. She knelt, staring into its black bead-like eye, regained her courage and scooped it in, the beak scraping once against her wrist and drawing blood. She held it to her, a desperate, dishevelled shadow peeled from off the earth and struggled back to her feet. Simon stood helpless and perplexed as she turned away from him, wounded wrist throbbing and with one long, loud groan to muster her remaining strength threw the bird high into the air. She lost her balance and collapsed, splayed out in the trampled snow looking up into the sky as the bird rose like a punctured, lop-sided ball. Tilting first one way, then the other, the ruined leg swinging wildly as the great black wings unfolded and the bird opened above her and began to beat the air. It pulsed up over the treetops, powerful wings pulling it towards the cloud cover then dropping a little to gather itself again. Another lifting, thrashing hard against gravity it ascended, a wounded, wind-torn phantom. The ragged vestige of a nightmare fleeing the daylight.

She sensed Simon standing behind her and knew that he was compelled now to see it through. He had wanted to show his father he could face up to some hard truth about living. A truth meant only for men that she had to be protected from. Uncle Hank would have seen what happened as weakness in his son but that was not the way she saw it and she regretted using his failing over Patch to blackmail him. She saw instead a kindness, like that of her father, who would have been more understanding of this reluctance. A compassion that came out of a reverence for life that she believed was the best in people. She wanted to tell him this, to let him know she admired his empathy for living things and that she was grateful that he had tried to protect her. She just couldn't find the words to tell him or to explain how it troubled her that it had been so easy to pull the trigger.

She had been astonished by the thoughts and emotions that flew through her simultaneously as she stood there, the whole world suddenly white with the sharp report of the gun bouncing hard against the sky. She had convinced herself that it needed to be done but she had not anticipated the distance that had opened when her finger touched the trigger. Nor had she expected the tinge of retribution that throbbed in her heart, as though Patch deserved this end for the betrayal of still being alive when her father was gone. It had seemed like a necessary act, but there were intricacies that went beyond the mercy of it. She felt like a mere observer as they worked in silence to lift the dog's body into an old flour sack, the lifeless head lolling with a trickle of blood seeping from one nostril. Then pushed it into a frozen hollow of earth where a big spruce had been uprooted. It looked too forlorn for Simon lying under the suspended roots and clods of dirt. He took the hatchet he carried on his belt and used it to trim some branches from a nearby cedar then covered the bundle with the limbs.

She felt more emotion now watching the raven fly into the distance, an unexpected sorrow welling up inside her. She had not cried for Patch, even when her mother had wept, but now tears rolled from her eyes. She did not want to turn and let her cousin see her crying or face his indignation over the futile release of the bird. A strange surge of energy pulsed through her, ready to explode with the need to escape, to somehow break out of her life. She began to run, driven by shame and an irresistible urge to follow the mutilated bird.

She took off as fast as she could and it was a few seconds before Simon realized what was happening. She began to sob in her pursuit, eyes and nose running, boots kicking the grainy snow up into the air, following the erratic flight path of the floundering raven as it flew up over the tree line, barely clearing the top branches and out over the frozen river.

She wept remembering the awful night when her father had

gone through the ice and disappeared from the world. Uncle Hank had been the one to bring them the news, forced to carry poor faithful Patch home over his shoulder because the dog refused to leave the ragged breach. He had burst through the door after tying the dog to his little house, carrying Sandy's broken axe, unable to speak, his eyes welling up at the sight of them while Patch barked wildly and threw himself against the night at the end of his chain.

Clarence had actually been the one to first stumble on the accident. Half-heartedly out hunting rabbits he had come across the dog on his way home late that afternoon when it was already growing dark. He had gotten close enough to see the ragged ring of thin ice and hear the muffled sound of water flowing underneath. With daylight fading swiftly from the December woods and Patch whining, fixed intently on where the river gurgled up into the frigid air it had made the hair on the back of his neck stand up. He raced to find his father in his office and blurt out his discovery and they had hurried back together. Along the way they had run into Monk Little, whose balding head had a natural tonsure since he'd returned from the war, heading home from his shift at the mill. Monk had been a stretcher-bearer, well-trained in first aid, in the same company as Sandy and Hank and he quickly agreed to join them.

Joe Pete and her mother stared up from the table where they sat just about to eat. Hank stood mute, his face pale, huffing like a locomotive in the dark train yard, each deep, rasping breath filling the whole space.

"What's wrong with Patch," Louisa had asked starting to stand, her voice betraying the fear trembling inside her.

Hank stared at Louisa, their eyes locking as he shuffled forward and let the cold steel head drop on the table between them. Mother and daughter started at the harsh thud and Hank reached as if to take it back and set it down more gently. It lay on the tablecloth, a mute and indisputable witness and Joe Pete saw the awful change in her mother's face.

"Lou..." He rested his index finger on the splintered haft. "Louisa...," he paused and then sighed heavily. "Monk's gone to town to gather some men to search..." He could not think of how best to put it.

Louisa's legs gave out and she sat back heavily.

"Where?" It was a soft exhalation.

"Along the river. They..."

"Where?" the same breathy imploring, her voice rising.

"At the rapids. Louisa, he's gone through at the rapids."

She remembered the crimson on her uncle's cheeks, how wet his eyes were and she had known it wasn't just the bitter wind. She knew as well as anyone that if her father had crawled from that hole Patch would have gone with him, not stayed on the river. She had snatched up the icy ruined axe from under Hank's trembling touch and fled to her room upstairs, stumbling on the steep steps. She refused to release the frigid dead weight, held it tightly against her chest in her crossed arms, though her hands ached and she bruised her shins against the rough stairs. She threw herself on her cot and heard her mother moaning as Hank explained what he had found.

"No," Louisa had cried out, half plea and half denial bolting from the table to grab her coat and rush out the door. Hank reached out to hold her back and she went limp in his arms.

"Stay with Alison. I sent Clarence to get Gina and she's coming over. Just stay here."

The rough implement grew warm and numbness spread through Joe Pete's fingers and arms into her chest. She felt the urge to rush out to call for him. If she looked, she thought, he would have to be there. But in the next moment an enervating weakness seeped into every fibre of her being and she was unable to lift the terrible weight of her body. She lay on her stomach resting her forehead against the chilled metal, squeezing her eyes shut and it was as if she was there somehow, at the jagged edge of that breach, under the cold eye of the moon. There was nothing but the night and a ring of deeper darkness at her feet and her lips began to move in a whispered appeal, begging for it all to be a nightmare. "Please," she said. "Please, Daddy." All her desire, her need for things to be different pressed into that one plea. Refusing to let him slip away, demanding that he hold on to life the way he had when he was wounded in the war, when it was the earth that had tried to claim him. She pressed against the steel head, attempting by sheer will to keep it from being so, waiting for it to disappear so she could wake, face buried in the comfort of her pillow, from the terrible dream. As if she could petition the day to turn back a few hours and the river spit him out, wet and gasping but alive. Or back even farther so that the ice would heal itself and Patch would simply pull the toboggan a few steps to the left or right passing by the treacherous weakness that had swallowed up her life.

She begged for God to yield him up, somehow miraculously alive downstream having survived the ice and the cold and the relentless black water. At one point she heard the familiar sound of the loaded toboggan being pulled over the snow and she sat up filled with hope and peered through the frosted window. It was only Clarence dragging it home, bearing the moose quarter her father had been bringing to them. In the days that followed, no one thought to look for the rest of the carcass and by then they knew the wolves had had it. They could never bring themselves to deal with the meat and Poppa Sam had given it away. All the rest of that night she rocked on her bed and petitioned for him to return, hardly noticing when her mother climbed the steep ladder stairs to curl up beside her, weeping and muttering her own prayers.

She kept the axe head with its short stub of broken handle under her bed for weeks, pulling it out every night before sleep to run her fingers over its keen edge and the splintered throat of the handle her father had carved. It was indisputable evidence of him, a symbol of his strength and self-sufficiency. She had often seen it employed to split firewood or cut poles for the tent or drive in a stake to set a trap. It was an indispensable tool for a man who made his living in the bush and she had watched him wield it with skill and confidence. Now it was an extension of him, a talisman connecting them, the last earthly thing to have known the touch of his hand.

She clung fervently to a kind of waking dream that had coalesced in her mind during the memorial service as she knelt, clinging to the back of the pew in front of her. A party of men from town had searched for ten days near the breach in the river ice, working a little farther north each day, but had found nothing. No evidence to suggest that he might have pulled himself from that hole and made it to shelter anywhere. The temperature had stayed very cold, hitting below minus twenty on a few nights. Even an experienced woodsmen would have found it hard to survive, wet, presumably injured and without provisions. They had stretched hope as far as it would go. There was no body to bury, nothing to which she might say good-bye. He was simply gone and there seemed to be no surrogate object to shrink the horrible emptiness down to a size she could apprehend. No corpse, no casket, no husk of any description to contain her immense loss. The sombre crowd of faces, the vaulted space of the church, the black fear squeezing through the vessels of her heart had left her in an altered state. Floating in place, head resting, cushioned against her hands, her face hidden by her long, black, neatly brushed hair. She heard the hymns and tried to listen to the words of the minister to draw some comfort from the sacrament, but the words held little meaning for her. When the minister asked the gathered to pray for her father's return she saw him alive and well, resurrected and stepping through the door, easing his pack from his back as she ran to leap into his arms. The sanctuary was full of warm light, sun streaming through the stained-glass panes and the soothing drone of the congregation repeating prayers lead by the sure strong voice of the minister. He spoke to reassure them all, family and friends, that whatever he may have suffered he was with Jesus now. Then she saw her father, arms splayed wide like the saviour on the altar, lifeless under the cold, relentless flow of the river. She tried to summon back the other image of him to be with her in the church but saw only fleeting shapes and sentiment, spectral flashes from her life. A blurred, disjointed vision of the past, fragments of other hours strobing behind her eyes. She seemed to lose her place, to be somewhere else without being anywhere, spiralling down into an insular dark. Then in a burst of light another apparition of him, on his way home, Patch pulling the toboggan with the meat on it, their heads down as they trudged along the river. She gasped when the ice split and dropped suddenly away and he and the dog fell through, plunging down under the water, his heavy pack pulling him deep. He came back up working his shoulders out of the straps, thrashing on the surface for a few long seconds as he worked the axe free. First heaving the scrambling dog up on solid ice and then swinging the axe to bite into the frozen surface and provide purchase to haul himself out. The angle though isn't right; the lower corner of the blade digs into the ice but the handle hits the edge and snaps. She sees him holding on against the insistent current that is sweeping him under, heavy in his drenched winter clothes, the broken handle clutched in his numb hand. The bright sphere of light that holds her vision begins to shrink and fill with black until there is nothing but a small perfect circle of open water and her father's face and then only stars in a dark portal of reflected night, blinking as if already adding this story to innumerable others held in their ancient memory.

It was only then that she started to cry, the stoic inertia that had suffused her body since clutching the frigid axe head leaving her and even this felt like loss. There was a rush of heat through her chest and arms and out through her fingers and she lost her grip on the polished curve of the pew. It seemed she was losing the only remnant of that bitter night, the final cold comfort of her father and it struck deep to the core of her being. His disappearance through the shimmering, liquid opening replayed in her mind's eye, as though watching him dissolve in the cold reflected light of the moon. She slid from her seat and sank to the floor convulsed by a deepening sorrow. Her mouth opened wide as though gulping for air and throughout the church women turned away from her wailing as she cried out for him, their hearts pierced through, though she would not remember making any sound. Only looking up into Poppa Sam's face as the weight of his hand pressed over her mouth.

She often welcomed the serrated anguish of this dream, conjuring it as she nestled under the covers in her small cot in the cabin on Indian Arm. She wanted the hurt. She wanted the pain over and over in the still hours of early morning, that tender time when she so often would wake to the sound of him in the kitchen below trying to be quiet as he stoked the fire and gathered his things, carefully pushing them down into his green canvas pack. Then, the lighter footsteps of her mother moving without a word or sigh to the stove to begin making his breakfast, her hand touching his shoulder or his hair as she walked by. She had peeked down from her loft to be reassured by these rituals. She liked to lie in the warmth of her bed, while these hushed acts of love played out and the day began in its familiar unassuming way. It was a comfort, a reminder to her that the things lost in the fire when the big house had burned down were not really the things that mattered.

Her father would gather up his pack and push the door open and Patch would pull himself out of his straw-lined house, stretching and shaking the cold night off his back. She would hear him talking to the dog, greeting him and fitting the hand-made harness around him while she raised herself up on one elbow and stretched to peer through the frost-etched window, watching till they were gone from sight. She remembered the last time, how small they looked trudging down to the frozen river under the winter sky. The stars still bright in that darkness just before dawn, her father on snowshoes carrying the axe in his right-hand and the white dog pulling the toboggan as they headed off to the bush.

In that fraction of a second between the trigger being pulled and the echo of the shot fading, pulling Patch away through a narrow tunnel of noise and scattered light she saw a thin sliver of hope. There had to be a reason for Patch getting sick, for the sudden strength that made her sure and steady and merciful. As her father would have been. As if he was there with her. So much could not be taken from her at once. First death was Patch still and bleeding in the snow. What had happened to her father was something else. Something much less certain.

Simon followed her tracks into a stand of jack pine, barrelling through with his arms raised to protect his face, and caught up with her on the exposed bank. They faced a white wide open plain marked by long curving lines and jagged ridges where the wind had sculpted the surface. Joe Pete pointed to something in the distance, a dark smudge low against the overcast sky. It seemed headed for Casey Island, a narrow, rocky hump which split the river just before it narrowed and swung into an elongated S as it meandered north. A funny, hollow croak that sounded almost like a query echoed against the flat silence. Then it faltered, deforming into an amorphous bundle that plunged down out of the sky to disappear below the trees.

Simon looked at his cousin puzzled by her faraway look and

single tear rolling down one cheek as she stood watching the speck of the raven.

"I shouldn't have done it, Simon." She wiped her face with the sleeve of her jacket. "But I didn't want to see it die. It was beautiful and I wanted it to fly again. I wanted to see it in the sky because I thought it had something to tell me. I thought somehow it would get better or change. Become something else."

He had a vague understanding of why she felt this way. It had something to do with the sorrow gnawing at her heart over the last three months and the stories told by Poppa Sam. The weird superstitious mythology he wasn't permitted to even hear. "Your stories are in the Bible and in your schoolbooks," his father would say. More and more he noticed Joe Pete invoking these old legends, making them part of their adventures, trying to see beyond the daylight world. A world that held no hope of ever seeing her father again.

"Joe Pete, what could a raven tell you? How could it change?"

She ignored his questions, remaining focused on the island that lay across the treacherous expanse of frozen river.

"We have to find it. We can't leave it to die like that." She paused. "Maybe I'm supposed to follow it. Okemah promised there would be gifts."

Simon threw his hands up in exasperation. "Are you nuts? It's just a raven! A stupid one-legged, half-dead bird. Why would we have to find it? What could it give you? It's probably gone off to die. It's probably lying over there all crumpled up and dead already." He grabbed her shoulders and tried to turn her to face him, terrified that she really meant to cross the river. He yelled in frustration, determined to get through to her, "You know we're not supposed to be on the river now, right? YOU KNOW IT!"

He stared in disbelief. Only minutes before he had offered to end the raven's misery and she had refused to allow it. Did she really expect him to cross the rotting ice to the island with her now and risk their lives for a bird?

"What is wrong with you, Alison? The current picks up around the island. The rapids are just beyond there and you've got Kokum Creek flowing in right there. That's always one of the first places the ice starts to go. We're close to where..." He stopped himself from finishing the sentence. He knew he had entered a territory as treacherous and uncertain as the frozen river.

"To where my father..." A moment's hesitation. "...went through? Is that what you meant to say, Simon? You think I don't know that? Why would the raven fly here, Simon? Why?" Her eyes had narrowed and her face was pinched into a tenacious look Simon knew all too well. She pulled herself forcefully from his grip and set off across the ice without looking back.

He yelled after her. "It's probably already dead," but she just kept going, leaving him muttering on the bank in frustration. He found it perpetually irksome that she always seemed to know, in a second, her course of action. Watching her pace obstinately, fearlessly, in a beeline for the island, he could not deny the grudging admiration he had for this stubborn decisiveness and he felt there was no alternative but to follow.

The moment he stepped onto the frozen river the day itself seemed to slow to a glacial pace. He felt the weight of each second in every step farther out, as though sensing the water deepening through the soles of his boots. It occurred to him that this in itself would split the ice. The impudence of the two of them crossing on such a foolhardy errand was more than the world could bear. After all that had transpired it was becoming clearer to Simon, with every inch away from solid ground, that Joe Pete must be made to fully accept her father's death. She had to abandon the improbable, desperate hope that he might appear, like some shape-shifting spirit from one of their grandfather's tales. Or like Jesus. In Sunday School they were preparing for the annual lessons of Easter and he had seen how intently she had listened to the story of the Resurrection. The angels rolling away of the stone. It occurred to him just then that angels were kind of shapeshifters like the manitous they talked about. He paused for a second fearing that this blasphemy might send a crackling spider web of splitting ice out from under his feet.

He had endured long difficult hours with her and his aunt as they mourned, while outside tree limbs popped in the frigid, black stillness of winter. He had watched helplessly time and again her face abruptly go blank after some memory of her father had been induced, often by something he had said and it pained him to know he had been the cause. After the funeral and the sombre meals with his family, after listening to his own father, drunk on whiskey, curse and pound the table with his fist and pace the kitchen with sorrow. After all that, she risks their lives on the idea that a crippled, hapless raven might offer some clue or message from her father.

"Where has he been waiting then?" he said aloud as he followed her. "Up in a tree? Under the snow like a partridge? Still under the ice, holding his breath for months, waiting for spring so he can pop up down by the Government dock?"

She turned her head a bit and he averted his eyes, afraid she'd heard him. What could she be thinking he wondered? What fanciful ideas had Poppa Sam put in her head? Perhaps this was what his father was afraid of after all, what made him so impatient with what he called Indian foolishness. Maybe he was right in discouraging any notion of this tradition in his family. "Superstition and fantastical nonsense," he muttered, mimicking his father's deep voice, "left over from a bygone era."

He tried to keep his eyes locked on his boots, puzzling over exactly what an era was and counting out each stride until the numbers began to take on their own weight. He noticed slush creeping into Joe Pete's tracks, water seeping up through a crack somewhere under the snow and the cold fear began to percolate down his vertebrae and drip into the hollow emptiness of his stomach. He thought of the coming weeks, of how the river would open and swell and people living along the banks would watch nervously as the turbid water inched up the bank. As the days warmed and the snow melted the drifts would shrink while the long, dark nights of the past season became liquid. The river would insinuate itself further into the low areas, filling hollows and depressions it had not visited for months. After the crest and a few dry warm days, the water would begin to subside and clear as the waking earth softened and the budding trees regained their thirst. Summer, he knew, always tamed the river, mollified it and swept away its morose nature, though it still could be dangerous. His older brothers, brash and audacious at their best, would go back to plunging in from the CPR bridge, wet limbs glistening in the bright sun as they clambered up the rough, wooden trestle to hurl themselves, bellowing down towards the deep cool centre.

He smiled reminiscing over hot July days when he and Joe Pete would make their way to the narrows, rambling along the hard packed path that paralleled the river, stepping over the bare rocks and roots and ducking under low hanging limbs and windfall. Stopping here and there to wade in where the gravel bottom was exposed to retrieve a few smooth stones and skip them across the water. They would swim in the swift current below the rapids, struggling upstream as far as they could before surrendering to let the rushing water sweep them back to a sandbar where they could lie in the sun until the persistent deer flies drove them back in the water. He marvelled at this change, from hidden, brooding force, gathering its rushing power to a welcoming coolness meandering through a lush green world.

He could not hold this reverie, and his face hardened again into its grim aspect around the certainty that at any moment he would plunge down under the deceitful ice, into the darkness to rest with his uncle's bloated, horrible corpse. He shook his head, repulsed by his own imagination and bumped one padded fist against his forehead trying to knock the terrible image out from behind his eyes. He was ashamed to look up and see Joe Pete, far ahead, trudging forward with absolute conviction, unaware of such morbid thoughts. He wondered if he could ever go in the water again, convinced, despite whatever unrealistic denials his cousin might possess, that her father's body lay decaying somewhere beneath the rippling surface. He saw himself on some future summer's day, slipping down under the sun dappled water, something brushing against him as he peered towards the murky bottom...

He wanted to call for her to wait up but the sound caught in his throat. He saw she had reached the island, wading through the heavy snow collected on its windward edge. He ran to catch up and became possessed by the feeling something was pursuing him. A crack in the ice or some malevolent spirit sprung from one of their grandfather's stories or his own father furious over their bad judgement. The faster he ran the more the fear grew and the faster he went until he was flying across the ice, croaking out for her to wait, desperate to reach solid land.

Joe Pete finally stopped, sinking down to one knee, her chest heaving with the effort it had taken to cross the river and clamber up through the heavy snow along the bank.

"We can't just leave it," she huffed and then collapsed onto her back staring up at the scattered clouds scudding across the sombre sky. Simon didn't hear her implication over his own heavy breathing and the resentment he felt over being left behind. He slowed to a plod, relieved to be off the river, his fear of crashing through the ice abating. His cousin was barely visible to him on top of the low embankment, nothing more than a thick shadow in the snow under the tell-tale wisps of her exhaled breath.

She was imagining how she might look to the raven, if he circled by overhead, trapped in the sky by his useless legs, a dark human figure splayed out below. She closed her eyes and surrendered to the feeling of deflating into the soft cold cushion of snow, as if she might sink down, through the crust, to the congealed ground, melting on through, past the burrowing tenacious roots and the geologic patience of stones. Flowing out into the lightless unending pilgrimage of the river, becoming liquid herself, dissolving in the relentless involution of water. Becoming something else. Anything. What would it be like to be a shape-shifter? To pull the black ink of the hidden river into another form. Wings and feathers and hollowed bone somehow swimming up into the sky. Metamorphosing into Kah Kah Ge Ow, riding the wind and looking down upon the winding white convolutions of the river. All the little creeks feeding in like capillaries, weaving through the undulating land. Searching the taciturn anatomy of the earth for some sign of her father.

"What the hell are you doing? Making snow angels?"

Simon dropped down beside her and she started at the sensation of suddenly coming back into herself. There on the edge of the island, arms and legs moving in her dream flight, snow melting in an icy trickle under her collar. She felt heavy now, pinned to the earth and on the verge of surrender. She listened to her cousin panting, the remnants of a recent cold rasping in his lungs. If he demands we turn back now, she thought to herself, then we'll go. She waited while he lay recovering beside her, preparing to concede to his sensible advice, unable to resist the gravity her life had assumed.

"You swore." She turned to look at him flat on his back, panting and the lenses of his glasses fogged an opaque white.

"What?"

"You swore and you never swear. You said you hate swearing?"

"Hooligans swear," he gasped. He'd heard this in Sunday school and had immediately thought of his brothers and other bullies in town and knew that it was true.

A sound from somewhere on the island caught her ear and surged through her body and she felt instantly revived. Her back straightened, her head rose and she snatched off the woollen scarf that had been wrapped around her head.

"Listen. Do you hear it?" There was a faint pathetic croak off in the distance. She leapt up and began to lope ahead.

Simon sat up beside her spread-eagled impression in the snow, pulling off his hat and relishing the cold air in his sopping hair, the heat of the day's exertions steaming off him, and rubbing his glasses clear with his thumb.

"Joe Pete," he yelled after her, petitioning for reason.

She was not listening to him but strained to catch any muffled squawk from the injured bird certain that it was more than a raven that beckoned her. Why else would they have discovered it under such peculiar circumstances? Why else would it lead her to this particular place? She pushed her way ahead through the trees ignoring the branches that snagged on her clothes and scraped along her face. The snow was softer now, the sun had appeared periodically between the dissipating clouds and the temperature had risen into the afternoon. Her boots sank even deeper and she was post-holing down as far as her knees.

Simon, stepping into her footprints, began to gain on her, the muscles in his thighs burning. He looked towards the sun and saw it high above the treetops to the west. They had originally planned to be back at the cabin for lunch time, they had not set out to travel this far and he was getting very hungry. He scooped a handful of snow up into his mouth to soothe his burning throat. If they didn't start back soon twilight would be upon them before they were home sucking away whatever warmth the day had mustered and leaving them in darkness.

Joe Pete stopped abruptly clutching at his sleeve and pulling him off balance so that he pitched forward onto all fours in the snow. His arms sank deeply into the drifts, his spectacles flying off his face and he flailed about helplessly for a few moments grunting like a snared rabbit as he tried to find some purchase

"What is wrong with you?" he shouted, rolling to one side to get his legs underneath him.

She nodded towards a misshapen stump. "I saw The Old Woman there."

"What old woman?"

"The Old Woman. The one Poppa Sam told us about." Somewhere close by two tree limbs were rubbing together in the wind and creating a low mournful sob. She leaned in close speaking in a harsh, impatient whisper, "The one that went crazy! Remember? Back in the old days, even before Poppa Sam, he heard the story many times. This woman, something happened, a matchi manitou, a bad spirit," she spoke haltingly, in quick bursts. "She was possessed and people were afraid of her, and some wanted to kill her, but some were afraid it might make things worse." She didn't have all the details but the way her grandfather had told it she understood the implications in an intuitive way, in her bones somehow. She wanted Simon to have that same understanding.

"So they put her on this island instead and for a time, people would see her along the shore, gathering wood or fishing. Some people left food and other things. To keep her happy. keep her on the island. Then they didn't see her anymore but sometimes they heard screaming and howling across the water and people said that now she was like a ghost."

Simon scrambled up onto his feet replacing his glasses retrieved out of the snow. "That wasn't this island. I thought that was some place way up north. Joe Pete it wasn't this island right?"

"Why do you think they call it Old Woman Island?"

"This is Casey Island."

She looked at him as though he were an idiot. "That's not its real name! Poppa Sam told me the real name is Keesayskwao. That means Old Woman. Casey is the white people's name."

He thought that she must be teasing him. Keesayskwao could mean anything as far as he knew and they often spooked each other by claiming to see strange things when they were out together. It was a game they played. They called them Manitous; apparitions that were glimpsed for only a second before they reverted to something more innocuous. One of them would stop suddenly and point out an old stump or a bent tree. "See that. That was a bear. Or, look at that rock; a second ago it was a wolf." Joe Pete was much better at it because she had the advantage of their grandfather's stories which often concerned mischievous, shape-shifting spirits.

"You know what that one is," she would whisper pointing out a jumble of broken limbs, covered in curled leaves, snagged high in some tree top. "That's Paguck. Paguck the flying skeleton man. He's always getting stuck like that when Keewatin, the north wind blows him around. Come out here when its dark, Simon and you'll hear his bones clacking together and see his dead eyes staring down at you. If you got the guts and climb up to free him and help him down he might do you a favour. Look away then look back quick...," she demonstrated her long hair flying across her face. She grabbed his arms at the elbows, staring into his face. "I saw him. Just for a second." Her eyes were wide. "All bony and white." Simon had peered over her shoulder, tensed and apprehensive squinting at the tangle of dead limbs afraid of what might appear.

Paguck had turned into its own game for a time after Joe Pete had found a collection of small bones in a sandy spot along the trail.

"Look," she'd said, gasping and when Simon looked, the hairs on the back of his neck stood up slightly. The white fragments seemed to take on the shape of an arrow pointing down the trail.

"It's him. It's Bone Man and he's left a clue we have to follow."

As usual, before Simon could say anything she was off, bent low looking for more clues. She found them soon enough. Odd footprints that might have been a dog scratching at the ground but might also be the mark of a fleshless foot touching down. Scrapes on trees that she interpreted as blazes. She saw what she wanted to see and looked at the world with an open and magical understanding that intrigued and enticed him. Somehow they ended up at a collapsed cabin, the site of some deserted homestead. They cautiously approached the tilted doorway. It was like a Hardy Boys mystery and their hearts pounded in their chests with each step. It was the power of her imagination that made it so real and it thrilled him.

"I think Paguck wants to tell us a secret," she said breathlessly.

There was movement behind the dilapidated wall, a scurrying and then a loud thump as something fell over. They had clutched each other and screamed before fleeing back to the main trail.

Simon steeled himself to turn his eyes in the direction Joe Pete claimed she had glimpsed the old woman and the syllables of Kee-shay-lo seemed filled with ominous connotations. He forced himself to look, cringing with a foreboding that rippled through him, expecting to behold an ancient lunatic, dressed in rags, bent and reaching for him with long, gnarled fingers. His glasses were wet and smeared from where he had wiped the snow away with his bare fingers and the whole world was blurred and distorted. He squinted to peer through the trees and gasped to see the back of the haggard old witch as she leaned on a crooked stick. He swiped frantically at the damp lenses almost knocking them from his face and when he looked again he saw the bottom of a rotted-out aspen, snapped off in a storm. He exhaled in a long sigh of relief and began to breathe again. The woods seemed unsound and hostile now, shadowed and rustling with spiteful intent. The wind was a chilly belligerence stalking among the naked branches and shaking snow out of the evergreens. The strange soughing of bark rubbing on bark was unrelentingly baleful.

"We should go," Simon said trying not to betray his discomfort.

She looked side to side, listening, but there were only sombre trees and drifting snow to be seen. Something indefinable hovered in the air, in the dull light that filtered through the stark limbs and the stillness that gulped in every sound. She was aware that Simon preferred to believe that the Manitous were only an amusement, a way of provoking fear for a little thrill because his father would perceive such beliefs as nonsense and scold him harshly for it. She knew differently. Poppa Sam had taught her that the world was a much more complicated place and you had to be open to it.

"Prob'ly it just flew down low and kept going." Simon said hopefully as if reading her mind. "I bet it didn't even land on the island."

"It was falling, Simon. It wanted us to come here."

Before he could ask what a raven could possibly want with them an odd noise emanated out of the distance. A soft plaintive moan from somewhere off towards the eastern side of the island. The line of sight was blocked by a low swelling in the landscape and a tangled stand of spruce and mixed pine that grew on its slight slope. It was difficult to gauge from how far away the sound had come but the island was not very large. Simon glanced reflexively towards the contorted stump to be sure that it had retained its innocuous shape then hurried after Joe Pete, who was already breaking trail up the hillside.

The wind was raw on top of the rise, pulling at their clothes as they squinted down through the trees. They could make out the blanched levelness of the river through the gaps. A nearby birch was adorned with a long scroll of bark hanging from its trunk that twisted and rasped with the breeze. Joe Pete thought she could make out what appeared to be some sort of unnatural structure standing in a small clearing down near the shoreline.

Simon called out a timorous "Hey" in half-hearted greeting as they approached the rough glade, thinking it best to alert whoever might be there of their presence and avoid any surprises.

Joe Pete shushed him with an elbow to the mid-section. She was listening intently trying to hear what was there under the wind. He heard it too, though it was barely audible, unidentifiable, a kind of moan or whimper that stirred the hair on the back of his neck.

"Joe Pete, I don't like this..."

She hushed him again, threatening another blow and then pointed. They were close enough now to see the black ring of a recent fire pit and beyond it a partly collapsed canvas tent. There were no signs of life, no smoke or movement and the tent didn't appear to be in any kind of usable state.

They moved in warily, recalling tales of trappers who'd lost their sanity on the line. Bushed, people called it, when loneliness and isolation drove some to act in strange and dangerous ways. Sometimes taking their own lives. Sometimes murdering friends or partners or other luckless trappers in a fit of paranoid madness. Some who merely vanished into the woods, swallowed up by their own insanity, by an evil created in their tortured minds. This camp was surely too close to town for something of that nature to occur it seemed to Joe Pete. It would have been easy enough to have walked to town and back in a single day. Train whistles could still be heard and earlier, out on the river listening for a faint utterance from the crippled bird, she thought she had even heard a woman singing. Something soft and soothing, familiar but elusive. She looked to Simon but he was a few yards behind complaining to his boots again as he trudged along. The harder she tried to hear the fainter it grew until she wasn't sure there was any sound at all, nothing more than an echo in her own head, perhaps a frail memento of the past flitting about her brain. Just the kind of trickery you could expect from spirits and shapeshifters.

They stopped on the very edge of the camp for a lengthy and cautious appraisal. The dingy tent was tucked in among a stand of alders and the brush had been cleared so as to leave a dense wall of trees and limbs along the side facing the river. Perhaps it was only meant as a windbreak, but it also served to hide the camp from anyone on the river. It was leaning forward so that the front end of the ridge pole was almost touching the ground. The top section of stove pipe seemed to have been jerked loose and was lying in the snow beside the dirty canvas in a lopsided halo of soot and blackened snow. They stood in front of the tent afraid of what might lay inside, certain that there could be nothing living. There was the faint familiar odour of decay in the chill air.

Joe Pete reached to wrap a hand around the rough pole and started to pull, tensing as the triangle of filthy canvas began to lift, ready to turn and run. It only came up a couple of feet before she met resistance. She adjusted her grasp and using both hands tugged hard as Simon took a step backwards. The canvas rippled taut but did not rise any further. The front flaps of the door were half-buried and frozen into the snow drift. She let go of the wooden support with a sense of relief.

Simon shrugged. "Just a dirty old tent somebody left behind. Some cheechakos packed it in, I guess." There were many strangers and transients these days passing through town looking to scrounge a living however they could. Living hand to mouth, desperate for any kind of work. Sometimes they would show up at the door asking if there was a chore they might do for a meal or a little money. Most of these men could be found in the makeshift camps near the tracks on the edge of town. Joe Pete and Simon and every other kid in town had been warned to stay away from strangers and bums, though when one showed up on the doorstep Simon's mother would often show them some little kindness even if it was only a piece of bannock and a cup of tea.

His father did not have the same patient attitude towards these men. He had been forced to deal with growing incidents of illegal trapping and poaching. Often from people in town but it was much harder to police your friends and neighbors who were just trying to get by. Instead, he directed his frustrations towards those he saw as criminal interlopers who only came north thinking they could make quick money in fur or live off the land through the hard times. He continually admonished his wife for her soft-hearted ways but there was something in her that could not bear seeing someone going hungry.

Only last week a man had shown up at their door late on a bitter afternoon underdressed for the weather, cold and asking to work for food. Simon had just arrived home from school and was at the kitchen table doing his homework. His mother was baking bread and it could even be that the tramp had been drawn by the smell as he walked past. There were days when every available surface in the kitchen would be covered by some kind of baking. Fresh loaves of bread and buns, pies and Johnny cake would all be laid out to cool. It was the smell of home to him. The moist, warm scent of his mother's love. They lived close enough to the tracks that on certain nights when the wind was blowing right the men could be heard around their fire.

Curious, Simon had followed his mother to the door and tried to peek around her for a look at the stranger. The man was standing in the windowless mud porch, an unheated annex where they kicked off their boots and kept the preserves. His expression betrayed some bemusement over his mother's appearance and after a brief pause asked if the lady of the house were in.

"I'm the lady," his mother affirmed shyly.

"Pardon me," the man said, though Simon thought he detected a note of sarcasm in his tone. He heard him ask his mother if there was some small task he could do in exchange for a bit of bread and a glass of milk. She paused for a few moments and Simon knew well she was troubled, not only by the prospect of Hank's displeasure if he discovered her generosity, but also over some previous difficulties they'd had with hungry men. He knew as well that she had experienced not having enough to eat in her past and in her years in Residential School and felt great compassion for anyone who was hungry. Anytime she thought Simon or one of his siblings was wasting food or being ungrateful for what was on the table she would let her displeasure be known.

She stood nervously, ready to slam the door shut in a second.

"Split enough to fill the wood barrel." She lifted her chin towards the big wooden drum in the far corner of the porch. "I'll give you bread." She closed the inside door and slid the bolt to lock it without waiting for his answer.

"I shall do, Madam," the hobo shouted through the barrier in exaggerated courtesy.

It was usually Simon's chore to keep it ready with a supply of fuel for the cook stove. He was glad to think that today he would be relieved of that duty but concerned over what his father would say.

His mother was busy making the evening meal. They could hear the man tramping about in the mud room and Simon noticed her pausing to peer out the window over the sink from time to time. He knew she was checking to see if his father was coming up the lane, afraid the tramp would not be done before Hank arrived home.

"Want me to go out and see, Ma?" he asked.

"You do your studies," she said impatiently.

He turned back to his Geography but the tension permeating the warm kitchen was too distracting. She should have just given him the bread, he thought to himself. There was a hard impatient knock at the door and he and his mother started. Simon went to unlock it after a look from his mother and the door swung open immediately.

"What's with the bum by the woodpile?"

It was Clarence and Henry home for supper, kicking their boots off back through the open door and into rough porch.

"Close that door!" She was glad to have her oldest son home

but embarrassed by his disrespectful reference. "That's just a man doin' some work for us."

"You know Pa don't like moochers." Clarence directed his comment at the door.

"He's doing work. Go wash up you two." She raised the large wooden spoon in her hand threateningly. "You got homework?"

"Nope," they answered in unison. Clarence gave the back of Simon's head a playful shove as he went past. Henry followed him sniffing loudly and running a finger under his nose.

"Don't look like he's workin' too hard." he said distractedly, looking at his younger brother. "What's up bookworm? Gettin' outta chores again, eh?" he leaned over the table to examine Simon's carefully drawn map and wiped something greasy off his finger on to it.

"Do as you're told, use hot water, then wake your sisters and bring them down. It'll be supper soon."

"I'm done, Missus," the man called through the door a few minutes later.

His mother was busy at the stove adding spoonfuls of dumpling mixture. She beckoned to Simon and he went to stand next to her.

"Have a peek outside Simon and make sure he did the work," she whispered as they stood enveloped in a cloud of heat and steam.

Reluctantly he opened the heavy door, wishing Clarence would come down and step in. The scruffy looking little man in a ragged jacket gave him a tight smile as he stood kicking his feet together to keep them warm. A cold blast swept over Simon as he glanced down at the hobo's worn inadequate shoes then peeked past him to get a look at the wood barrel in the corner and saw it piled high with freshly split pieces.

The man stared at him with an expectant sort of smirk. "Bring the bread, Sonny and I'll be gone."

He asked the man to wait in the porch and slipped back through the kitchen door, his glasses fogging again.

"He did it, Ma."

"Did he do a good job?"

Simon tilted his head down to peer above his blurred lenses and nodded. His mother slid a plump, fresh loaf out from under the tea towels and handed it to him.

"Give him this and say thanks."

He took the bread to him and said, "Thank you, Sir."

The man grabbed the beak of his cap and said pleasantly, "Oh no, thank you, Laddie." He ruffled the boy's hair, tucked the loaf inside his jacket and slipped out the door.

Simon hadn't even had a chance to sit down when the kitchen door which had just closed behind him swung open. It was Poppa Sam who came over every Wednesday for supper. Gina always felt a pang of sorrow thinking of him alone in his house out on the arm. She smiled from the kitchen, "Come on in Poppa. I made a nice stew for us."

The old man came quietly into the kitchen and sat at the table where his grandson was intently colouring a hand drawn map of Europe. He watched him attentively for a few minutes and Simon used his elbow to cover the ugly smear left by his brother and pretended to be very involved in his studies. There was a certain unease between them and it seemed they never knew how to be with each other. Finally Gina spoke to break the tension, "Simon, tell your grandfather what you're doing."

The boy lifted his head a bit but didn't take his gaze from his workbook, "Geography."

The old man nodded and reached out to lightly touch his grandson's shoulder, "You're smart you to study so hard. Be educated, hey. You don't wanna live like me."

Simon liked the praise but it was too close to his father's constant advice and it still irked him slightly. Poppa Sam moved his finger to Simon's carefully coloured map. The boy looked at the dark brown hand, the thick stubby finger resting on Spain.

Strong and capable, it was everything he wasn't.

"Is this Overseas?"

"Yes. Europe."

"Which one is France?"

Simon pointed to the country, coloured in light blue. The old man lifted his finger from Spain and rested it on the centre of France. "My son Daniel is buried here. Trench Fever they said. He was my oldest boy. His brother's used to call him, Ohomeiseohtastahmeik."

Gina opened her mouth as if to say something and looked nervously towards the door.

"You know what that means? That's Owlface. He always looked too serious."

The door to the back porch slammed and Gina jumped a little and dropped the hot pot lid she had just lifted to stir the stew. It clattered noisily on to the stove top and she adjusted the tea towel protecting her hand to retrieve it. Simon heard his father stamping his boots and involuntarily shifted away from his grandfather as Hank came through the kitchen door.

"Who filled the barrel?" he demanded without greeting them.

His wife couldn't meet his gaze.

"Why do you ask?" she said spooning dumpling batter into the stew pot.

Hank fixed his son with a stern look, "It wasn't you was it, Simon?" It was more of an assertion than a question.

"No Sir," he answered simply, but it felt like he was betraying his mother. There was a long uncomfortable silence.

"Was it Clarence?"

"It was a hobo. He was hungry. He did some work."

"What did he do?"

"Just filled the wood barrel. I just gave him some bread."

He turned and stomped back out through the porch. They could all feel the bitter chill sweeping in through open door. "Come out here," he said. "Both of you."

It was already dark and there was no light in the room except for that spilling in from the single overhead bulb in the kitchen. They could see him standing beside the barrel with the wood stacked high above its rim.

"See..." Gina started.

Hank pushed against the barrel and it tipped easily to one side. Most of the wood spilled off and tumbled on to the unfinished floor. The barrel had been turned upside down and covered with pieces balanced on top.

"How much bread is that worth?" he demanded, his anger barely contained.

She looked at her father ashamed to be so easily tricked. "So I fed a hungry man. Does that make me bad?" she asked defiantly, knowing Sam would understand. They had been a family that had known real hunger.

"No, but it doesn't make you too smart. Can't cheat an honest Indian, is that it? That'll be a good laugh down in the hobo jungle tonight."

Whenever he was frustrated or disappointed with her, he managed to work in some reference to her heritage, though with his children he refused to ever acknowledge it. He knocked the wood barrel over completely. Simon, his face flushed red with embarrassment, walked to the overturned barrel in his sock feet and stood it upright shaking his head as he looked apologetically at his mother.

"Weesaykayjak, I think," Sam said playfully, a wry grin on his face.

There was an outburst of derisive laughter and Simon turned to see Clarence and Henry with their heads stuck through the half-open door chuckling over the incident.

Hank threw his hands in the air. "Where were you two idiots?"

"We was lookin' after the girls upstairs." Henry answered frowning.

Their father snorted at this and, unsure of who he was most displeased with, gave his father-in-law a long hard look the old man didn't turn to confront. Then, shooing the older boys out of the way, he paced passed them and went in.

Simon watched his grandfather and mother exchange a subtle look and it seemed to him that it was his father who was missing something. Some hidden angle of the world.

"I'll fill the barrel Ma," he offered.

His mother nodded her head thankfully and said, "Go put your coat on first."

"I'm okay," he'd answered, slipping into his cold boots hoping to prove something to his grandfather. Then he and the old man began to pick up the chunks of wood scattered about.

"Dad you don't have to..."

He waved her away. "You go look after supper and me and the boy will earn our meal."

Simon remembered how they had worked quietly together in the star lit dark, the glow of the past day still faint above the western horizon. He had carried the wood in from the woodpile while Poppa Sam worked at the chopping block swinging the axe to split a few down to kindling and smaller pieces that would be useful in cooking.

"This is the biscuit wood," he said. "When you need heat quick."

Simon had watched as the blade rose and fell with easy efficiency. He'd already broken two axe handles since the fall and put a good nick in his left shin. Sam neatly split the last slender stick then turned the axe head upside down on the block to lean on the upturned handle. Kneeling on the snowy ground, gathering the wood into a bundle, he had looked up into his grandfather's face and for reasons he didn't fully apprehend wanted to confess to him. To reveal how sometimes he felt like he was a Ghost or a Manitou from the game he played with Joe Pete. That he never felt like he completely belonged, always shifting somewhere in between and that he too was fascinated by the old stories. He wanted to hear them the way his cousin did, not second-hand through her. They frightened him in ways he could not grasp, but so did not knowing them. Like never knowing a part of himself. Just then the inside door opened and his father called out to them.

"Come on in. Supper's on and we're feeding the hungry today."

It sounded somewhat conciliatory and he put his hand on his father-in-law's shoulder as he went past.

"Hope you brought your appetite, Sam."

Chapter Five:

The Killing

There was something disquieting about the deserted, partially collapsed tent but Joe Pete's curiosity had been aroused. The only sound was the loose canvas rippling in the wind and reassured by this she worked her way around to the back where the material had been pulled taut. She opened her coat and slipped her knife out of its rabbit-hide sheathe. Poppa Sam always kept it sharp for her. 'It's a dull blade that cuts you,' he would say, working the whetstone rhythmically across the keen edge. She stuck the point through and ran the knife down the canvas then pulled the edges apart and peered inside.

Snow had blown in before the tent had buckled but other than that there was only a pile of dried out pine boughs, several empty wine bottles, some bits of firewood, and a small cast-iron stove like the one her father had hauled with him in winter.

Simon called for her, a rising note of panic in his voice, and pulling her face out of the crude opening brought a sense of relief. Touching the filthy material left a feeling of contamination. She found him pointing across the clearing to a reddish brown, amorphous lump in the snow. There was an unnaturalness about it and scanning the open ground she spotted other visible mounds and tufts of fur spiralling around on the snow. It seemed that for some reason whoever had occupied the camp had high-tailed it without taking their pelts. They approached the nearest moldering heap and as they drew near the wind lifted the stench from it. Clearly it was more than a stack of hides.

They crept tentatively to the first forlorn heap and found only the skeletal carcass of a medium-sized dog. The eye sockets had been plundered and the long snout was only exposed bone and yellow teeth, the mouth gaping in caricature of a snarl. It was surrounded by a jumbled nest of hair and a tight circle of small paw prints.

"Fox, I think," muttered Joe Pete examining the tracks.

The belly had been opened and emptied of all tender organs and the frozen eviscerated dog, outlined in fur and crystallized flecks of blood, seemed already a part of the earth, as if it had erupted out of the ground. The scuffling and scrabbling of hungry animals tugging at the soft tissues had exposed parts of the chain that had tethered the dog to a nearby tree. Simon was behind her and it sickened him to look at the dead creature.

They moved along the line, relieved the next ravaged corpse was tucked in under a small pine bush, partly covered by drifts and they were spared the gruesome sight. There was a space and Joe Pete found a rope which she pulled up out of the crust. A broken leather collar hung at its end and it seemed perhaps one dog had escaped. The last one though had been severely mauled and both hind legs had been gnawed up to the knee joint. A portion of the tail had been broken off and blown into the brush to lay like a giant woolly caterpillar wrapped around a sapling. Simon felt his gorge rise looking at the mangled limbs. A large leg bone had been snapped in half and the jagged end stood out at an odd angle like a broken arrow. Something had been tearing viciously at the animal. Joe Pete squatted next to the ravaged body and sliding her right hand out of her mitt reached to stroke the forlorn head. It was the smallest of all the dogs, and she guessed from its grizzled chin probably the oldest. She was repulsed by how cold and stiff it was, the fur like bristles on a brush.

"See," she said, "how the chain is stretched out tight."

Simon looked, swallowing hard, at how the loop that held the dog had been yanked up as far as its ears, like something had tried unsuccessfully to drag the dog out of its tether and away by its back end.

"This is strange." Joe Pete was shaking her head. She pointed to the emaciated but largely unscathed body. "It looks like something big tried to haul this one away but..."

A low menacing growl started up and she pulled her hand back, startled. They retreated from the inert dog, Simon shaking his head in disbelief as a few yards beyond the grotesque corpse a grey hunchbacked shadow began to rise up out of the snow. A tremor shook through the apparition and crusted snow fell away to reveal a large salt-and-pepper mongrel struggling to its feet.

"Shh," whispered Joe Pete. "Shh. It's okay. It's okay."

The animal seemed too weak to pull itself to full height and could only manage a kind of half-crouch teetering on its front legs. It bared its teeth and a low rumbling started again only to catch in its throat. The dog swallowed hard and licked its lips reflexively. There was still a semblance of power in its focus and demeanour. A glimmer of havoc in its cold blue eyes. Simon was relieved to see a length of rusted chain hanging from around its neck and disappearing under the snow. He could see a slash of blood from an open wound on its hind end near the tail as though something had started prematurely on the weakened, dying dog.

Joe Pete was down on one knee slipping her arms out of the straps of her backpack. She began creeping forward, keeping low to the ground at the dog's level and speaking to it in soothing tones.

"Joe Pete..." he reached out to grab her boot and pull her back from the snarling, mangy animal.

She jerked her foot free of his hand and tossing her long black hair looked back at him and hissed, "This dog's worn to a nub. He can't hurt me."

"Sure looks like he has a different opinion," he replied sullenly.

She ignored him and inched closer continuing to offer reassurance to the dog in hushed tones, "Okay, Atim. It's okay puppy."

Simon stared at the trembling beast, heard the growl begin again, the menace softened by an undertone of whimpering but still salient. He could see that the dog had been tied, probably by lucky accident, where it had been able to stretch close enough to reach the carcass of the other dog and tear away enough nourishment from the meagre corpse to sustain itself. Driven by desperation, mad with hunger it had stretched out the old chain, the loop around its neck pulling tighter and tighter, until it could bite down on the thin tail of its dead companion and tug it near enough to sink its fangs into a back paw.

Perhaps that explained the condition of the untouched dogs. The scavengers hadn't dared to come too close while it still had strength. Then, both chains stretched to their limits, it was unable to reach any further on the scrawny cadaver. He could see how the restraint had cut into the dog's neck and bloodied the fur around its throat and where the snow was rutted and packed hard, as the animal strained, pacing back and forth. Clawing down to the frigid earth, desperate to pull one more bit of thin sustenance from the snow. Eventually, unable to get anymore from the ravaged carcass it had retreated and curled into the snow for warmth, waiting to die. It was pitiless and cruel and hit him like a blow to the stomach. He could only hope the smaller dog had been thoroughly dead when the other began to feed.

"Alison! Alison don't..." He was again overcome with misgivings he could not articulate.

The dog's hind legs gave out and its back end collapsed heavily onto the ground. It managed another short, deep snarl and then fell onto its side with a whimper, the last of its strength spent. She was close enough now to reach out tentatively as the mongrel watched through narrow brown, inscrutable eyes, the black sinuous border of its upper lip pulling back just enough to expose the tip of a dull yellow fang. She paused with her left hand held above the dog's head, fingers quivering, and Simon could see she was trying to decipher the thin slit of the animal's eye. Then she closed her own and turned her head, half expecting the jaws to suddenly snap down around her wrist as she let the hand drop gently onto the animal's head. The dog, too weak for any other response, shut it eyes and accepted the stroking. Simon exhaled noisily.

Joe Pete lifted the dog's head into her lap gently massaging between its flaccid ears while her cousin stood watching impatiently. They had been there a long time now. The afternoon shadows were stretching across the crusted snow and the sun was plummeting through the treetops.

"See what you can find there." She pointed, directing him towards what was left of the small dog and ignoring his discontent.

"What do you mean?" he asked, afraid of the answer he would receive.

"This dog needs something to eat."

He started to protest, then groaned wearily and went reluctantly to the pile of emaciated flesh and bone. Arguing would only be a further waste of time. He used a stick to poke at the forlorn corpse. Everything seemed frozen and unyielding.

"Use your jackknife," she ordered impatiently. She ran her hand along the big dog's side, appalled to feel every contour of bone down to the protruding hip. Tufts of fur stuck to her hand.

He produced the black-handled knife from his pocket tucked his mittens in his arm pit, clumsily opened out the three-inch blade with cold fingers. He'd watched animals being skinned many times and helped Joe Pete with their snared rabbits but usually she used the blade because she was more skilled and had more practice. He forced the point into the naked belly feeling the urge to vomit and sawed up towards the ribs. A vile smell emanated from the slit and he stood up stumbling backwards, holding his wrist against his mouth. Joe Pete pushed past impatiently taking out her belt knife and slicing a larger opening. Even she gagged as she worked at the opening, prying and hacking with the big blade until the frozen organs spilled out. He knelt beside her, retching as they worked together scraping away what bits of flesh they could, gritting his teeth as the jagged end of one rib scraped across his knuckles. She took what they had managed to collect and tried to feed the animal the thin strips of meat and viscera. The dog seemed too weak to even chew now, worn out by its last feeble act of defiance.

"You're bleeding," Joe Pete said matter-of-factly.

He looked down at the back of his hand and was shocked to see a trickle of blood running across the knuckles to drip into the snow. He'd hardly felt the cut, his hand anesthetized by the chill air. She tenderly took his hand and reaching into her back pocket pulled out a simple white handkerchief, made from a ruined bed sheet. She took hold of his fingers, wound the cloth around his hand and tied it in place, the knot sitting neatly in his palm.

"Don't worry. I only used it once today." She helped to slide his mitt on over the bulge of the makeshift bandage.

"Thanks," he said. It was beginning to throb against the stricture of being jammed in his mitten.

She made her way swiftly to the rear of the collapsed tent, a new tactic already forming in her head. She pulled at the canvas, wrenching the stiff material as wide open as she could, her anger over the cruel treatment of the dogs renewing her strength. She slipped inside and after some grunting and thrashing came out struggling with the small cast iron stove separated from its chimney. She made it only a short distance and fell to her knees, setting the heater down heavily on the snow-covered ground. She looked up at Simon who stood dumbfounded clutching his injured hand.

"Get wood to burn," she barked.

Simon hurried to a low, neat pile of sawed and split logs stacked between two trees near the tent, almost tripping over the grinning carcass of a dog, its eyes sockets picked clean. In the fading light it was even more grotesque, heightening his urgency to be homeward bound.

Joe Pete rummaged through her knapsack and pulled out the billycan they used to make bush tea and retrieved the sheath knife from where it lay next to the butchered canine. She went to the dog and examined the chain around its throat. She could see a raw loop of torn skin under the crude collar from the dog's desperate efforts to survive, twisting and turning its head in torment as it struggled to feed or be free. She held some slack near the dog's abraded neck and with her other hand pulled the length taut so that it snapped up out of the snow to where it was looped around a half-rotted birch, a deep pale groove worn halfway through the punky wood. That effort must have given the dog the extra inches he needed to reach the carcass. A large bolt held the loop closed. She couldn't see how the other end of the chain was fastened, it lay under the dog and she had to rotate the rusted metal links to bring it around. The animal's eyes flickered open, its tongue licking reflexively along its upper lip before it let out a barely audible whimper. She was causing pain but felt compelled to free the dog even though it might be an empty gesture.

There was a simple metal snap hooked through one of the links and she released it letting the chain go slack and fall back into the snow. Easing it out from under the wounded neck she flung the whole length vehemently back against the birch with a hollow thud. The dog flinched slightly at the sound, shifting its head as if checking for the chain and revealing something slender and black that caught her eye.

Hearing the metallic rattle of the chain colliding with the tree,

Simon looked up from the stove where he was nursing the fire he'd dutifully started. A frisson of fear shivered through him and he started to say something in protest but relented. The dog seemed incapable of posing a threat to them now and Joe Pete would not have heeded his warning at any rate. He went back to poking at the fire with a slender stick and muttering under his breath into the flames. Not a complaint but a selfish petition for the animal to expire quickly so they could be free of it, for which he immediately felt contrite. It frustrated him that she would not listen to his advice when he was the older one. Hadn't she noticed that lately he had acted as man of their house? How he often stayed with them on weekends and helped with the outside chores? He had even spent two Saturdays working with Joe Pete, washing floors and windows when she was the one who had been sent to houseclean for Poppa Sam. Didn't she always come to him for help with her homework?

The sun was beginning to set, the temperature plummeting as the shadows deepened quickly around them. They still needed to make their way back across the unpredictable ice and follow the lightless paths through the woods back to their homes. Contemplation of this dreadful prospect was interrupted by the sound of heavy blows.

Joe Pete was using the axe from her pack. She was swinging it now, with both hands, down onto what was left of the ribcage of the gutted dog. There was a loud crack as one split and a chunk of bone and sinew spun out into the gloaming in a crystalline spray of bloody tissue.

Simon threw up his hands and exploded in confused frustration. "Alison! What are you doing? That dog will die. It can't even eat. We can't help it. Let's just get out of here before it's too dark." His voice rose throughout the appeal until he was nearly screaming the last word.

She calmly reached down and held up what she had found for him to see. A single ebony feather.

"What's that?" he asked, though he was sure he knew.

"A feather. From Kah Kah Ge Ow," she responded, as if it were all self-explanatory. She repositioned her grip on the hatchet and swung again as hard as she could. There was a loud snap and a triangular chunk of hide flew off and landed half way between them as bits spattered across her face.

"A crow feather."

"Raven."

"So what?" His exasperation was growing and he had no patience for ridiculous stories.

She let the arm wielding the hatchet drop in mid-swing. "Don't you see? The bird we followed was only a Manitou. It was leading us here. Bringing us to this dog."

"Alison," he implored, emphasizing the use of her given name, hoping to bring her back to the real world. "That's a game, Manitous. Most of the time I don't even see those things. They come out of your head and I just go along." He hung his head. "It's fun. But today I saw you hold a real bird. I saw the blood. It was real and it flew off to die. Don't you see? You couldn't save it and you can't save this sad, stupid dog. It is HOPELESS." The effort exhausted him. He leaned heavily against the trunk of an old yellow poplar his head hanging, close to tears.

A moment of fury flashed through her at this admission but was replaced quickly with compassion. He looked so pathetic propped against the tree. Beaten. She knew she had asked too much of him.

"I'm making marrow soup. He's too weak to eat meat. It's what Daddy did for Goliath." The hatchet came down again and a slab of three partial ribs came loose with a flap of skin. She turned to him. "I saw a cast iron frying pan hanging from a nail on that tree by the tent. Please get it for me and fill it with snow and put it on the stove. Then you better go."

"I can't leave you." It was said in defeat, almost a whisper.

"You should go. I want you to go. Everyone will be worried

now. And ask Oki..." She did not want to provoke him anymore. "...ask Poppa Sam to come with his sled."

"Alison..." They were less best friends and more like relations when he called her that.

"I am going to look after this dog, Simon. I don't know if I can help but I know he needs food. He needs something to live on." She looked into his eyes, releasing him. "You go get help." She spoke with calm assertion as though it was the only sensible plan. As if there was simply no other choice.

Even though much more prudent alternatives were swirling frantically in his mind, he knew she would accept none of them. He reluctantly undertook what had been asked while she continued grunting over the bones, smashing them open. The dog, slightly revived by the smell of raw flesh, had claimed one of the larger pieces that had landed near him and lay with a paw draped over it licking weakly at the exposed marrow.

Simon worked till he had melted enough snow to make half a pan of water and then gathered himself to leave. In a last gesture he picked out two of the best chunks of firewood and placed them carefully on the fire to keep it burning well as he did for them at home. It had grown dark but it was a fairly clear night and a waxing gibbous moon could be seen rising just above the treetops. He watched her collecting up the bits of bone and ragged gobbets of flesh, dropping them into the abandoned frying pan on the stove while the dog tried to follow her every move. He felt duty bound to make one more appeal.

"We could come back first thing in the morning. My father might..."

"Go. Your father will be very angry. he would never let us cross the ice again."

He capitulated without another word. She was busy adding more snow to the pan and using a stick to stir her rough soup. He trudged off following their tracks and found that their path had grown much firmer with the cooling evening. As he departed from what remained of the campsite he remembered where he was and it filled him with doubt and fear as the night closed around him. He didn't want to leave her. In some part because he was worried about her alone there with that starving, half-mad dog but also because he didn't want to make the solitary return trip. He paused at the crest of the knoll where they had first spotted the encampment and looked back. Tongues of flame licked out of the open door on the abandoned stove. The fire was burning fiercely under the pan and he could smell the marrow beginning to cook. Flickering light danced around the rough glade and he could see her half in grim silhouette crouched over the mutilated dog. She was using her knife, hacking into the open chest cavity, pulling out bits to add to her gruel. He watched mesmerized for a few seconds as she worked alone under the winter stars, the undulating flames throwing huge stark shadows around the ruined camp. She pulled something dark and spherical out of the frigid body with her bare hand. It made him think of a story, a fairy tale about a jealous queen and a heart in a box and then the eerie history of the island itself. An involuntary shiver trembled through him accompanied by a resolution to help and get her safely away from the island.

It was a realization of how much he needed her and how out of place he felt in the world. How different he was from his brothers and cousins and his own father. Here he was, once again unable to do what should be done. Afraid to go back, afraid to go on alone. He clenched his fist and hammered it against a nearby tree calling forth all his will to set off for home.

His courage threatened to flag as soon as he stood on the tortuous shoreline facing the level terror of the river. He had thought that crossing in daylight had been his worst nightmare. Now the ice groaned and cracked all around, contracting in the cold, hardening and constricting through subtle changes in pressure and purchase. The deepening night settling down on the cryptic peril of the river. He had only taken a few steps before his foot shattered a thin layer that had formed on top from melt water during the day. Convinced he was plunging through to be swept away under the ice, never to be seen again, he let out a high-pitched, pathetic yelp. Then he realized he was still on the surface, standing in a small puddle and he looked about sheepishly before plodding on, imploring God or one of his angels to lift him, transported instantly home.

He came upon an area that had been purged clean by the wind, the exposed ice smooth and shimmering in the moonlight. It was speckled with fringed white dots like flowers where bubbles had formed in thinner ice and crisscrossed by patterns of cracks and striations. He couldn't keep from imagining his uncle's face frozen there, exposed, dead eyes like the pale frost blossoms, ashen skin fissured and seamed. He shut his eyes and tried to force the tormenting image from his mind. He looked back seeking some sign of Joe Pete's fire, the frayed outline of the island barely visible to him against the contoured horizon of the far bank. He peered intently and his heart skipped a beat. Against the pale drifts, where the island sloped to meet the plain of ice, there was a vaguely human shape standing out on the shoreline. He stood watching for any perceptible motion. A shifting of weight or a raised arm. Perhaps his cousin calling him back or signalling him to wait. Maybe she'd had a change of heart.

The apparition remained utterly motionless and he knew it was not Joe Pete. Nothing human could be so still. He couldn't shake the unnerving sense of being watched. The more he squinted the more ominous its immobility became. Almost predatory, like a lynx gathering itself to bounce on a hare. He thought of the mad woman that had given the island its name and it left him petrified, convinced the old witch was waiting to pursue him the moment he turned away.

Steeling himself, he forced his feet to take a few steps forward then whirled around, blood pounding in his head. Was it in the same place? Was it closer? Bigger? Was there something different? He felt a tingle along the nape of his neck under his collar and it was compelling and paralyzing all at once. He was convinced that if he fled headlong it would give chase, cackling and skimming across the ice to claim him. He was afraid to look away, sure that it was his blurred scrutiny that held her in place. He willed himself to turn and keep going and not to look back even though his ears strained to hear the slightest sound. Was it the ice shifting, the crust collapsing deeper into itself or was it footsteps? A loud snap reverberated out of the darkness behind him and he bolted, his leather-soled boots crunching in staccato bursts on the frozen surface, echoing off the approaching river bank. He was certain now that something malevolent was pursuing him, closing in and a low continuous moan began to emanate from his open mouth.

He came up against the other bank but not where they had crossed. It had been hard for him, with his weak eyes, glasses fogged from his own breathing, to distinguish the exact spot where they had made their way on to the river and he'd lost any sense of it in his headlong flight. The shoreline was a single featureless smudge in his bleary vision. It was steep here and cluttered with fallen trees where the sandy ground had been eroded from underneath them. They jutted out at diverse angles and tangled with the naked underbrush. He looked back over his shoulder, heart pounding, and saw nothing, the island invisible now, the whole horizon only a muted contour between the river and the sky. In the darkness nothing looked familiar and he suspected he had moved too far down river in his crossing. He began to follow the bank back to the north, head swivelling around, every sinuous shadow rippling with potential peril. He blundered his way along over the roots of trees that stuck out like long fingers from the crumbling frozen sand and tripping over dead heads whose perverted shapes plunged down under the ice. He looked back across the river again, once more trying to get his bearings, scanning the wind-swept ice for the wraith that hunted him. He turned and began to scramble up the steep bank frantic to get off the river and find the trail home, fighting for purchase, snapping off dead limbs, his feet sliding down the frangible bank. Then something grabbed his sore outstretched hand and his mouth gaped in pain and terror as he was hauled bodily up into the air. He screamed and felt his knees buckle underneath him.

"Son, you make more noise than a brain-addled moose in the underbrush."

Chapter Six:

Mecowatchshish and Neikahweh

Month by month Mecowatchshish had watched Neikahweh's belly grow and it thrilled him to feel the living thing that moved and kicked against his mother's stretched skin. Striking out so hard, that sometimes he found himself wanting to hit back. His mother always seemed to sense his agitation and she would lay her hand gently across his and soothe him with a gentle smile. In such moments he would feel his entire being there between the warm patience of his mother's touch and the urgent thrust of the life pushing against his palm.

A few days before Nootahweh had slaughtered a sow bear and Mecowatchshish had gasped in surprise when his father pulled two smaller versions of the mother from its opened belly. They slid wetly a short ways across the snow, clouds of steam from the last tender heat of their mother's womb, rising off the small, inert bodies. Forlorn, almost naked, they laid side by side melting temporary graves down into the drifts, drawing close to the frozen earth, to the world they would never know. How had they lived in there? He looked at their short, stubby legs. Imagined them like puppies rolling and wrestling and chasing each other about inside their mother's sumptuous body. Kicking the way the life inside his mother kicked. Couldn't his father make them live? Let them be free? His brothers, who were older and had seen such things before, elbowed each other and snickered when he began to softly weep.

His father touched a hand to his back and when he looked up, laid a finger against his own cheek in a sign that Mecowatchshish knew meant to pay attention and learn. His father arranged the tiny dark bodies neatly beside each other before moving back to dressing the sow. He found the beast's heart and cut two large pieces from it and placed one section in the mouth of each cub.

"Why?" the little boy asked with only a look. His father had already anticipated the question because Mecowatchshish was at an age when everything was why.

"It's what has always been done." An answer he often gave his sons, usually with a look of patient exasperation. There were things he saw done, rituals that his own father and others did in a faithful way but did not or could not explain. Their people had worked and traded with the whites for generations and had long ago adopted their Christian ways. Many of them, as it was in his family, were of mixed blood and had forgotten or abandoned the old ways. When they were in the bush, away from Waymeisteikoshoow they would feel the pull of these half-remembered customs as though something had been abiding for them there, among the trees that ran on forever and the lakes and rivers known only by their ancient names.

Nootahweh had been very lucky to come across the den so close to their camp. They had only meant to go out and check a trap in a nearby beaver pond when their father had caught sight of the merest wisp of steam rising out of a small opening melted through the snow cover. The bear had dug in under a cluster of roots and torn up earth where an immense spruce had been blown over. Mecowatchshish had looked at the stiff crooked roots that seemed to writhe up into the sky, clots of dirt and naked white boulders suspended between them, the great bulk of it crowned with snow. It was like something caught in the midst of pulling itself from the ground or a monstrous bug that had died burrowing back to its homeland. There was something baleful and unfinished in its tilted, lop-sided attitude, broken roots fanned out against the sky like fat snakes slithering up into the air. The round speckled stones seemed like cold, dead eggs, ripped from the nest and trapped between these rigid contortions. He knew it was only wood and rock and earth ripped up out of the ground by the immense weight of the falling trunk but there was something in it which he didn't fully understand and that filled him with alarm. He felt its gnarled presence behind him, the hairs on the nape of his neck tingling as he helped Neistes and Wahpistanoshish load the meat wrapped in the bears hide onto the toboggan. He was afraid to look back. Fearfully he would see it shudder and begin to move. Angry they had killed his friend and her unborn children. He was very relieved when they started for home and was soon anticipating with his brothers the feast they would enjoy that night.

When Neikahweh began preparing for the arrival of the baby, Mecowatchshish could not help but recall the carcass of the she-bear; pale and all-too-human looking without its hide. The pitiable bodies of her cubs on the cold ground beneath that awful totem of sinuous roots and displaced earth. At that very moment his mother was lying on a lush pallet of muskrat fur, her body covered by a rabbit blanket preparing to give birth. It was an event he did not fully understand and it filled him with apprehension. If this was how all things came into the world, why could he not remember tumbling around inside his mother's belly? And how did the right creatures get in the right bodies? He knew from the stories Nootahweh told that once all living things were the same and spoke to each other and lived in the world as equal beings. What if it was a bear in there? What if it was someone from another family? He could sense that no matter what happened, one way or another, everything would change. Neikahweh would change and Nootahweh and his brothers and he, Mecowatchshish. He was anxious and excited and kept trying to get a peek at what was going on. "Please don't cut her open Nootahweh," he had pleaded when he saw him putting his sharp knife down near the birthing bed.

"Don't worry," Nootahweh had said. "Oshkeiwahshish has their own way out. I just have to cut them free." The words were reassuring but Mecowatchshish could sense a particular uneasiness in his father's voice and manner.

His brothers pulled him back to their corner and tried to distract him with the small wooden figures of animals their father had carved for them. Despite their assertions to Mecowatchshish that they had seen it all before they too were curious and a little afraid. Wahpistanoshish really didn't remember his little brother's coming into the world and his playing was only half-hearted as his attention wandered back to his mother. He tried not to show it, to look after his brother as he had been asked.

"Shouldn't we wait for Auntie?" Wahpistanoshish blurted out. "Isn't Auntie coming?" Neistes gave him a stout cuff in the back of the head for asking the silly question.

"No time," said their father.

Mecowatchshish heard his mother moan, then grunt in pain and it shocked him because he had never heard her make such sounds. He scurried on all fours to where she was lying.

"Pull him back," Nootahweh called impatiently and Neistes scampered forward to seize Mecowatchshish by the foot and drag him away. Wahpistanoshish remained where he was, arms folded tight, still pouting and on the verge of tears over the unjust blow dealt to him by his brother. Mecowatchshish slipped free for a moment. He lunged to grab the edge of the blanket covering his mother just as his frustrated brother got a firm grip on his long hair to wrench him back. The blanket went with him and was jerked off their mother who was wearing only a short tunic, her lower half revealed. She tried to retrieve the covering but was hampered by her condition and fell back on the furs pulling her legs up as she rolled onto her side.

Both boys stared, stunned by the scars on her naked legs, frozen in their peculiar attitude, the younger one on his hands and knees, head pulled back severely, Neistes genuflecting behind him, one hand locked in his brother's hair the other outstretched for balance. They looked like acrobats posing at the end of a difficult stunt. They could not take their eyes from the wide, pale, bands that ringed their mother's exposed calves. Deep, corrugated indentations that circled her legs a little below each knee and bled short peninsulas of yellow flesh. She always wore deer-hide leggings that went above her knees and were covered by long skirts.

"It's all right, boys. Let your brother go." She was very tired. Two nights previous it seemed as if things were starting and then had stopped. She had never been alone before, without another woman to help and she was worried. She had not slept well and wanted just a little more rest, to maybe slow things down a bit and allow her sister-in-law time to arrive.

Wahpistanoshish, alone in his corner, had begun to weep softly overcome by all the turmoil and his own hurt feelings. "It's all right," she said with as much serenity as she could manage for her middle son. "It's from a long time ago." Her face clenched in the grip of another powerful contraction and Mecowatchshish saw the muscles in her legs contort and the strange patterns on her flesh tinge with purple. He did not know that in those long seconds it was not the pain of birth that concerned his mother, but rather the remembered agony re-igniting in those scars.

Neikahweh was then still a girl, living with her younger brother and father and his wife. She was not yet a mother, not yet Neikahweh but called Victoria after a faraway queen. She was thirteen that spring and would soon be preparing for life as a woman with her own family. Her father had taken in the woman who was their stepmother five years before; three years after her mother had died giving birth to Joseph her little brother. The difficulties that had caused their mother's death had also left a legacy for the boy. He developed slowly and it became apparent that he was afflicted with a weakness on his left side that would never get better. She was very proud of her father, Malcolm Goodwyn, who was an excellent and reliable hunter and had become a lieutenant in the Home Guard. It was the responsibility of these men to provide fresh meat for the people of the Factory.

He was well liked among the English not only because of these capabilities but in part because his own father had been an admired Company factor. Angus Goodwyn had loved the North Country and its people and had taken a Cree woman as his wife. Not just a Country Wife as most did, but as a full and legal partner. He had been held in high regard by all who knew him, white and Indian alike, as a fair and just man and there was a keen sadness that lingered decades after he had drowned in a rapids with two of his sons, the youngest only eleven. They had been on an expedition to build alliances and coax trade away from the growing competition in the west.

Neikahweh and her family lived in a small cabin on the edge of the settlement. The woman, Mary, who was their stepmother had come to be with them after the white man who had taken her as a companion returned to England. She was not Cree but Chipewyan, from the Hoteladi people and he had brought her there after guiding an extended reconnaissance somewhere to the west. When she spoke Cree there were still traces of another dialect and there was a rumour she had been brought as a slave out of the north as partial payment on a debt. When this man left for home, she had only a well-worn dress and shawl that he had provided her and nothing else. She had been alone for a while, fending for herself, when their father took her in to cook and care for them while he was away hunting. Before too long they began sleeping in the same room when he was home and soon without any kind of ceremony or announcement she assumed the function of their new mother.

It was a practical, very matter-of-fact measure, a development out of necessity and their father had not the slightest inclination to justify any of it to them. Mary simply began living there and assumed a portion of domestic authority with complete deference to their father whenever he was home. For the most part, in the beginning, it seemed she was determined to provide a happy home. She could not always hide her impatience over Joseph however, despite his sweet nature. He was much loved by his father and sister but was dependent on his family and would never be able to hunt or trap or make a life for himself. Victoria did not overtly dislike the woman but neither did she ever feel any genuine warmth towards her. Mary had a dour bearing that kept people at arms-length. She mostly let her long black hair hang freely and kept her head tilted forward as if in deference to the world. When she had to go out among people she pulled her shawl up, well-forward and held it under her chin to form a kind of cowl. Victoria had surmised that this withdrawn behaviour was to hide the deep smallpox scars on her cheeks and forehead. She had a hard narrow face with a nose that swerved to one-side having been knocked off-centre by some blow in the past. When the light was dim, one or two candles burning after the dishes were done, and the shadows smoothed the contours of her face Victoria could see that she had once been quite pretty. It was the harsh impress of life that made her otherwise.

Whenever their relatives were in the house, because Mary had none of her own, she was diffident and stayed silently ensconced in the corners. After a few years it became apparent that she, who had not had any children in her previous marriage, was not going to have any babies with their father. She would never provide him with a healthy, able son to care for them as they grew older.

Victoria perceived a bitterness in her stepmother that festered as time passed, though Mary did her best to keep it hidden whenever Malcolm was around. She was quick with a harsh word or a slap and there was often an icy aspect in her eyes as she watched her stepson move about dragging his crippled leg and drooling from the corner of his mouth. Victoria became aware of a growing envy in the way her stepmother regarded her as she matured out of childhood, nearing the age when she would be marrying. She knew that men found her appealing and she was already enjoying at a distance the attentions of many of the young Hudson's Bay men and the native trappers who travelled to the post to trade. It was inevitable that one day she would leave with one of them and Mary dreaded the prospect of being left alone with the burden of Joseph.

"So easy to be pretty," Mary said to her one day as she braided her hair and made ready to go out. Her stepmother stood at the table making bread, without looking up, as though talking to the dough. She pounded her fist into the pale, moist lump. "Men will forgive you."

"You're pretty," Victoria said as she reached to open the door. She wasn't trying to be sarcastic but she couldn't stop from biting her lower lip after she spoke.

Mary raised her head and looked at her with narrowed eyes. "I know what your father thinks. I'm not a fool. He's disappointed. Soon he'll be stuck with an ugly woman and a useless son and what will happen then."

For her thirteenth birthday Victoria's grandmother presented her with a pair of fine beaded moccasins she had sewn with her own hands. They were soft and supple with a rolled fringe and multi-coloured beads that covered the top of the foot in elaborate circular patterns that rippled elegantly up the entire front in alternating stripes of white, red, black, and yellow. Mary had feigned admiration, cupping them together in her hands and running her thumbs over the stippled designs, her expression hidden behind the curtains of her thick loose hair. Victoria glimpsed the bitter jealousy harboured in her heart when she abruptly handed them back and then, in her aloof manner, served the tea.

There was no love lost between the two older women. Her grandmother was a devoted Christian and did not try to hide her disdain for one who had come among them as a kind of property and who chose to live in sin with another man, even if it that man was her own son. She still grieved the passing of her daughter-in-law greatly and Victoria understood that the old woman had suffered through much loss in her life. Not only her beloved Angus and their sons but the very winter after that tragedy her own father and mother and a young niece with a small baby had frozen to death, caught in a three-day blizzard on their way to the post. This was the swift and certain power of the land, like some petulant beast, in a moment swallowing up what you loved. Afterwards she had plunged ever more deeply into the Presbyterian faith inherited from her husband. Her name was Ruby which Victoria thought was beautiful but there was no one left who called her that. As far as her granddaughter knew she was always addressed as Mrs. Goodwyn and it seemed another part of the misfortune attached to her.

Whenever she thought of the love she had for Nokomis, with it came the harsh awareness of how the years can fill up with pain and travail. This knowledge left Victoria with an anxious sense of foreboding for her own life. She had expected so much anguish would cause someone to question their faith but it only made the old woman more devout. She was aware that her stepmother also knew the hard edge of life and wondered why it was not a bond between the women. Mary never looked her husband's mother in the eyes. Victoria knew well how Nokomis' sharp, naked gaze could pierce down to your heart and that to her grandmother Mary would forever be nothing more than her son's housekeeper.

Neikahweh moaned deeply. The dim, warm space of the cabin an indistinct territory on the edge of her consciousness now, her family only shadows. She could feel the soft moosehide of the moccasins on her calves again and she smiled recalling the intricate beadwork flowers that decorated them, then frowned deeply remembering how duplicitously Mary had gushed over their beauty and after took every opportunity to reprimand her stepdaughter for not showing the proper respect for such a precious gift. They were splendid but there was a terrible fear that came with that splendour, a sinister apprehension that transformed every bead into a pinpoint of pain. As she lay there on her billet of muskrat, the new life inside her pressing to be born, she could feel those designs from the past sinking into her flesh like rows of sharp teeth.

She was that pretty young girl again, swinging a pail in her right hand as she went to retrieve some milk from the Post for her stepmother, a privilege for the families of the Home Guard. She was holding her brother's hand as he hobbled along beside her, his left arm folded against his chest like a featherless wing, the hand turned in against his collarbone, his left cheek resting on the knuckles, that side of his mouth a grimace that exposed his teeth. He walked on the ball of his left foot, the knee permanently bent and rigid. Even though the sun had come out they could tell it would only be a brief respite, but still it drew them out towards the river where men would gather to smoke and tell stories. There was that anticipation that grew as the days became warmer and the river opened and ice retreated. The goose hunt had begun and soon the Inlanders would begin to arrive after the long winter of trapping, bringing furs to pay their debts to the Company. Young Mr. MacBurnie, one of the Factor's clerks saw them and shouted out, "Hullo, Step-and-a Half," but when they looked his eyes only met hers and she turned away shyly from his smile.

Neikahweh hovers above it all now like a great white gull over the harbour and it is vivid with awesome portent, like a recurrent dream. The so-brilliant flash of sunlight, the swift clouds filling the sky the way caribou spill across the river in spring flood, driven by need and terror. The shouted greeting, the sense of change that came with breakup and boats in the harbour being loaded with supplies for the other posts. The cold black water, the mud-stained slabs of ice driven onto shore and the putrid body of a seal rotting on the far bank.

It had all turned suddenly, in a shift of time impossible to measure, all the promise of the day withering before them as they hurried back the way they'd come. Now it was different. She was trying to hide her trepidation even as she pulled at her brother when usually she was very indulgent with him, content to move at his pace. James was wet and her handsome moccasins soaked. They had been down along the river, watching the preparations.

Distracted by the excitement, they misjudged the slick slope. The bank underneath crumbled into the brown turbid water when Joseph, searching for the strange spiral figures etched in some of the stones, had ventured too close. The water had been cold, not too deep, but easily enough to drown someone small who could not pull themselves up off the soft murky bottom. She had leapt in immediately without thinking, her heart racing, and pulled him out. So quickly that only the crippled side of him had been soaked, the rest of him merely damp for the most part and not wet through. It had divided him again into two hemispheres, one water stained and dark and the other dry and remarkably untouched. They were surprised to find themselves sitting back several feet from the shore, not quite sure how they got there, the fear still arcing through their bodies. Joseph's eyes were wide. "I jumped like a fish," he said, flapping his good hand in the air, a thin line of drool dripping from the open left corner of his mouth. Then they burst into laughter falling against each other until they realized in almost the same moment that her moccasins were saturated with mud and brine.

She remembered the look her brother had given her, the alarm and guilt that was there in his face. He knew the wrath she was sure to face at home and that it would be because of him.

"Your mucc thins..."

It hurt her to see the pain in him, hear how he had to struggle to even say the word. She wanted to protect him and say something reassuring but couldn't find the words. A chilling gust blew off the bay against them and she saw him shiver and knew they had no choice but to hurry home. She reached out and with her thumb wiped away a thick filament of drool that hung from the corner of his mouth.

"Come, Joseph," she said. "We have to go."

There was a noise, a metal door scraping shut and Neikahweh opened her eyes. She was in the cabin; her husband had just added wood to the fire. She felt the warmth of the small place, felt the contraction leaving her and saw her sons staring. It felt as though she had been away a long time, visiting another world, but now her senses were coming back to her along with the familiar heat and expansion as her body prepared itself. That connection to the being who came through her into the world, and she knew everything would be all right.

She looked from her boys to her husband and no words were needed.

"Boys," Nootahweh coaxed. "Come on. Help me get more wood. We need to keep this place warm for the little one who comes tonight."

The boys stayed fixed on their mother and their father had to collect them and herd them towards the small, hide-covered opening that was the door. He helped them dress and the whole time they watched their mother keenly aware that a transformation was taking place. Then he held back the moosehide closure for them to go out. The older boy bowed out through the opening and stood in the cold waiting for his father and brothers to follow. Mecowatchshish bent and started to leave then stopped and looked back at his mother just beginning to sink down into another contraction.

"Where are we before we are born?" he asked.

Neikahweh opened her eyes wide, surprised by the impulsive question. "With the stars," she managed through tight lips.

Then his father pushed him out into the night.

Now she was alone and shrinking down again, the darkness closing in, the space changing with her family gone, becoming hers. The story from the past insinuating itself, the ghosts returning to her though she didn't understand why. Maybe it was something the one to be born brought with them from beyond the world. A gift of pain. A purging. A drawing out of poison.

Mary had assailed them the moment they walked in the door, at first only over the condition of the boy as he stood protectively in front of his sister trembling and dripping on the wooden floor. She herself had made his clothes and now they were sullied by a thoughtless act. Nothing invoked her ire as much as ingratitude. Then, mouth gaping, she took a step back, eyes riveted to the soaked, muddy moccasins, and pounced the width of the room, slapping the young girl hard across the face so that she dropped to her knees in astonishment. The blow had ruffled James' hair as it passed over his head and he withered to the floor like something broken beside her, crying and throwing his good arm up. The enraged woman kicked her hard in the ribs knocking the wind from her, the force of the blow transmitted to the boy, pitching him over onto his back.

There was the sense of something unleashed, something elemental flailing loose, like a tether torn free in a high wind. She shrieked and howled, raining blows on them from all directions as they cowered and tried to twist away from her fury. Victoria covered her head and heard, as though from far off, Joseph trying to plead with her, trying hard to explain that it was his fault, but it came out as a long garbled, gurgling lament. There came the sound of a sharp, well-placed blow and then silence and a sudden calm. Victoria pulled her tousled hair away from her face.

Mary had retreated a few feet and stood hunched and gasping, her arms hanging loosely, shoulders trembling, a thin streak of blood trickling down her left cheek, loathing and revulsion smoldering in her eyes. Joseph was propped awkwardly against the wall, half-turned with the left side of his face flattened against the rough wood, his good right hand quivering, still extended in front of him. He had struck her with all his strength, the momentum propelling him off kilter to slam into the wall, a fingernail from his half-closed hand raking her face.

Victoria started to plead for clemency, for a chance to explain, but it didn't matter because their stepmother was beyond hearing. She came at them shrieking, driving Joseph to the floor with her closed fist like a hammer on top of his head. She whirled and grabbed the girl by the hair and dragged her through the house to their bedroom in the back. Victoria, dizzy and in pain, collapsed in the doorway and Mary propelled her into the room with another vicious kick to her side that lifted her off the floor and onto her back. The breath exploded out of her and a brutal agony ripped through her chest. Joseph, already scuttling after them, determined to try and protect his sister, was seized by the scruff of his collar and flung bodily onto his sister. The door shut after him.

They had witnessed her temper growing shorter and more unpredictable in the past months. The longer their father was away the more mercurial she became. She would strike out at the slightest provocation and Joseph was sometimes beaten with a stained bit of leather from an old tumpline for spilling his food or moving too slowly. Last summer while their father was away helping guide Company canoes on an expedition to the north-west, she became increasingly agitated and despondent as the days passed. Three or four times they had overheard her talking to herself in a harsh conspiratorial whisper. When Joseph stumbled and accidentally spilled a pot of potatoes onto the floor, she snatched up a long boning knife she was using and turned with a feral look in her eye, screeching and shaking her head like a rabid dog.

"You do these things on purpose. You punish me. You know he has another family, don't you? You know another woman is out there giving him children. Good children. Not a bent, weak little boy. Not a silly, useless girl only good for the Englishmen."

She had been between them and the door and Victoria, terrified by the malevolence she saw in her stepmother's twisted face, quickly pulled her brother into the backroom and lifted him out through an open window. They had fled together to their grandmother's and remained with her until their father returned and came to get them. Their stepmother was able to convince him that they were exaggerating the whole thing. That they had run off to be spiteful because they were lazy and she made them do their chores. He had never witnessed any of her rages. He admonished them for being so much trouble and told them he had better things to do than to deal with children. Victoria could see how tired he was and she did not argue further when he impatiently waved off her protests. Still, he must have said something to Mary because she welcomed them back in an exaggerated manner and things were tranquil for weeks afterwards.

For a few moments she had no sense of where she was or what was happening. It had been a violent fury beyond anything she had ever known, a hateful wrath she had not expected in her own home. In her confusion she even found herself worrying over the safety of her stepmother as though the thing attacking them was something else, something separate from the woman she knew. She wrapped her arms around her brother and hugged him, her eyes closed and then gently she began to push his weight from her.

"It hurts," she whispered, and she rolled onto her side pulling her legs up as far as she could. She was sure a bone was broken on her left side, or at least cracked, and her head throbbed. The door flew open and she tensed waiting for more blows.

"I see you, Macheimunto! Wicked One," the woman hissed. "Wicked. Wicked. Don't look at me with your evil. You go back to hell, you!"

She opened her eyes slowly, not recognizing the voice that spoke to her and peered through the tangled mess of hair clotted over her face. Mary was standing over her, holding the thick debarked tree branch that was used to prop open the door to the root cellar.

"Don't take those moccasins off. Don't change your clothes. Don't mess the bed. You stay there. On the floor like that. Like someone's dog. I want your father to see you for the dirty thing you are. I want him to know how wicked you are. Don't look I told you!"

She saw her raise the cudgel and weakly crossed her arms over her face. She heard Joseph whimper and then felt a single hard blow near her elbow that made her cry out and her lower arm went numb so that her hand dropped onto the floor like something dead. The door slammed closed again.

"Are you well?"

Neikahweh opened her eyes. It was very warm. She rolled the rabbit blanket down to her waist. Her youngest son was beside her, his runny nose almost touching her cheek trying to peer into her half-closed eyes.

"I'm fine, Mecowatchshish." She gently pushed him back and saw standing behind him her husband's concern etched on his face.

"It looked like you were crying." It was Neistes squatting just inside the door.

"It hurts a little," she answered, smiling to ease any fears. "Where is Wahpistanoshish?"

"Outside pooping," said Mecowatchshish with an enthusiasm that made everyone chuckle. The humour subsided into a strained silence for a few seconds and then the middle-brother burst in through the hide door still adjusting his pants which seemed slightly twisted. The laughing began again over this unintentionally comical entrance and swelled with the puzzled look that came over the face of Wahpistanoshish as he tried to figure out what was so funny. It might have gone on longer but Neikahweh sighed with another strong contraction.

"It's alright, my boys. This one is taking their time. They are bringing me a long story."

"What story?" asked Mecowatchshish.

"A brother's story. Maybe I'll tell it someday." She spoke through clenched teeth and exchanged a look with her husband.

Nootahweh pinched the shoulder of the little boy's coat and tugged him up onto his feet directing him towards the exit. "Come now. We'll go to the river for water. Neikahweh will be very thirsty." He pushed them one after another, back out into the night, then paused before ducking through himself, to offer his wife a reassuring smile. Her eyes were closed, her lips pressed together in a grimace of remembered pain.

She was not sure how long she had slept, Joseph curled tightly against her but when she woke, strong beams of light were filtering through the shuttered window. She wanted to scream in agony. The moccasins were drying and as they did the leather shrank and constricted around her legs. Her fingers went to where a rawhide lace closed the top of the moccasin against her shin. She clawed at it with the hand of her uninjured left arm, but the ligature had pressed deeply into her skin and caused the flesh to swell where the blood flow was restricted. She grunted and moaned and scratched, one of her nails broke and some of the bead work came loose and spilled on the floor as she tried to loosen the excruciating grip. She was afraid her stepmother would hear and come back to beat her some more and her hand felt frantically along the rough planks to scoop up the bits of coloured glass and hide them under her body. She felt her brother stir beside her.

"Do you hurt?"

She reached with her good arm to stroke his hair. It made her weary and she let her hand fall onto his crooked shoulder. They were like wounded birds hiding in the shadows.

"My arm is aching and my moccasins...They are so tight. My feet feel like wood."

He pulled himself around and felt with his right hand where they were tied. He tried the right one for a few moments, then the left but could not loosen them. In frustration he tugged sharply on the lace and pain shot through her whole body.

"Stop, Joseph. Don't move me. It hurts."

"Can't. Too tight." He spoke in wet truncated sobs.

She didn't like to hear him cry and she was sorry for upsetting him. All she wanted was to lie motionless and wait for the pain to ebb or to ride its crest back into the darkness.

"Just lie close," she said, fighting to keep the anguish and fear out of her voice. "Papa will come. Or Kokoom. It'll be all right."

She could sense him beside her listening and trying to control his breathing.

"Quiet...Victoria. Quiet...quiet. Maybe...sleeping. Maybe... gone." Each word separated by an inhalation.

He was listening again, turning something over in his mind.

"Knife," he made a sawing motion with his hand, his whispering even lower now, barely audible. His breathing quick and shallow as if something compressed his chest. "I'll," Breath. "Cut." The last word as fragile as a blown kiss.

"No, Joseph. No. Just stay with me. I'll be fine." She was giving him permission to be afraid. To wait it out.

She felt the fingers of his good hand tracing the top edge of the moccasins. It felt now as though that was where her legs came to an end. As if the moccasins and that part of her contained in them had coalesced and become desiccated. Broken off like dry sticks.

He lifted his hand from her bloated calf and held it, warm

against her bruised cheek then crawled towards the door, left foot dragging. It nudged her deadened foot and she whimpered with the tremor it sent through her.

"Joseph."

"Shhh." She heard the latch lifting and the swish of the door scraping lightly along the plank floor, but she could not summon the strength to turn over and look. She sensed him slithering out through the opening, pulling himself along on his good side as he used to do when he was very young. It took him a long time to learn to walk. He fell, over and over slamming down against the world and she had admired his determination. He kept moving about, not feeling sorry for himself, refusing to give in to his infirmity. Then she recalled a mouse she had seen tortured by a cat, trying to drag itself away, a pale sliver of bone protruding from one hind leg.

She half-turned to look towards the door and fire surged through her in a scorching wave. She pulled into a foetal position, trying to become smaller than the pain and for a time that was all there was in the world. The agony of her body curled around itself, doing what was necessary to endure.

With a sudden terrible clarity she became aware of a depraved sharp-edged shrieking that seemed something other than human. Her only thoughts were of Joseph, set on helping her, defiant at first, determined to face the creature that howled and railed against them. She forced herself to turn and begin to sidle towards the door; she could see faint light where it stood ajar. There were no fires burning. No lamps lit. All the windows shuttered tight and sealed. Had she been sitting there in the cold darkness waiting all this time?

She could hear the sounds of them scuffling and she knew Joseph would be no match for her.

"Don't hurt him," she managed in a hoarse, beseeching whisper. A murmur of dried blood and dust.

The only answer was a high-pitched shriek from her brother

that startled her and seemed to corkscrew through the marrow of her bones. She clawed at the edge of the door, pulling herself up off the floor with one arm but her lower legs were numb, the hide of the moccasins contracted powerfully around them. It was as if two voracious snakes had begun to consume her, pulling her apart. The pain forced her down onto her left side and she struggled out through the door using her one good arm, compelled by the gurgling cries of her brother.

It became still all of a sudden. The shadows seemed to thicken and close in. Then something slammed hard into the half-open door and she was flung back into the small room, into the deepest darkness. Swallowed whole.

Mecowatchshish, his brothers and his father walked now towards the river making their way easily by the light of a waxing moon. His father carried the metal pail and said they were going to retrieve water, but even little Mecowatchshish understood that this was only an excuse. There was a full kettle steaming on top of the stove and a small wooden keg brimming with melted snow just inside the door where it would not freeze solid. Still, it was exciting to be outside, the four of them filled with anticipation, breathing in the cold crisp air. Fresh snow was heaped on everything and he was pleased by the way the muffled shadows of the trees lay across the unmarked drifts. It made him think of drawings he had seen in books his cousins brought with them on their visits. Especially the one he liked best which showed a team of dogs pulling a sled on a winter's night. There was the white snow and the bright circle of the full moon and everything else was black ink and stood out starkly against the background as if all the figures had been cut out of the winter night. The running dogs, the sled, the man in his hooded coat and the whip rippling through the air over his head.

He could hear the falls off in the distance. Even though much of the river was frozen already, water still cascaded over the brink and churned down through the cataracts below. Could it ever get cold enough to make the whole river sleep?

"Wastahwayahnaskon," exclaimed Nootahweh, pointing up into the sky.

Mecowatchshish had seen the spirits dancing among the stars before but on dark nights when they seemed brighter. Tonight though they looked as close as he could ever recall, moving in a shimmering supple wave over their heads. He stared open-mouthed and could hear a low rasp-like chattering, as if they were trying to talk to him. He stumbled along the rough path behind his older brothers and his father, staring up, mouth agape, straining to listen to the whispering spirits and trying to make sense of the sounds drifting out of the sinuous river of lights. He was amazed by how much the world could give in a single night. How it filled his heart sometimes to be alive, so that it swelled and ached inside his chest. He could feel the throb of it through his whole body and the luminous vision appeared to move now to this beat. As if his heartbeat was the drum that turned the world. He felt as if he himself was glowing, as though he was about to turn to light and drift up into the sky when something cold and bristled hit him stoutly across the cheek and nose and he cried out as he fell back hard onto the packed trail.

He lay stunned, eyes watering, nose stinging, the aurora writhing far above him, a shimmering smudge that seemed to make the treetops swirl and twist

Who had struck him? Why had he been punished?

His father came and lifted him back to his feet and wiped the tears from his eyes with one warm thumb. Off to one side he could see Wahpistanoshish standing with his hands behind his back and a pine bough still trembling near him. It was a game they often played with each other on long walks through the forest trails. The idea was to catch whoever was following in a moment of inattention, bend back a tree branch as you passed and then let it go, timing it so that it whipped back to catch the daydreamer off-guard.

"Hey," Neistes called from farther down the path. Impatient for them to catch up. "Coming," Nootahweh assured him and gently pushed Mecowatchshish ahead along the trail. He went quickly, ashamed of his tears and when he looked back over his shoulder his father was stopped and looking down at his brother who in turn looked at the ground. No words were spoken and soon they were once again on their way to the river. Mecowatchshish glanced up to the sky but the lights seemed farther away now, less vibrant, and the only sounds were the falls and their own footsteps.

Chapter Seven:

Hank I

Hank had fully expected to meet the inconsiderate cousins hastening towards him along the darkened street. His last words as he left the house slamming the door and shrugging his heavy coat into place, "Don't serve the Goddamn pie 'til I get back!" A slice of his wife's crab apple pie and a cup of tea didn't seem too much to ask for at the end of a long day. He paced along over the frozen dirt road rehearsing the speech he would use to scold the pair. Nothing as severe as what the boy's intractable brothers regularly received but something unmistakeably firm; something suitable to serve in place of a good swift kick in the ass. He had committed to act less out of irritation, as had been his tendency in the past with the older boys, but rather take a more measured and mature approach. He felt especially lenient towards his niece who still mourned for her father, the memory of his lost brother-in-law and best friend tempering his wrath. It was still hard to accept that Sandy was gone and a bitter melancholia churned in his stomach, dissolving his appetite in a sudden wave of grief and trepidation. The truth at the heart of it was that he was afraid for the pair and angry that they had brought this fear upon him. His steady footfalls resounding off the frozen ground and echoing along the empty streets was a plangent tolling.

"Goddammit, Sandy. Goddammit," he muttered.

He resolved to be a better father, less rigid, particularly with Simon who was more sensitive than his older siblings and not so in need of such a firm hand. He would strive to be a more tolerant parent to his younger children and a benevolent guardian for Joe Pete. Punishment, he decided, would be meted out in a calm and considered manner, not a reaction driven out of anger.

After an unsuccessful half-hour he circled back to the house and kicked his recalcitrant sons back out into the streets to search the town. He had vainly attempted to avoid leaving his plate and exacerbating the ache that had been festering in his haunch all day by sending Clarence and Henry out earlier. They had returned after only a few minutes, sullen and smelling of tobacco smoke. He doubted they'd gone further than the back of the woodshed.

"All right, Mother," he'd ordered, "dish it up and they can damn well go without."

It hadn't worked. Gina served them but had refused to eat. Instead, she retreated to the kitchen muttering and banging pot lids and clattering dishes in the sink. She paced out to check on the twins in the playpen Hank had built in the front room and then to the front door to fling it open and peer out into the street before stalking back to the sink to thresh about the pots and pans. By the time he gave up and threw down his fork Gina was on the verge of tears and followed on his heels wringing her hands behind him, her unspoken worries filling the front hall with apprehension. He put on his good boots and mitts and pulled his department issue flashlight from his rucksack. He considered saying something comforting but instead went out without a word, deciding it would do her good to stew for her persistent leniency with their youngest son and ruining his meal.

He trudged out to the cabin on Indian Arm but found his

sister-in-law's place dark and cold, so he followed the path across the point to Sam's and spoke with his father-in-law to find out what he knew. The old man told him that they had been on their way to check their snares for rabbits to trade and hoped to go to the moving pictures in the afternoon. It was his understanding that after the matinee Joe Pete was going home with her cousin for supper because Louisa would be at the Turkula's cooking for them and expected to be busy all evening with her mid-wife duties. The last he saw of them, hours before, they were headed out towards the trails along the river where they had their sets.

Hank asked him to go over to Turk's and see if Louisa knew where her daughter or Simon might be and he would head out looking for them on the trails. He had advised them on placing their snares, telling them likely places to seek out along with a stern warning not to cross the river to the Park. Emphasizing that it was dangerous and illegal and that he didn't want to have to arrest his own family for poaching out of the game preserve it was his paid duty to protect. He made his way through the growing darkness with a bitter wind gusting in off the river.

He found one freshly dead rabbit and worked it free of the wire noose, stuffing the small body down into the deep pocket of his coat. It would be his lunch tomorrow, a punitive tax on their tardiness and there wouldn't be any outings to the picture show for a while either. At least now the walk would not be a complete waste. A little farther on he found the place in the snow where someone had wrestled something from a trap. In the weak light from his flashlight he could make out a few spots of what he took to be blood and a large dark feather. As he bent to retrieve it from the ground a sharp twinge of pain jolted through his hip. He straightened with an involuntary grunt and the feather slipped from his hand. He swept the area with the weak beam from his flashlight, making a mental note to order new batteries from Head Office. The feather had settled back near the overturned trap.

Even in the insufficient glow of his light he could see by its general condition it was not one of Sam's. He surmised that perhaps they had been caught pilfering someone else's catch and were perhaps in hiding somewhere.

He located where they had bushwhacked through the brush towards the river's edge and he followed their track with the inconstant flashlight flickering on and off. He shook it and smacked it against the palm of his hand, and as he waited to see if the bulb would stay lit he heard someone blundering along the tangled bank in a panic. The clatter among the dry branches reminded him of the tangle of bones he would find occasionally, rattling and clacking together in the wind, offerings left hanging in the trees by the superstitious Indians. In the quiet of the woods, when he was alone and had been out for some time, it often sounded like chattering human voices, a distant argument or invocation. He knew that even Sandy, as he had been taught since childhood, would return the bones of beavers that he trapped to the ponds where they had been caught. He dismissed this ritual as a credulous bit of whimsy. Harmless except for the time and energy wasted in doing it.

He turned towards the frantic clamour, sure that it was the errant cousins in a heedless headlong rush now to get home. They had probably been worried about the consequences of interfering with someone else's trap or just lost track of time, caught up in some nonsense game. Hank fretted over the boy, his thin-skinned son who was so susceptible to being pulled into the fantasies and ghost stories of his cousin. So unlike his raucous, hard-headed older brothers, he seemed ill-suited for a life in the northern bush. Another stab of pain in his right leg brought him up short and his hand pressed down hard, probing his hip. He was sure he could detect something there, a new lump in the landscape of scar tissue. Something had been gnawing at him for months now, growing more insistent. Another token from the war. The notion that after a decade and a half he would have to go back to Toronto for more treatment worked to feed his impatience as much as the pain itself. Could there really be anything left? In the years after the war, he had been to the Dominion Orthopaedic Hospital on several occasions. Sometimes just to receive physical therapy but also for surgery to remove shards of shrapnel that had skulked about his flesh since the war. This visit though, he reflected sadly, would be different. He had not been back for years and now there would be no Rebecca, his old and secret friend. She was an artefact of the life he might have had if things had been different. If perhaps he had made other choices.

He moved cautiously towards the steep shoreline as the sounds continued to draw nearer though he could think of nothing other than wayward children making so much noise at night in the bush. Certainly not poachers. He slipped the malfunctioning light into his pocket and peering through the tangle of branches watched his son claw heedlessly up the incline toward him. He took a vengeful pleasure in startling the boy half out of his wits when he reached to yank him bodily up over the bank and had to bite his lip to keep from bursting into laughter at Simon's gaping expression in the moment before realizing it was his own father that had seized him. The boy came along slipping and tripping awkwardly, one boot working free so that it was hanging off his foot, pulling the thick woollen sock with it. Hank struggled to right him and hold his weight while Simon gained his feet, but the boot flopped around and the boy flailed about attempting to keep his half naked foot out of the snow. A constant pain throbbed along Hank's leg from hip to knee. He let the boy drop to the ground with a gesture of impatience and Simon landed with a thump on the hardened crust fighting back tears.

He could hear the boy quietly sobbing as he wrestled the frozen knots with one hand and pull at his sock with the other. Hank felt some compunction to offer something soothing and at the same time despised this weakness in his son. His discomfort hardened his heart and put more anger in his words than he intended.

"Pull yourself together for Christ's sake. Quit jackassing around and get that boot on. Where in the hell is that foolish little cousin of yours?"

Simon pointed out towards the river. "There. On Kei Sha...I mean Lundy Island. We found a dog." He snuffled wetly and ran his sleeve across his nose.

"You went out after a dog? On that ice?" He shifted his weight off the aching leg, gritting his teeth and stifling a groan.

"No. We...we chased a bird..."

"What?"

Their eyes met and even in the darkness Hank could tell his son had decided to leave something out. He wouldn't press him for the full story now.

"There were some dogs, dead dogs. They were tied to trees. One still alive. Joe Pete wouldn't leave..."

The man dropped to his knees, grunting under his breath and jerked the boot from his son's grasp. The knot in the laces had been reefed together into a frozen, insoluble lump. He slipped his belt-knife out, parted the lace and slid the boot forcefully back onto his son's foot though it caused him some discomfort to do it. Crossing the dangerous river, staying out to look after some abandoned mongrel, some madness about a bird.

"When you get home you find something to tie that up properly," he barked. He pulled his handkerchief out of his pants pocket and roughly wiped the boy's nose. "You get straight back; I'll deal with you there. This better not be any more of your cousin's imaginary gibberish. Enough is enough. Your goddamn supper has been waiting for you, you know that. Your mother's very upset. Tell her I've gone to get Alison and I'll bring her back to the house if I don't kill her first."

He grabbed the shoulder of Simon's jacket and towed him back the short distance to the logging trail. It was well-packed but he knew it would take some time for the boy to make the outskirts of town. He thought of Gina waiting anxiously at home and had a momentary urge to send him on his way with a kick in the pants after all, but restrained himself, deciding that it would hurt him more than it would his son. Instead, he handed over the flashlight knowing it would offer some comfort if nothing else. Then, like a magician, he pulled the dead rabbit out of his pocket and held it in front of the boy's face. Simon stared wide-eyed.

"Take this home and clean it before you even think of going to bed." He shoved the limp animal into his son's arm. "You clean it. Not your mother." He wanted him to have blood on his hands that very night.

"Go," was the only other leave-taking he offered.

Blue fire pulsed back and forth between his knee and hip as he zigzagged through the trees and made his way along the riverbank. He wanted to cut more directly across to Lundy Island so as to minimize his time on the uncertain ice. He had seen how large stretches could open up overnight and he had no desire to end in the river like Sandy. Who would care for their families then? He stopped short once to beat his fist against his thigh trying to hammer the pain out of the muscle, then limped on. Distracted by the throbbing and unpleasant thoughts of another hospital visit, he missed the trail he wanted in the darkness and he came out on a rocky point with a steep drop to the river. It was a bleak territory that had been burned-over a decade before in a determined fire that scorched more than six hundred acres and ruined a lot of timber. Hank had helped in the rescue of some men trapped at a logging camp and that work had put him in good stead for the Game Warden position. A fierce windstorm had swept through more recently and many of the charred trees had been broken and left standing mute and blackened. Vague twisted shapes that brought back memories of No Man's Land.

He was loathe to retrace his steps and opted for a direct approach down to the river. The sooner he would be home, sitting alone in the dark kitchen, the house at peace, sipping whiskey and nursing his throbbing hip by the woodstove, the better.

He stood gathering himself for a second and spoke to the frozen river waiting implacably below. "Damn you, Sandy for leaving me with this. If it was anyone else I'd drag my sorry ass back to town and send the brat's own father out after them."

Reaching out, seething, for what he thought was a small tree but was only a long dead limb sticking up out of the snowbank like a spear, he plunged off the bank. The incline proved much steeper than he had judged, obscured by a deep, yielding drift, and unimpeded he crashed headlong down onto the frozen river. His long woollen scarf fluttered down coming to rest over his face like a condemned man's blindfold as he lay in a nebulous abyss, the wind knocked out of him, his body cold and remote, parts of him seemingly aflame. He rolled to lie on his back, the cold creeping up into him out of the frozen river, not soothing but at least anaesthetizing. It brought back a well-known terror, a razor-edged memory that was at a distance now, but rebounding like something that had backed away only to gain momentum. It was returning for him, he could feel it and he heard an old familiar echo, like the slow, solemn beat of a drum.

The blast that maimed him was lost in the cacophony of noise and havoc that consumed the world. Gunfire. Exploding shells. The screams of men. He remembered the noise and clamour that came before, the terror and anguish that clawed at him as the creeping barrage pounded across the torn earth. The way he seemed to shrink in his uniform, all the swagger withering away till he was just a scared boy again. They had hunkered down in the bunkers as it passed over, shaking the ground and rumbling through them, turning their guts to jelly. The whistles and the counter barrage and then they were scrambling out to their positions in the dugout. He was last through the opening and a trench mortar struck nearby forcing him down into the dirt. Then he was up, weaving among the dead and dying, focused on the singular need to attend to his duty and get with his crew, the heavy reassuring ballast of the ammo boxes pulling his arms straight as he scurried, bent low towards the forward position of his mates. Through the smoke and shell bursts he could see his comrades huddled down behind the Vickers. Priest, whom he admired, at the trigger, face grim in concentration as the barrel spit measured bursts of fire. Next to him was the new man, Victor or Vinnie, he had already forgotten. Just another kid, brash and full of bravado standing now in the kind of stupor that comes over everyone their first time in the maelstrom. Fox was feeding the belt into the gun as Sandy stood to one side sighting down his rifle, ready to help if someone fell or they needed to replace an overheated barrel.

He was advancing across the broken ground, the covering barrage meant to soften them for the attacking troops was winding down and their own artillery and mortars were firing into the charging horde. Above the unrelenting din he recognized the sound of a short round. It would not carry to the enemy lines and he wanted to shout to the crew, but then there was that space he could not really recall. He knew it existed because it echoed still somewhere inside of him. The men disappearing in a funnel of black earth and noise as he half-turned from the storm he knew was coming. It was a sudden ferocious, smothering darkness, shrapnel peppering the left side of his body as though some giant beast had seized him in its jaws and was shaking the life out of him. It tore at him with hot metal teeth and tossed him so high it felt like rising right out of the world into the profound emptiness that is the space between the stars. The earth dropping away from him as he spun, weightless, into a black void. Then it all came asunder and bits of that lightless void lodged throughout his left side. Little scraps of death burrowing into his flesh, nestling against the gnawed curve of his bones.

The world came back as a single repeating reverberation. A distant uneven tolling that stretched all the way back to the earliest memories of childhood. At first he felt only a deep, ambiguous nostalgia which he could not identify. Then a puzzling flash of blue, on and off, pulsed in front of his eyes. He recalled no pain, only emptiness. A feeling as though somehow he was detached from his body, his limbs distant and unresponsive. The bright azure awareness flaring behind his eyes, a black bottomless terror pulsing in between and the only sound was the steady, hollow beat. Gradually he came to realize he was on his back, his eyes open to the bright summer sky but peering through an opaque liquid haze. He could feel the muscles on one side of his face twitching uncontrollably as though trying to crawl off the bone. He wanted to reach up and lay his hand over them, to calm them but he couldn't connect the thought to the actions necessary. Then unconsciousness flooded back over him.

He came back to the tympanic nudge repeating through his skull but this time in complete darkness. He could sense the sun on his face as he felt himself jostled back and forth, a familiar rhythm that evoked the beginning of a dim awareness. It started with one word. The oldest word. The first connection of sound to meaning when he was a child as his father carried him on his back to the barn where the beasts stood in their stalls, snorting and stamping. Huge and powerful. Horse. He reached out his small hand to brush his fingers against the soft nose, felt the heat of the animals breath, and said the word, the magic of it in his mouth. Horse. That single breathing syllable and the smell of them and the way the muscles rippled along their flanks. The hulking Percherons that worked on the farm, the old nag in town that hauled the milk wagon, his grandfather's liver-chestnut mare pulling them through the snow on a cutter all wrapped and snuggled and warm.

Now he had seen too much, too many mangled body parts loaded like refuse, shifting and trembling as they were hauled away on the wagon for the dead. Again and again he had seen the bodies of the animals themselves bloated and putrefying, all that proud flesh ripped open and filling the world with the thick stink of death. Pulled into a gruesome pyre of limbs and hooves and bloodied manes, doused with gasoline and set ablaze. The smell of burned meat and petroleum as the greasy black smoke smeared across the sky. Now that old familiar clop filled him with panic because he knew what it meant. He was on the meat wagon, piled in with the dead. It was a frightening, discordant thrum without the old familiar rhythm. He wanted to shout and declare himself but his throat was dry and closed, his lips sealed together with blood. He raised his arm to try and signal that he was still alive, and something struck him. Only later did he learn that it had been his own hand. His arm had gone up but he was too weak, too numb to hold it and it fell back onto his ruined face with a loud slap. That was what alerted the stunned wagoneers and saved his life.

The wavering light of the fire burning in the abandoned wood stove surged to flare high against the naked trees around the campsite. The compact, doorless heater had settled unevenly, tilting over to one side but was now too hot to shift. Joe Pete had to hold the cast iron pan in place to prevent it from sliding off and spilling its soupy contents on the snow. She glimpsed the tremulous silhouette in her peripheral vision first and kept watch out of the corner of her eye where it lingered at the outer edge of the illumination, leaning heavily against a tree. In the inconstant shadows, the two things seemed joined. The dark figure elongated, becoming starker as the flames rose and sank back into the trunk, an amorphous incarnation reluctant to come into the world. She wasn't frightened and smiled warmly, certain that it was another messenger, like the raven or perhaps the spirit of her father returning. She had read the signs correctly and the raven and the sick dog and her belief had coalesced to become the magic needed to bring him back.

"Alison! What in God's name are you up to?"

Her face dropped at the sound of his voice and a little of the broth she was stirring slopped to sizzle on the stovetop. She stared, crestfallen, as her Uncle Hank began to limp towards her before turning to the pan dejected.

"What happened here?" he was pointing towards the pathetic hump of fur that was the dead and butchered dog. The white-hot pain seared up into his hip and across his lower back. The river crossing had been a forced march, one foot in front of the other in fixed determination.

She moved the pan to a couple of logs placed nearby and added a handful of snow to the mixture. She sat with the canine's huge head in her lap, spoon feeding him the warm thick soup she had made from the smashed bones. She had struggled to slowly drag the animal close enough to the stove so that she could feed the fire, tend the pot and minister to it all at once. Pushing aside his upper lip she poured sustenance in through the grim teeth, the dog's tongue lapping and working to get it down.

"Eat, Mohegan. Get strong," she said.

"That's not a wolf."

"I know that. Mohegan is his name. I named him." She had hoped he would simply disappear like one of the Manitou's in the game.

"You shouldn't have, Girl. It will only make it harder."

"He needs a name. I have to call him something," she said, ignoring the implication, perturbed by his persistence in remaining there. She was sure the presence of someone else would spoil everything.

They held their positions, the dog in between them, doing its best to intimidate with a low snarl but stopping every few seconds to lick its lips as pain flickered in its eyes. She shifted under the weight of the dog's head, preparing, and the man took another step closer.

"I came to help, Joe Pete." He used her affectionate nickname. "The dog won't live. You've been a foolish lass, risking your life and Simon's. I know you've been confused by your..." He paused seeking the right word "...upbringing. Fairy tales told to you in good faith. But no human life is worth an animal. Your father knew that. You can see its suffering."

There was something untrustworthy in his calm attitude, like holding a trap that has been set and the tension in the spring is a potential that makes your fingers tremble. Not just the immediate danger but the knowledge that you hold a bit of impending death in your hands. She was disturbed also by the mention of her father which in itself seemed a betrayal.

"He's not. He's fighting to live, that's all."

"He won't live."

She hated the way he said it. The cold certitude.

"He will. You don't know. I know." She spit the words across the space between them trying to match his confidence, arms trembling with the weight of the animal against her and the need to protect him.

"I know you want that but saying something don't make it so."

She bent to cradle the dog's head. "He wants to live. He wants to be with me. That's why I found him."

He started to move towards them and the animal struggled to raise its head and bare its fangs.

She shouted, pointing at him, "You stay back!"

She saw his leg tremble, a spasm of pain and exasperation convulsing across his face, "I'm tired of your insolence, Girl. There's already been more than enough trouble over this."

He lunged forward and grabbed the shoulder of her coat to wrench her away forcefully. She hugged the animal and the dog growled with all the menace it had left. She felt him set his feet trying to yank her away and she grabbed two fistfuls of fur so that even the dog was lifted for a moment. Then Joe Pete lost her grip and the man was able to pull her away but with more force than he intended so that she was sent tumbling over the packed snow.

He took a step towards her where she lay her face buried in her folded arms sobbing.

"Alison, I'm sorry. I didn't mean to hurt you. You're not giving me a goddamn choice."

"Leave him alone. He wants to live. I can help him. I need to help him. Okemah told me..."

"Your Grandfather is an old man who lives in the past. Foolishness and spirits won't do you any good in the real world."

She looked up at him, her eyes narrowing. "You owe us. You owe my father."

She was desperate and looking for some leverage. Two winters before he had lost his goggles and they had found him wandering snow-blind across Atikameg Lake.

"Little Girl, you have no idea of what went on between your father and I. You just don't know. I'm doing what needs to be done and you need to respect that. Your father would..."

"My father told me to always remember Life is sacred. He believed in spirits. He would give him a chance."

She could see that he was done arguing and a sudden emptiness surged through her as he reached for the bone-handled knife on his belt.

"You start back and I'll wait till you're off the island. It'll be quick and this creature won't suffer anymore."

"What about me?" she sobbed. "I'll suffer. I'll still suffer."

She saw that the dog had hauled itself up onto its feet, head held low, lips pulled back, the dull canines exposed. It meant to fight, protecting her as much as itself. Hank paused for a few seconds to contemplate the defiant dog. The fire was burning down again, the faint light shimmering in the dog's eyes and on its teeth. It tried to look daunting and dangerous but it was obvious that it couldn't stand long on its trembling wide-splayed legs.

She hit him hard and low from behind, not trying to tackle him, only to push past and get between the knife and Mohegan. Man and dog both toppled at once though only her uncle made any sound, an agonized grunt as his bad leg gave out underneath him. Joe Pete was shocked by his collapse and the pain she heard in his voice. She had not meant to hurt him, only to buy some time to plead for the life of the dog.

Big white flakes were beginning to filter down through the naked branches and accumulate on the thick matted fur of the dog. Hank pulled himself into a sitting position and shifted to the left sliding the big knife back into its sheath.

"The hell with it," he said wearily. "But I am not carrying that thing home. You come back with me and we'll see what the river's like in the morning. It can die slowly if that's your choice but mark my words you're coming with me if I have to tie you up and drag you across the ice."

"We could use the tent to make something and pull him..."

"Goddammit, NO!"

She jumped at the vehemence with which he shouted and felt the tears and fear welling up inside of her again. A familiar figure moved towards the weak circle of light cast by the guttering fire.

"Okemah!" She leapt up and ran to greet her grandfather as he trudged forward pulling his old hand-built toboggan. She threw her arms around him. He hugged her with his free arm and his eyes met those of his son-in-law for a brief moment, trying to assess what had occurred.

Hank pulled himself painfully to his feet, "Well, Sam. You're just in the nick of time."

Her grandfather said nothing, only stood surveying the ruined campsite and the bodies of the dogs. "Shame," he said, shaking his head. "Shame, shame."

Hank nodded. "It is a shame. A damn shame and what's more of a shame is that dog is still suffering. Your granddaughter is determined to help that hopeless case over there." He pointed to the prostrate form of the dog, breathing hard as snow gathered along its heaving flank.

Joe Pete smiled as she felt the old man's hands on her shoulders, "We can try."

Hank shrugged with resignation and weariness. "Okay. You try. I'm going home."

She went to kneel beside the exhausted dog, petting its head as her uncle gathered up his aching bones and begin limping towards home.

Chapter Eight:

The Island

"You were most fortunate."

She woke not knowing where she was or how she got there or who was speaking to her. She woke in an unfamiliar bed to soft daylight diffused through the lace curtains of a pair of tall windows in a room she didn't recognize. She could hear someone quietly singing a hymn, her grandmother's favourite, "All Things Bright and Beautiful." She tried to sit up to see where she was but pain surged through her and she collapsed back onto the mattress.

"I'm afraid your arm is broken."

The voice seemed more familiar now and her vision became clearer. She looked up into the youthful handsome face of Mr. MacBurnie. Then the stern face of her grandmother appeared and the young clerk was sharply elbowed aside.

"Victoria. How are you? How do you feel?" There was something there in the old woman's staunch tone that she found unnerving. Something more than the expected concern, a darker colour than the old woman's accustomed matter-of-fact inflection. It frightened her and she struggled to clear her head and recall how she might have come to be where she was.

She inventoried her discomfort and became aware of the tight bindings around her calves. She remembered the strangulating moccasins and the desperation of her confinement returned and she tried to reach with her good arm to release her legs from the strictures.

"The moccasins..."

Her grandmother leaned in. "We had to cut them away." She smiled and summoned a little humour to comfort her granddaughter. "It was like skinning a rabbit too fat for his skin." Concern reappeared over her countenance. "Don't worry about that..."

It took all she could muster to turn onto her side and throw the bed clothes aside. It was not the moccasins binding her legs but bandages, wound in a wide bloody band around her calves.

Mr. MacBurnie reappeared hovering over the old woman's shoulder. "That's where you were so fortunate Miss Victoria. We've had the benefit of Doctor Simpson this past winter. He arrived with last year's supply ship employed by the Company as our new physician. He had a great deal of experience in South Africa with The Royal Army Corps. He dealt with some truly horrendous injuries inflicted by the Boers. Poisoned bullets and..."

A grunt exploded from his lips and she saw him grimace and knew Gramma Goodwyn had caught him in the ribs with another elbow. He stepped back again nodding apologetically and rubbing his bruised sternum as the matriarch briskly snapped the blankets back into place and smoothed the covers. She felt tears begin to flow down her cheeks. "Jo..." she choked, her dry throat seizing around the second syllable of the question she was afraid to ask.

Her grandmother was weeping now as well, an occurrence Victoria had never witnessed and the redoubtable Mrs. Goodwyn made no attempt to wipe away the tears. It was, somehow, the most upsetting and most reassuring thing the girl had seen in her short life.

"He was very brave."

"No!"

"You should know..." the disembodied voice of the young Englishman came from somewhere behind the old woman, presumably at a safe distance. His enthusiasm and eagerness to share were all too obvious and Victoria could not help but wonder what she had ever found appealing in him. "...that some men have gone out seeking your stepmother. Though none of the Indians would go. Not even the half-breeds. They are convinced she is a, I believe the word is Wit...Witacho." His time among the natives in the colony had suddenly become much more intriguing.

Gramma Goodwyn winced and snorted at this mispronounced invocation. "The Devil has many names."

MacBurnie's disembodied voice carried on. "They are concerned for the well-being of their own families. I find it a fascinating idea really. A flesh-eating creature, blood turning to ice. Ridiculous, but I see it as a kind of crude metaphor. If you know what I mean." He was really talking more to himself now. "What else would you say about someone who could commit such brutal, inhuman acts but that surely ice must flow through their veins...?"

Gramma Goodwyn turned to look at him and it was not hard to imagine the daunting visage that confronted the young clerk. The girl was grateful; it put an end to the young man's prattling.

"Perhaps I'll go find Doctor Simpson and let him know she's returned to the land of the living."

Joseph had not been strong enough to keep her from taking the knife, but he had been determined to rescue his sister and Mary had to stab him many times. Perhaps it was the copious amount of blood or wounds she suffered to her own hands in the struggle that dulled her madness and caused her to flee. She seemed to take nothing with her, not even the knife which she dropped next to the boys crumpled body, the tip broken away and lodged somewhere in the pathetic form. She stumbled out through the door leaving red footprints and a crimson handprint on the floor where she had slipped. It wasn't until the next afternoon that Gramma Goodwyn came and found the slaughtered body of her grandson and then her unconscious granddaughter sick with fever and pain in the bedroom.

When the news reached Malcolm Goodwyn, already on his way home, he dumped a sled packed with provisions onto the trail and did not allow the dogs to stop until he was back. By the time he had arrived the body of his wife had been found naked and frozen solid not far from the Factory and Victoria was up and learning to walk again. Her legs were stiff, hobbled by the healing wounds and compromised muscle and she could manage only a few painful steps. She had been fortunate and the surgeon had been quick to excise all the infected tissue. She was mutilated but not crippled.

Malcolm Goodwyn had no words to say to his daughter. His face was raw and creased from the wind, his cracked lips trembled, his jaw clenching and unclenching, and his eyes full of remorse. He could not hold her gaze. He pulled her close to bury his face against her shoulder then turned abruptly and left, almost knocking over Clark MacBurnie. Victoria staggered across the room to the south window, tears streaming down her face. She pulled aside the curtains and pressed her face to the thick warped glass to watch as he strode to the powderhouse where they had stored the bodies of his son and Mary, each wrapped in a shroud of sail cloth.

It was quiet for a few moments, the day was cold and bright, and a few men of the post stood around unsure of what to do, blowing long plumes of breath through their hands. Then she saw the heavy metal door propped open and her father came out, a long heavy ramrod in one hand, pulling the exposed corpse of her stepmother by the hair. She was rigid, still locked into the grotesque attitude in which she had been found. He tugged her roughly down the stone steps and out a few feet onto the hard packed ground and before anyone could react he raised the heavy metal bar and smashed in her head.

Victoria had turned away at the last second and did not observe the impact but the sickening crunch had echoed through the cold air. She let the draperies fall back into place and turned away, the back of her free hand across her mouth.

It was the young clerk who later told her how her father had bound the body onto his sled, the head cracked open like a piece of pottery, and borrowed a fresh team of dogs. He left by way of the village, travelling through its centre with his horrific cargo openly displayed. He was gone for days.

Rumours began in the village about evidence of an unusual fire along the shores of the Moose River, not far from the mouth of James Bay. Someone had gathered a large pile of driftwood along the bank and the blaze must have burned for more than a day. It was reported that a shattered, blackened human skull was among the ashes and charred wood along with other bits of bone. Someone, it was surmised, had sought to destroy a terrible evil, though none would name it or give voice to their shared suspicions. The Cree hunters and trappers avoided going anywhere near the place or even speaking of it. The next year a large ice dam blocked the river and the spring freshet flooded the land and afterwards no evidence could be found.

The fire in the wood stove had burned down to embers and, except for their faint glow, night had seeped in at every opening to fill the little waskahekun. She was glad for this; there was heat enough from her own body from the effort of giving birth and the enveloping dark made her feel safe and hidden away. She was squatting now and she knew the time was close, that the baby had shifted, preparing for its release. She felt herself moving as well, away from the place that had been the source of so much terror and pain. She was grateful to have been alone with the story she could not tell, had never told to anyone but her husband and even he had not heard every detail. There was too much irreconcilable regret that needed to be purged before she would have enough strength to reveal it all. It was a burden she had carried all the days since. The cruelty of people that can fall upon you without warning, the way a fox might seize upon a rabbit. No, much worse, because it comes without reason. A fox needs to eat or feed its young. An animal kills in the name of life, not just to take. She pursed her lips against the pressure of the child coming into the world, her hands between her legs to receive this new gift, she felt the rings of deep scars like hot bands around her calves. She wept with the release, as she had with each birth. With each beginning, she relived the ending of her crippled brother's afflicted life.

All four stood studying the rounded silhouette of their silent home. Nootahweh was holding the bucket of water, a rime of ice coating the rim and the side that had been dipped into the swirling eddy below the falls. Mecowatchshish looked up at his father wondering why they did not go in. He could not smell smoke and it was obvious that the fire had burned very low. The night was still, the hut seemed a part of the landscape, like a lump of earth and the trees around the clearing like taciturn guardians. Even his brothers made no sound. Nootahweh seemed almost frightened. Then a fox barked somewhere close in the night, seeking a mate, and the boy saw his father jump so that a little water sloshed from the pail. Another answered it far off in the darkness and it seemed his father was about to call out, to pierce the shrouded uncertainty that lay before them, but before he could there was a soft cry. It seemed distant and dislocated and at first Mecowatchshish thought it was the fox again but Nootahweh recognized it. He dropped the bucket heedlessly, the water spilling into the snow as he hurried forward and there was another cry. The boys hesitated a moment, looking at each other. The cry became a wail and they rushed in jostling to be the first to follow their father through the door.

There inside, barely perceivable in the contained darkness, in the fading warmth, a naked mystery in the arms of their mother, they found their little sister.

In the Field Hospital they had done only what was necessary to keep him alive and get him ready for transportation to the Casualty Clearing Station, pulling out the larger bits of shrapnel and closing his wounds. In the operating theatre in London they had opened him again and extracted all the metal they could from his body, even using a magnet to coax a tiny shard out of his eye. It had not saved his vision but it kept the fragments from working their way through nerves and tissue and into his brain. Still, sharp mementos remained, transient in his flesh, travelling through muscle and sinew, somehow propelled by his living in slow, secret wounds, sometimes working their way to the surface to appear as hard little lumps under his skin. These could be removed by the local doctor and needed only a stitch or two. Other shards remained stubbornly deep. "We can't just go digging around your body like it's an Easter Egg hunt," a surgeon had told him. Lying in hospital after an early operation, he had come up with the notion that they were incremental dividends of penance. Penalties to be paid for coming out of it alive.

The pain woke him early, when it was still dark, well before it was time to catch the train. It seemed beyond reason that such mementoes of the war might still be pulled out of him more than a decade and a half later. He shifted, seeking a more comfortable position and grunted in frustration. Gina stirred beside him, rolling away and swinging her feet out onto the floor as she sat up on the edge of the bed. He sensed intuitively she had been awake for some time, lying there waiting in silence. She pulled her housecoat on, without a word, and shuffled past his suitcase which she had packed the night before to go and make him breakfast. He had said things in anger after he'd stumbled home, things he regretted. She repaid the slights now with silence and duty.

He pulled himself from bed, stiff from his tumble down the riverbank, back muscles in spasms. He bent awkwardly and, clinging to the brass bed knob for support, he was relieved to be left alone. He balanced on his right leg, the left all pins and needles as he shook it to get the blood flowing. When he put weight on his bad leg it threatened to give out. He stood, one hand holding onto the round knob of brass headboard and stamped lightly to get blood flowing in the reluctant limb before hobbling towards the bathroom to shave. He gazed a long moment into the oval mirror above the sink, preparing for what lay ahead over the course of the next few days. The Department was no longer as patient as they had once been with these medical excursions. The War, after all, seemed like a long time ago and with the Depression affecting everyone's daily life there were more immediate concerns. His time away would be unpaid and he could not afford to be off work more than necessary. This time there would be no Rebecca to soften things, no tea at the café around the corner sharing a few laughs, a taste of what his life might have been had he not become so lost and impetuous in those years after the trenches.

In such moments of despair, it seemed that the only good that had come out of it all was Rebecca. She had been some consolation for the things the so-called Great War had taken from him. They had been schoolmates growing up in Fallowfield, not really friends—his family certainly did not share the same social status—but more than passing acquaintances. He had a very fond recollection of a Christmas holiday sleigh ride with a group of their classmates, ten or twelve of them piled in among the hay bales and loose straw. An old farmer, smoking continuously and muttering French around his pipe stem, drove the horses along through the fields while they all jostled and joked, pushing each other off the sleigh into the powdery drifts and laughing as one or another of them leapt up covered in snow before running to catch up.

Eventually they were all soaked and exhausted and on the way back the chill began to get to them, so they hunkered down into the shelter of the bales and formed a kind of contiguous warm continent under the thin light of the December stars. Someone, probably Jimmy Schmidt who always seemed to be able to produce a flask of some kind of hooch, offered him a drink and he took a long pull and passed it to Rebecca. She smiled and he noted how pretty she was and the way her blonde hair flowed from underneath the knitted tam she wore. He watched entranced as she took a quick sip, even as the thick liquid still burned in his throat, and grinned when she coughed and held the back of her gloved hand to her lips. They sang Christmas carols, the bright silver flask flashing from hand to hand and the more he drank the less he felt like a farm boy. He found himself next to her, his leg pressed against hers, their damp wool clothes transmitting the touch with a keenly tactile awareness. He tried to act with the same air of insouciance they all presented but he was paralysed, afraid to lose the connection. She made no effort to move away. He could feel her muscles tighten and relax, the wet fabric transmitting every subtle shift and implication as the sleigh rocked and bumped along the rough trail rocking them against each other. An intimate quiet settled over the entire group. There was only the sound of the bells on the traces jingling and the sibilant gliding of the runners over the packed snow and the deep resonance of the horses breathing.

A couple near the back of the wagon, half-hidden by strategically placed bales, were kissing. Her warmth seemed to pulse against him as though he was wrapped in her heartbeat and he could smell lavender in her hair. He was surprised to discover his hands and arms rigid at his sides. He contemplated moving a hand to rest lightly on her waist and the thought made him swallow hard. Then the sound of a loud drawn-out fart from one of the horses broke the stillness and filled the night with a less pleasant anticipation until Jimmy sang out, "A farting horse will never tire and a farting man's the man to hire," and they all burst into raucous laughter.

Breakfast was a grim affair. He made no attempt to coax his wife out of her sullen muteness even when she tempted him with a weary sigh or two. He ate with determination, drank his tea, and gathered his things to leave. She followed him to the door and stood behind him as he put on his overcoat till he had taken his Pullman case in hand and reached to turn the doorknob. She then moved in to stand on tip-toe, hands in her apron pockets as she offered her cheek. He gave her a perfunctory peck and pulling on his cap opened the door to step out into the chill morning.

Sam was standing there, one hand raised as if about to knock, a look of surprise on his face.

"Catchin' the train, eh? Bit early though I think."

"Everyone safe and sound?"

"Oh yeah. That's what I come to tell you. The girl's in her bed and Louisa is there with her. She's pretty mad so I didn't hang around. You know that dog is awful skinny but I think he's gonna live."

Gina squeezed into the doorway to take her father's arm and begin to pull him inside. The two men shuffled around each other wordlessly and when it was done, Sam was standing in the hall with his daughter and Hank was outside on the porch. Gina began to push the door closed.

"Have a good trip," Sam called sheepishly through the narrowing opening.

It seemed like a longer walk than usual to the station, switching the heavy bag from hand to hand, grimacing and trying hard not to betray a limp. When he looked at the clock on the wall over the train schedule he was astonished by how early he was. He bought his ticket and exchanged a few pleasantries with Roger the station manager who said, "Hell, Hank, you got time to go home for another breakfast. Another little good-bye smooch with your sweetie."

Hank grunted, turning on his heel.

The hard wooden benches in the waiting room didn't look inviting and the events of the previous night were on his mind, so he began to make his way out onto the platform. It felt better to be walking anyway. He carried his bag to where the luggage trolley was parked and threw it up beside a few crates already loaded and waiting. He strolled slowly up and down the long wooden platform under the overhanging roof and thought of his niece on that island. He felt the anger in him dissipate, replaced by a grudging admiration for her tenacity. She had brass there was no denying it, he had thought, moving towards the circle of light before the dog's low growling had given him away. So much had been taken from the girl and he felt a profound appreciation for the reverence towards life that was the legacy of her father. Still, it was tainted with bitterness because he had been left alone to deal with it.

"Bit early ain't you, Hank? Headin' to main office to meet with the high mucky-mucks?"

It was Heinrich Shultz who worked as a brakeman for the railroad.

"Naw, Henny. Going to The Big Smoke to see the sawbones about my leg."

"Hospital again? They can't still be pulling the war out of you?"

Hank only shrugged.

"Hey, I haven't seen that Pinky on my caboose for a while, the ol' hobo. Always stealin' my lunch that dog."

"He's dead. Distemper," Hank said bluntly

"Aw, hellfire. I liked that dog. Never saw a dog smart enough to catch the train by himself before. Used to wait out by the junction and hop on when we slowed down, then beg for leftovers. Damndest dog...Shit."

There was an awkward silence. Heinrich's mood had soured. He pulled out his railroad watch.

"Well, you still got some waiting, Hank. Warmer inside."

"I'm good here, thanks."

"Suit yourself. Good luck with the leg."

The train rumbled across the countryside.

The world was flashing past, bright and distant and then suddenly shadowed and close. White plains that soon would be lakes again dotted with the tracks of animals and then a blasted wall of granite inches from the glass. Frozen bogs and fens and swaths of cut timber, yellow tamarack and a pair of ravens sitting high in a naked ash squawking over the stark shadow of the train slithering along the ground.

He sat slouched against the side, his head resting close to the big window, his cap pulled down over his face as if he was asleep. The pain in his leg was only a dull ache now and there was something soothing in the rough rocking and clamour of the train. It meant he was moving away, heading south alone and he could relax. With each mile he felt the tension leaving him.

As he sat, drifting into sleep, the memories of the hospital train began to coalesce in his mind. It was only sound and smell to him that first night with his whole head bandaged and swollen, the rocking pulse of the steel wheels as they rumbled across the countryside reminding him he was alive. Occasionally the cars would grind and jerk around a curve or have to slide into a jolting unexpected stop and men would moan and curse or sometimes scream out loud. He thought of his days as a boy walking the high raised spine of the K and P line to go fishing and picking up the round nuggets of a pig iron that had spilled out the rail cars and made excellent slingshot ammunition. And he thought of Rebecca.

Nothing ever came of that night. She had a beau; Daniel Higgins who was two years older, scion of a rich lumber family in Nepean who had already left Queen's to join the war effort. By early spring Hank had enlisted too, despite his mother's pleas for him to finish high school. He remembered that youthful eagerness, the fear that he would miss out on the war, with bitter ruefulness now and thought of his impetuous son Richard. The memory of that winter night and the nearness of her body in the lurching, seismic intimacy of the sleigh had been with him in the mud and stink of the trenches. When the end seemed imminent—the many-headed beast roaring and flailing, flinging lives away all around him, and he was certain that he would be ripped from the world at any second— he had invoked the intoxicating implication of how sweet life might be with her. Huddled in the deepest shadow of Death he imagined an entire lifetime with her in vivid detail. Saw their children at the kitchen table, the lawn he would mow, the way she would look, golden and shimmering, walking towards him on a summer day, her small hand holding her hat to her head against a warm breeze. She could wash the blood from his hands, rinse the grit and mud out of his mouth. He would hold her and bury his face in her hair and her scent and finally lose the putrid stench of the funk holes where he tried to hide from the war.

Crouched clinging to his rifle, bayonet fixed, waiting for the whistles and the call to go over the top, he would promise himself that if he made it back, if he survived the war, then he would find her and marry her. Rich Captain Danny Higgins could go to hell if he wasn't there already. In the lulls when he sat in the sunlight with the other men smoking cigarettes and brewing tea and they talked about their wives and girlfriends, passing around pictures, the fantasy could not be sustained on the strength of one high school sleigh ride and it would slip away from him. He doubted then that she remembered him or even recalled for a second that evening of hay bales and damp clothes when they had nestled together like secret lovers. Then a darker daydream would seep into his brain and leave him brooding and morose. Daniel Higgins returned home, an officer, wounded and proud, a decorated hero with a secure position in his father's company. A wealthy husband admired by all, who could care for her and give her the kind of life she deserved.

This he came to discover years later was closer to the truth than he might have imagined. He had not thought about her for some time and then there she was volunteering for The Dominion Orthopaedic Hospital, a facility built to care for the multitude of maimed and crippled returning from the war. The surprising thing was that she recognized him first, or perhaps it was his name that she recognized. He was embarrassed partly because she found him limping along with his cane and his pirate eye-patch feeling sorry for himself after undergoing what the Doctors told him was an enucleation. They had removed his dead, clouded eye, leaving the muscles intact and eventually, after some healing, it would be replaced with a glass prosthesis. At the same time, he felt some contrition because there were so many others there who had suffered devastating injuries that made his seem trivial. In the reception area on the day of his arrival he'd witnessed two chaps in their uniforms standing arm-in-arm, amputated leg against amputated leg, bracketed by crutches tucked tightly against their good sides, posing for a nurse with her box camera. They held each other with obvious affection, joking through clenched teeth as they smiled for the photograph. Then with easy dexterity of young men, briefly hopping on one foot, switched their crutches back to the side that needed support and shook hands in farewell. Even across the room he could feel the change in atmosphere, the sudden influx of fear as they looked to the exit and the rest of their lives. The loss of sight in one eye, a few shards of iron in his body, a little stiffness in his joints. These seemed minor inconveniences by comparison.

She greeted him in a very formal way, warm but with professional aloofness. He was grateful for this, too much familiarity and he may have blurted out his gratitude for the illusions that had helped him through the bleakest times overseas. The resolve he'd felt crouched in the mire and filth to one day thank her for the hope she had unknowingly provided shrivelled down to an insipid romantic notion. Standing with her in the bright antiseptic hallway, recalling a vision of himself curled in a muddy little niche behind a drooping poncho, it seemed pathetic and adolescent.

She worked mostly with amputees helping to properly fit prosthetics and assisting with patients in the first weeks of their adjustment to an artificial limb. He saw her wedding band, the elegant engagement ring that had been hidden under her woollen mitt that winter's night from another lifetime, and he had heard from his mother about her marriage to Captain Higgins, but he didn't ask about him. Not even when she inquired if he had heard about Jimmy Schmidt and Bud Lawrence who had both died during the Hundred Days Offensive.

"Yes, I heard. At Amiens," he answered simply.

He had seen her a few more times during his stay, which lasted over a month until his eye socket had healed enough to accept the glass prosthetic, but they had only exchanged a smile and a wave.

He was back a year later for more surgery to remove a large fragment in his lower back that had shown up in x-rays. This time he didn't see her till after the operation. Waking in recovery he had the sense of coming from somewhere much deeper than previous operations, a depth he had not visited since he had been tossed on to that stinking wagon for the dead in France. For a few seconds he was terrified that he was back in the field hospital, that everything since the beat of the horse's hooves and the intermittent sky had been a dream. He tried to cough but didn't have the strength or the spit.

Someone held a cup of water to his lips, and a hand supported the back of his head. It took some effort to pull his lips apart, which seemed glued together. The first sip was only a drop or two and only increased his thirst so that he thrust his head forward and took a bigger gulp. It stuck halfway down his throat and he sputtered and choked as most of the water ran out of the corners of his mouth.

"Sorry," he croaked.

"It's fine. Take your time."

It was her. Surprised, he turned his head, still cupped in her hand, and tried to focus.

"Rebecca?"

"You're in Recovery, Mr. Baer. On the second floor. You gave us a bit of a scare." She lowered his head onto the pillow and it came to rest at an awkward angle that left him looking up at her out of the corners of his eyes, his throat stretched and his mouth agape like a frightened horse.

"The surgeon went a little deeper than expected and you were under a long time. There was a lot of blood loss and you may have reacted adversely to the anaesthetic."

He continued to stare blankly, trying to reach back to a solid place in his memory as a wave of vertigo washed over him.

"Where..."

"You're in the Dominion Orthopaedic on Christie Street, Mr. Baer. You've been here before after all."

"I dreamt...back in the trenches...huge rat...on my...on my chest." He gasped between each phrase.

She adjusted his pillow so that he was more comfortable then offered the cup again and he was able to drink with less difficulty.

"I saw your mother in church last week while I was back home and she asked me to look in on you while you were here."

She wiped the corners of his mouth and they sat for a while in awkward silence.

He recovered quickly and saw her two or three more times in the following week. She peeked in just to say hello, barely setting foot in the ward, before turning to be on her way. Then, after therapy one day, he had hobbled across the street to the Whizbang for a cup of tea and a smoke. It was a warm April afternoon and a few other patients were there, crutches propped against the sun-warmed bricks as they sat outside to enjoy the agreeable weather and chat. He was wary of these casual conversations that so often turned to the war and comparisons of exploits and adventures. The names of the dead conjured up in cigarette smoke and laughter as though it had all been a lark.

He understood the inclination, even felt a warm affection for them because of it. Legless men in wheelchairs, men who'd learned to roll their cigarettes one-handed, the blind and disfigured. A vast assortment of broken young soldiers who weren't ready for the rest of their lives. He greeted those he knew, nodded to the rest and sat at a table a little ways off by himself with his copy of *White Fang*.

"Back to the farm tomorrow I hear."

He peered over the top of his library book. The brilliant April sun was high behind her and the winged hat seemed like a crown in silhouette.

"Mrs. Higgins." He started to pull himself up from his seat

but this put pressure on his bandaged hip, sending a sharp jolt of pain through him and he sat back heavily, forced to grab the edge of the small round table to keep his high backed chair from going completely over.

She gracefully ignored this. "May I join you? And no need for old friends to be so formal off the ward. Please call me, Rebecca."

Embarrassed by his infirmity he reached to lift his hat. "I'd be honoured, Rebecca."

She pulled back the only other chair and ordered a tea for herself. "Nothing like a little sun to speed recovery," she said smiling and removing her long gloves. "It's even warmer than I had expected. Would you have a cigarette?"

"I could roll one if that's all right?" he said pulling the makings from his jacket pocket.

"Please. That would be fine."

She watched while he nimbly manipulated paper and tobacco into a neat cylinder and self-consciously ran his tongue along the edge to moisten the glue before handing her the finished smoke. He was charmed by the confident way she took it, staring as she placed it between her lips.

"Light?"

"Oh shit, of course. Sorry. Sorry." He said it twice, apologizing for his soldier's vulgarity as he slapped his pockets to find his trench lighter and lit her cigarette.

"They did a lovely job with your eye. The colour matches perfectly."

He took this as a personal compliment, though it made him self-conscious about his scars and he ran a hand up over the side of his face.

The waiter brought her tea and she sat back while he placed it on the table, drew heavily, then exhaled a long, thin plume of smoke in an exaggerated sigh.

For a few long minutes they drank and smoked and talked

about the weather and smiled at each other. She asked about his parents and he asked about her husband and then they began to reminisce about their school days and this naturally lead into talk about the war. He sensed she shared his reticence in these discussions. She had lost two cousins and an uncle over there and he could hear the passion in her voice when she spoke of the poor treatment many of the returning veterans received.

"We're all sick of it, Hank. Sick of that stupid war and so many want to forget about it and get on with life. We kept our chins up through all the death and grief and no one wants to be reminded. People keep talking about our 'after the war' problem. How will we deal with all these pensions and invalids? We sent young men over there to be mutilated by the thousands. But now we do not want to give them proper treatment?" She glanced over at the cluster of other tables, the maimed, crippled men clinging to whatever brief brush with glory they'd endured. "I see these boys, watch them forming their one-armed baseball leagues and such and it breaks my heart."

She stubbed out her cigarette; her second which she had rolled herself just to prove how well she could, grinding it into the thick glass ashtray. Without looking up she said in a most matter-of-fact way, "So much has been lost. Hasn't it, Hank?" and he sensed she was speaking of some very personal loss. She looked up at him abruptly. "Do you have the time?"

He was unsure of her meaning. "I beg your pardon?"

"The time. What time is it?"

"Oh, of course." He pulled out his pocket watch and flicked open the case. "Ten of two."

"Oh sugar! I'm late. I have to get back. Thanks ever so much. It was lovely to speak with you. Keep well, Hank. Are you going home then?"

"Briefly and then I'm thinking of going up north to visit a friend from my unit." He almost said, 'He's an Indian' as if this might offer some special insight into his motivation but then decided against it.

"Enjoy your trip, then. And I don't want to see you here again." She was smiling brightly as she said it and he nodded in acquiescence but something sank in his chest.

He watched her turn to leave and he had the impulse to jump to his feet and ask, "Do you remember that Christmas hayride in senior year?"

He imagined her turning back, head tilted, blushing slightly, maybe making an offhand remark, something like 'not really' but when he looked into her blue eyes he would see it was a disguise. And thinking of the sulphur poisoned nights when he shivered and prayed and counted each and every breath, gratitude flowing through him to blur his eyes he would tell her, "That hayride got me through the war."

But she was already gone, striding purposefully across the street and he sat back and opened his book and began to read.

Chapter Nine:

Mecowatchshish Says Good-Night

The death of Wahpistanoshish changed everything and Mecowatchshish could not escape the keen edge of his absence. Looking up into the swaying treetops as the restless air moved among the naked branches, he searched for something that was not there. Lying on his pallet snuggled against Neistes, in the soft light of the banked fire, he could detect a melancholy space in the breathing of the other sleepers. At times in the darkness, when the hide door would stir though no one had moved, he would close his eyes, waiting to hear a familiar giggle and anticipating cold feet against his back. But the playful chill did not come.

Neikahweh often wept softly in the night, turned against the rough wall, trying to keep the deep hurt from her family. Nootahweh would whisper his reassurance, words Mecowatchshish could not hear as he lay there in the darkness wishing it could just be a dream and they would all wake together in the bright morning, reunited. He sensed that her dead children, the deep grief of losing Wahpistanoshish and the secret tragedy that was linked to the scars on her legs were a crushing toll on her. In the morning as they woke to begin their day, he felt the weight of these losses amongst them, a burden that had to be put away with each beginning.

The long winter had seemed to settle in under their skin and the illusive sun hid its face from them but eventually the days began to brighten and grow longer. That spring Neikahweh was afflicted with a fever and persistent coughing that left her so weak she collapsed to lie stricken, unable to rise. It took weeks for her to recover and it wasn't until the beginning of summer that she began to regain real strength, though there were still times when she tired easily. Nootahweh relied on his boys to help with the many tasks while he was hunting and to care for their mother and sister. Little Neisheem had grown into an inquisitive and mischievous little girl who brought an exuberant joy to their hidden lives and looking after her was a kind of respite from the relentless worry.

These familiar affections and the warm summer sun started to make the world seem right again. During the dark days, Nootahweh had talked to his wife of taking the family and leaving their place in the woods to travel down river, back to life in the village where there would be help for her sickness. Relations who could watch over the children. Neikahweh, despite her flagging vitality, was defiantly determined to stay, convinced it was the only way to keep their family together. She pleaded and argued against leaving until Nootahweh gave in. It was a good summer and there seemed to be reason to hope that the sickness had passed.

With the approach of fall the weather turned cold and damp and she began to falter into another decline. She tried her best to hide it, trying to suppress the rasping cough that started whenever she exerted herself, pretending it was only a cold but soon she was languishing again. She tired easily and took a hard tumble on a day of freezing rain. Nootahweh suspected she had cracked a rib. The next morning she could not get up and the coughing persisted taking a turn for the worse, each spasm causing a jolt of pain. She stubbornly pulled herself from bed the next day, limping and sore and remained chronically weak, deteriorating over the next few weeks into bouts of wet hacking.

It was a brutally cold winter with deep snow, made more difficult because the rabbit population was at a low ebb and game was scarce. It took its toll on all of them and Nootahweh began to fear more than ever for the well-being of his wife. She became gravely ill and this time there was blood with her coughing and a high fever and she spent many days gasping and too frail to get out of bed. Mecowatchshish saw the fear in his father's face and felt he must know something of this lingering disease but he would not name it now. He did not travel far to hunt, afraid to be away for any length of time and they survived on dried fish and small game.

Once the worst of the spring flooding had passed and the river was safe enough, Nootahweh's brother Franklin travelled with his oldest son Willy to visit, though it was a long journey from where they lived in the south. They brought with them flour and sugar and other supplies including tobacco which were welcome gifts. Nootahweh was especially grateful having smoked even the last of his mullein which he had dried as a substitute. Willy was 17, very quiet and whenever they spoke to him in Cree he answered in English. Uncle Franklin had not seen them for over a year and a half since the fall before Wahpistanoshish had died. He did not try to hide his tears when he saw Neikahweh's condition and recognized the sorrow in her face. He was heartbroken over the loss of his nephew and very concerned for his sister-in-law. Once she fell back into sleep, exhausted over the excitement of visitors, he began earnestly trying to convince Nootahweh that the only sensible choice was to take his stricken wife to the south, to the hospital where she could be treated. He promised that they would be welcome on the reserve and he would help them as much as he could and perhaps he might even find work for Nootahweh with the railroad people while she was being cared for. Both Franklin and Willy wore beautiful new clothes and store-bought boots now. He told them he had been working for some time for the railroad, guiding for the survey crews as the rail lines expanded. He had brought out gifts of canned fruit, hard candy, and a new pipe for his brother. The time for living in the bush was over he said. Mecowatchshish was surprised to hear his father agree and to see the relief in his face. Together with Uncle Franklin, though, it took three days of determined effort; they convinced Neikahweh that it was for the best and then, after many tears, only with the promise that it would only be until she got better. As the men and Willy began planning the trip, Mecowatchshish felt the deep dread of being poised on the edge of days he could not predict.

The trip up river was long and hard. It took over three weeks to reach the Killdeer reserve where they were to live with their Uncle and Aunt and cousins. Twice they had been forced to stop along the way because of heavy rain and Neikahweh's frailty. Mecowatchshish remembered how small their waskahekun had seemed the morning they left, no smoke coming from its chimney. A melancholy loneliness settled over him and he thought of his absent brother and the time they had shared in that quiet place. A breeze moved through the treetops so that they bent and swayed together and whispered something in the language of the wind. Already that life and their arduous journey seemed far in the past and he found himself somewhere he did not want to be. He wished to flow with the same ease as the river, back through time to their own secluded world safe in the woods.

In the first days he had paddled urgently, as hard as he could, driven by the desire for it to be over. The need to get there as fast as possible burned in him as if he alone bore the responsibility of finding the help that would save his mother. He stroked obsessively towards each turn in the river. Paddled and prayed that when they rounded the next bend there would be some sign of hope. All he wanted was for his mother to be made well again so they could return to their home in the woods and things would be as they once were.

Nootahweh had tried to warn him and encourage him to save his strength. Neistes had shaken his head and given reproachful looks. He ignored them and paddled till his arms were worn out and painful blisters erupted on the palms of his small hands. The next day they tore open and because of the pain he could not paddle at all. Instead, he sat with his throbbing hands in his lap and focused his wrathful gaze on Neistes who paddled in the bow at his usual measured pace matched by Nootahweh in the stern. His brother seemed to be enjoying the trip, pointing to things along the bank and asking questions, unconcerned that every stroke, every bend in the river took them farther and farther away from their sanctuary in the woods.

It took a few days to give in to the cadence of the journey and accept each methodical mile as it came. He could not quite put away the frustration he felt, often directed towards his brother, though he knew Neistes was not to blame. In places, moving always against the current, they had to line the canoes around white water or, where it was too shallow, he and Neistes would walk along the shore carrying some of the bundles to lighten the load. Sometimes he was overwhelmed by regret as he felt the growing distance between them and home and the next moment, as well as the anxiety that they moved too sluggishly and would not arrive in time to save Neikahweh. His mother seemed to sink down lower each day, settling to the bottom of the canoe, covered by a square of canvas that Nootahweh had rigged to protect her, sick and dripping with sweat. When they were on the water, Mecowatchshish dipped a cloth in the cool river to soothe her brow. One day, feeling small and powerless under rain that was unrelenting, soaking his sick mother as she lay coughing and slumped over the packs in the canoe, he howled up in anger at the roiling sky. Even Neistes did not tease him over this but knelt hunched in the bow paddling grimly on.

Every portage proved to be a gruelling ordeal. Neikahweh valiantly attempted to walk the first few, adamant that she would not be a burden. Neistes had tried to help, ignoring his mother's protests but it was difficult on the rough terrain. The ground was soft and muddy still from the spring floods and there were narrow flooded spots where he could not manage the extra effort and his own load. The carries were slow and laborious and they had to trudge through swamps and rock gardens. On the third morning she had fallen hard, tripping over an exposed root, scraping her knee and aggravating her old rib injury which had never properly healed. From then on Nootahweh carried her on his back. It meant even slower progress and more bundles for Neistes and Mecowatchshish but they did not complain. The final portage was long with a steep climb at the beginning, but it finally put the river behind them, skirting a series of narrow rapids, jammed with deadheads and taking them to the northern tip of Lahwaynahkon Lake. They left Neikahweh resting under some trees and Mecowatchshish stayed to watch over her as they carried the first loads to the other end. Mecowatchshish kept the kettle with him and gathered some dry wood to make tea for his mother. They tried to convince Neisheem to remain but she was too restless and would not be left behind. She picked up a paddle to prove her usefulness and skipped off down the trail. When they returned after some time to retrieve them and the final burdens she was still dragging the paddle behind her.

The tea and rest did little to revive Neikahweh and she slipped in and out of consciousness and had to be carried. Nootahweh used his tumpline to support her weight running it underneath her and up across his forehead. She became delirious and tried to fight her way out of her bonds so that Nootahweh had to stop and bind her too him with a leather strap. It was precarious just the same and he was afraid to fall on the rocky, uneven ground and injure his wife. Neistes and Neisheem were far ahead, the little girl, having abandoned the paddle which was now in Willy's charge, was running from tree to tree with a stout carpenter's pencil that Uncle Franklin had given her, pretending to write her name on each one. She had watched her oldest brother carve his into a large aspen earlier in the trip. Mecowatchshish had hesitated and then ran after them, unable to bear the anguish of his mother's feverish struggles.

They waited at the head of the rapids and while his siblings laughed watching a mink slip in and out of the turbulent current on the far shore, Mecowatchshish sat with his eyes closed listening to the water as it spilled down over a series of ledges, the sound reminded him of the falls near their home and he could almost see the empty waskahekun sitting in the deserted clearing. How silent it must be without them. It shocked him how little of the trip lived in his memory. It was like one of his mother's fevered dreams, the water endless and hostile as they struggled against the current. A sudden, overpowering fear swept over him and he imagined the ghosts of his dead brother and sister. Would they look for their family there and be sad and become lost because they were gone? Maybe they would join the other spirits who lived in the dark crevices around the cataracts. He heard a shout and looked to see Neistes pointing across the river. The sleek mink was pulling a fish up onto a flat rock on the other side, its jaws locked firmly around the head as the silver body jerked and curled trying to escape. Neisheem giggled and clapped her hands and it made him want to look away. He turned his head and saw his father approaching, his mother slumped over his back and

Uncle Franklin and Willy, each with a canoe balanced on their shoulders, following patiently behind.

The sun was low in the west as they began the paddle up the long eastern arm of Lahwaynahkon Lake. There was a steady forceful breeze blowing straight up the long arm against them. They still had a long way to travel on the big lake before they would reach Uncle Franklin's home. They were weary and it was late in the day but they kept on till dusk and then stopped at a large island where Willy said there was a trapper's cabin that would not be occupied at that time of year. It was small with a low roof but it had a stone fireplace at the far end and they settled in quickly and were soon asleep.

It was cool and clear the next morning. Neikahweh appeared a little better at first after a warm night bundled up by the fire and sat to sip a little tea but was soon shivering with chills again. She wanted to try to be more helpful and pulled herself up to her feet, "I'll make some bannock," she said, then was racked by rasping coughs that caused her to spit up bloody froth before collapsing. It was painful to hear and see, and Mecowatchshish turned away while Nootahweh tended to her. They lingered a while and ate the last of their oatmeal and cooked bannock on green sticks over a fire that Uncle Franklin and Willie had made outside. The men conferred for a time and then decided they would push on and try and make the settlement. Nootahweh tried to reassure his children with a smile and then he and Uncle Franklin carried her down to the shore. Neistes stood uncomplaining, knee deep in the frigid water, to steady the canoe while they settled her in and packed the gear around her.

A cold wind swirled around them in petulant gusts like a spiteful presence determined to keep them from their destination. For the first little while as they set out the canoes side by side, Willy, speaking in short bursts between the strokes, said that when they saw the high cliff face, known as Hobgoblin Point where the Maymayquaesihwuk lived, they would know they were close. "There's pictures...on the rocks...ancestors drew...them things sit up there...in the dark places...no noses, hair everywhere...if they're feelin' mean...the waters rough...supposed to leave tobacco...no time today...your Mama's pretty sick so...paddle hard for the other side."

The wind seemed to be snatching the words away, then a big swell rolled up between the canoes and broke over the sides splashing them with cold water. They moved farther apart, the wind buffeting hard against them, there was no more talking and the paddlers dug in. They were familiar with stories of the spirits who lived in hidden places beside the lakes and rivers. There was a deep crevice close to the falls near where they used to go for water and one evening Neistes had claimed to have seen one. A momentary glimpse through the mist thrown up by the churning water before it disappeared right into the massive stone wedge that split the falls. He had told his younger brothers that if they got too close to the slick granite edge above the tumult the creature would push them in. With his mother, pale and groaning on the bottom of the canoe, his family so far from home, it hurt to remember the way Wahpistanoshish had laughed at this and shaken his fist at the falls.

The blisters on his hands had begun to form into calluses but his palms were still tender. He did not mind; he welcomed it, gripping the paddle tightly, feeling the dull ache with every stroke. For a while he concentrated only on this rhythmic twinge of pain, matching his brother's pace in the bow and helping to keep them turned into the waves. None of them could swim well enough to make the shore in such a rough chop. When he looked up Uncle Franklin and Willy were well ahead and he could see the long arm opening up into the main body of the lake. Neisheem, as was her habit, was leaning to one side to trail her hand in the cool water but her little face turned back towards them was set and serious. Uncle Franklin had teased her when she had done this on the river, telling her a big pike was going to come and latch on to her tiny brown fingers. Then he had made a big splash with the blade of the paddle and she had squealed and clutched her balled fist against her chest as their Uncle's deep rumbling laugh echoed through the river valley.

To the north loomed the tall granite face of the point that marked where the lake split into two elongated bays. The wind had begun to pick up and the waves were becoming choppy. Mecowatchshish looked to where they broke, splashing up high against the grey wall of stone and water. Painted ochre figures could be seen glistening where the rock was wet. Strange forms that filled him with dread. High above on the cracked stone face was a deep crevice where the imposing edifice had split apart. Neikahweh stirred, shifting to one side with a moan and the canoe tilted sharply to the right. Startled, he shot his arms up and out for balance and missed his stroke.

"Easy," said Nootahweh.

Neikahweh moaned, then let out a loud angry grunt and Mecowatchshish twisted to look at her. She lay with her head towards the stern covered by the grey cloth tucked in around her. Her face, soaked with sweat, suddenly contorted in a pained grimace as she kicked her legs out, sending the end of the tarpaulin flying up off her feet. It caught in the wind and folded back over itself, covering her face. She began to thrash and fight harder so that the canoe rocked and veered. The next wave hit broadside and threatened to tip them into the cold water.

He grabbed the gunwale, dropping his paddle into the churning water. His eyes met those of his father and without Nootahweh saying a word he knew what he had to do. They would never survive being dumped; his mother would sink like a stone. He and his brother and father might thrash on the surface a while but Uncle would never be in time to save them all, and what would become of Neisheem. They were still a long way from anywhere they could safely land and the sheer face of Hobgoblin Point rose out of the water a hundred feet to its tree-lined precipice.

He twisted to throw himself back, keeping low and stretching out full length to cover his mother. Her knee came up and glanced off the ribs on his left side so that he grunted and half-turned, almost slipping over the side. Neistes was drawing at the end of his stroke to help swing the bow directly into the rising waves and paddled with all he had to propel the canoe away from the rocks, towards the far shore. Mecowatchshish squirmed towards centre trying to pin down his mother's arms as she flailed and struck his head and shoulders with desperate, poorly directed blows.

"Mama. Quiet, Mama. Be still. We're in the canoe."

He gripped her forearms and fought to restrain her. His long hair hung down and the bitter wind off the lake fanned it across his face. Suddenly his mother's eyes focused on him, brimming with terror and rage.

"Go back to hell!" she croaked. She was wracked by a paroxysm of coughing as she arched her back trying to throw him off. Blood appeared on her lips and he could feel the strength leave her. "Let... him...be..." it was a barely audible plea, each word punctuated by a gasping fight for air. As he let his full weight rest on her in a desperate embrace, he found himself looking back at the ominous cliff wall with its painted figures. High up, in the half-light of the crevice he thought something moved.

He turned his face trying to fight off the rising panic and saw the other canoe pulling away, his uncle and cousin paddling for all they were worth to cross the wide expanse of water and reach the safety of the settlement on the far shore. Beyond them in the distance he saw that the people of Killdeer had become aware of their predicament and were gathering on the beach. He knew that Uncle Franklin and Willy could not help them out on the treacherous water. The waves seemed to come from three directions at once and it was if they were being held in place. He saw Neistes shoulders droop and could tell there was no strength left in his arms. His father was weary from the long journey and too tired to do any more than hold them steady and keep them off the rocks. The effort of getting Neikahweh this far had worn him out.

He watched the other canoe as it shrank into the distance and hoped that his little sister would be safe. Willy and his uncle worked relentlessly until they were in shallow water where two men waded in and steadied the boat. Neisheem was lifted free and carried high above the waves. He thought he could hear her cry out over the howl of the pitiless wind. The paddlers tumbled out exhausted into shallow water and others who'd been lined along the narrow beach came to help them and empty the canoe. Three young men leapt in immediately and headed out onto the lake towards the floundering boat. The sky grew darker and the storm more determined. It felt like they had been there for a very long time and Mecowatchshish closed his eyes and rested his head on the chest of his mother. It seemed he did not breathe until he felt someone leap into place between him and the weary Neistes. There was a tense few moments with the two canoes wallowing together in a trough; men grunting as Neistes was transferred, plucked bodily out of his place as they rose on a wave. It seemed they would capsize and Mecowatchshish twisted on top of his mother, the craft tilting until the gunwale dipped low so that his face was practically in the water. Then the stranger took up the paddle and began to stroke in a powerful rhythm that drove them swiftly across the turbulent water. Nootahweh summoned the last of his strength and did his best to match him.

There was the desperate heaving turmoil of wind and waves and the efforts of the paddlers and then they crossed an unseen border where a peninsula protected the small cove and into a sense of being let go. Everyone catching their breath together. They scraped bottom just behind the rescuers who were pulling their canoe out of the water. He was lifted bodily from his mother and set aside in the wet sand. He stumbled a bit, finding himself so suddenly on solid ground, and stood watching, heedless of the waves breaking over his feet as others moved to take Neikahweh and carry her farther up the beach. They set her down on a blanket spread out on the sand and used it as a makeshift stretcher to transport her. Someone, he did not look to see who, pushed a pack from the canoe into his arms and gave him a firm shove towards shore. He went slowly, in a kind of daze, surprised to be suddenly among so many strangers. He watched as his father gripped one corner of the litter blanket by its rolled edge and joined the group of men shuffling forward as they carried Neikahweh off.

He was unsure of what to do with his little family scattered among people he did not know. Everything had happened so fast, so much new territory and everyone moving with such purpose. He took a few tentative steps, clutching the bundle in his arms. Out over the lake, bright rays of sunshine pierced through the thick clouds and the fierce squall seemed to abate, the day turning over. Mecowatchshish stood, wet feet numb with cold, a little boy remembering the river, envious of the running water that would flow back over all the long miles they had travelled. Past the place in the woods where he and his siblings had been born and cheman had lain hidden peering out with its black open eye. He looked for his family and it seemed almost everyone had gone. A woman, squat and plump with a round pleasant face, was in front of him and he realized she had been waiting patiently the whole time.

"I'm your Auntie Isabel. Last time I saw you, you wasn't even walking yet. Come on they're takin' her up to our place. We set a tent up there for your family. We'll take care of you all don't worry."

She took him by the wrist and led him through the village. The little cabins with their smoking chimneys seemed too close together. People everywhere and everyone curious about them. Children staring. Dogs running up to bark and sniff. He felt drowsy and disconnected like an animal pulled from its winter sleep. He resented Neistes who had seemed excited all along by their journey, happily anticipating being among their relations, renewing old acquaintances. Their Uncle's family kept chickens and he scowled when he spotted his older brother laughing as he leaned against the wire fence surrounded by enthusiastic children. They were giggling and demonstrating how the ugly birds would scramble to compete and peck at each other over a few blades of green grass tossed through the gaps.

Neikahweh had been brought to a walled tent close to Uncle Franklin's small house just as dark clouds closed overhead and rain began to pelt down. She was laid on a comfortable pallet inside. Willy had been using it as his own to escape the crowded cabin and his younger siblings but for now had gone to stay with other relatives. Soon he would leave to spend the summer working in the bush with the survey crews anyway. Someone had brought in their gear and prepared beds for them. Little Neisheem was taken to sleep in the house with Aunt Isabel's youngest daughters.

Mecowatchshish squatted inside, heavy with the long weariness of the journey, his head resting on his knees as he listened to his mother's hoarse breathing and the downpour percolating on the canopy. He still had not spoken a word aloud, not even to Nootahweh. The sound of the storm on the stretched canvas became a sanctuary and he felt concealed inside the drumming. Hidden from the world. He drifted off and was surprised to wake the next morning, the whole night passing in the blink of an eye, stretched out under his blankets, the tent full of soft light. His father was there kneeling by the bed and feeding his mother some milky oatmeal. He rose still in his clothes and went out barefoot, blinking against the full sun, to relieve his bladder in a nearby stand of bushes. Water dripped from the trees in a broken echo of the rain that had greeted them. When he came back, Nootahweh was waiting outside the tent holding his moccasins and he led him over to a group that had gathered around a fire. They were cooking some freshly caught fish and frying eggs. He sat down on a log bench and Aunt Isabel fetched a tin plate with a serving of pike that she placed in his lap.

He felt the others watching him and though they weren't staring he was frozen like a stalked rabbit by the scrutiny. He was not used to the presence of so many people and wanted to retreat to the tent but felt this would be seen as rudeness. Suddenly something else caught their attention and the conversation became excited. He looked up from his lunch to see an old woman, walking with the help of a stout carved stick, coming along the path that led up from the beach directly to them. She was acknowledged warmly by the community as they congregated around her, one by one taking her hand and calling her Nanny. A boy with his hair tied up in two long braids followed close behind her, eyes on his moccasins. He looked to be about the same age as Neistes and was called Daniel. Uncle Franklin stepped forward out of the group and introduced Nootahweh to her. Nanny nodded as they helped her to a place by the fire and the boy squatted on his heels next to her. It was lucky that she had been called to the village to tend to an old man with a bad leg infection, though it was said of Nanny that somehow she was often exactly where she was needed.

Nanny was short and sturdy and her grey hair, held back by a faded red kerchief, was streaked with strong bands of black. On more than one evening during their journey, as they sat around the fire after a long day on the river, Uncle Franklin had spoken of her with much hopefulness. She was a powerful healer, he told them, an Ojibwa who had married an Oji-Cree man named Peter Hannah and come to live on the reserve as a young woman a few years before Uncle Franklin had been born. She and her husband became renowned as medicine people and lived alone in a small cabin on the edge of the village and never had children. Peter, Uncle

Franklin told them in a hushed conspiratorial tone, had taken his own life some years before after a long and painful stomach cancer. All their potions and poultices could do nothing to help and it grew inside him until it got to where he could not even swallow soup. Knowing there was no hope, failed by his own powers and before he grew too weak, he went out into the woods with his shotgun. After that, Nanny had gone to live alone in a different place and though people asked, for a long time she did no healing. Some said that someone had put a curse on her husband and that was why she had left. Then in recent years she had started travelling with the young boy, though no one could say where he had come from, and she had started to practice her medicine again.

She spoke quietly, lips hardly moving, and the boy sat mutely beside her, clutching a hide bag decorated with a sunburst of painted porcupine quills. Uncle Franklin, face lit by the leaping flames, had revealed a few of the many rumours around the mystery of how the boy had come to be with her. Some claimed he had been given to her or that he was abandoned in the woods as a baby, because he was silent from birth and did not coo or cry. Others whispered he was an adopted bear cub, that Nanny's magic had grown strong during her self-imposed exile and that the lonely old woman had transformed the creature into a child who could make no human sound.

Nootahweh invited them to eat and Nanny nodded and said, "Megwhich." She took the portion offered to her and passed it to the boy who immediately began stuffing chunks of fish in his mouth, accidentally dropping the bag on the ground. It flopped open and Mecowatchshish could see it was stuffed with cattail roots and mullein leaves and other things they had gathered that were not so easy to identify. Nanny swatted the boy on the back of the head and he stopped chewing and looked up long enough to bow his head to Uncle Franklin in mute thanks.

Mecowatchshish, who had never been struck by his parents, studied the old woman with reproach. She was squat, dressed simply in a dark skirt with a muddy hem and water stains up to the knees with several layers of shirts all partially hidden under a patched woollen sweater. He watched as she brought a small brook trout to her mouth, holding it by its crisp, fried tail. Her hands looked strong, the tendons standing out, the fingers bent over a little to one side by arthritis and there were thin black ribbons of dirt under her nails. She had a gap where two teeth were missing on the upper right and he found something loose and slightly repulsive about the way her mouth moved as she chewed. Another medium-size beaded bag rested on her hip, the strap slung over the opposite shoulder. They both wore moccasins stitched in the puckered Ojibway style. He found the woman and the boy somewhat disappointing in comparison to the mythical beings of his Uncle's stories. He suddenly became aware that Daniel was watching him with hostile regard, his face set, eyes unflinching. Nanny reached out and laid a hand on the boy's shoulder then rubbed gently the place on his head where she had struck him. She looked across the fire at Mecowatchshish.

"Daniel. You know the story of Daniel?"

She spoke in Ojibwa but slowly so he could catch the meaning. He thought she referred to the boy at her side.

"It's about a boy made to sleep with lions. Gitchi Manitou," she raised her open hands up towards the sky then clutched the boy's shoulder pulling him in close. "He protects Daniel. I heard it long ago. It's a good story."

After they had eaten and had tea, she pulled herself with great effort up onto her feet. Nootahweh rose as well. He pulled a pouch of tobacco from his pocket which he offered to Nanny and she accepted by clasping her hands over his and giving a slight nod.

She slipped the pouch into her bag and they went together into the tent. His father could be heard speaking to her in a quiet voice over the pained coughing of his mother and then Nanny began to speak in a very deliberate way. His father wandered listlessly out to sit by the fire, his face in his hands. An incantation began to filter through the canvas starting softly but building steadily and though Mecowatchshish could not understand the words there was something mesmerizing in the quality of its delivery. She paused and called out for Daniel who snatched up the bag and brushed passed into the tent. When Mecowatchshish looked down he noticed the piece of fish he couldn't bring himself to eat was gone from his plate.

Soon the smell of white cedar being burned drifted out and the singing started up again and after some time the boy came out and then the old woman backed through the flaps of the tent. For Mecowatchshish it was like waking from a dream. He shivered and became aware of where he was and as he watched the old woman intently felt the great distance of the last few weeks and knew it was only the beginning. She carried a goose wing fan in one hand and a mussel shell with something smouldering in the other. She paused for a moment, lips moving, eyes closed, and then she sprinkled the ashes from the shell across the entrance to the tent. She told Nootahweh she would make an infusion from the inner bark of aspen mixed with maidenhair fern as that might help a little with the coughing. Uncle Franklin stood and pulled his hand from his pocket to offer some of his railroad money but she shook her head and pushed his hand away. It was said that she would accept nothing that had come from the whites, except tobacco which after all had first been a gift from Gitchi Manitou.

Nootahweh handed a plate he had prepared to Mecowatchshish and told him to carry it inside to his mother. He looked down at the tin plate in his hands. Some bannock and a bit of fish his father had minced to make sure there were no bones and so his mother would not have to chew. He took the plate inside and his father followed him in with the special tea and milk in a bowl. Neikahweh smiled up at them from where she lay. There was a trickle of bloody sputum drying on her chin and her husband wiped it away with his thumb before taking a pinch of the soft white meat in his fingers and pressing it to her lips. She ate slowly and he offered her another morsel while Mecowatchshish held the plate. When she had swallowed this he took up the tea and held it to her mouth whispering his own prayer as she sipped. With his free hand he took the plate and instructed the boy to go and fetch his brother who was down by the river playing with his cousins.

They gathered in the tent, a single low candle burning on a plate perched on a block of wood. Nootahweh, Neistes, Mecowatchshish, and Neisheem who sat on Uncle Franklin's knee. Mecowatchshish could see the plate by his father's side and knew she had not eaten much.

"Your mother is tired," Nootahweh said. "I want you all to say good-night to her."

Neisheem got down and crawled in beside her mother and hid her face against Neikahweh's breast and Mecowatchshish shuffled in on his knees to hug them both at once. It lasted only a second and then she began to hack and choke and the bucket was held for her to spit into. The little girl began to cry and Mecowatchshish started to scold her but stopped when he felt his father's hand on his shoulder.

She settled back onto her blankets and looked up to Neistes who still stood back, his face hidden in the shadows.

"My brave one," she said and he rushed to her kicking over the unfinished plate as he fell into her arms.

After a short while Auntie Isabel, Uncle Franklin's wife, came in to take Neistes and Mecowatchshish to her home. He looked back as they went and saw that many people were gathered close around the fire beyond the tent. There was a loud crackling and by its rich scent he knew someone had offered some sweet grass onto the fire. In the light from the leaping flame he could see Nanny was there and Daniel leaning drowsily against her. Mecowatchshish slept that night in a big bed crowded with three of his cousins and his little sister slept with his Aunt. Sometime, late into the night, he stirred in the strange darkness, one of his young cousins snoring wetly with a cold beside him and listened to the men around the fire, singing their prayers.

They buried her in the old way, wrapped in birch bark with her feet pointing to the west. A small fire was kept going by the grave for four days. Nanny and the boy stayed for the feasting that was meant to celebrate Neikahweh's life. Auntie Isabel's relations supplied a bull moose, an old sow bear and a few chickens for meals. When the old woman left, she came to each of them in turn. He would always remember how surprisingly soft her wrinkled fingers felt on his cheek as she spoke her quiet blessing and though it seemed the words were not meant to be understood by him, he knew it was more than a kindness. He watched, standing with what was left of his family, as she and Daniel loaded their canoe and began to paddle to the east. Then he turned and looked north and knew in his heart that they would never return to their faraway home.

Chapter Ten:

Spring/Simon

It was an inclement spring that arrived in a turbulent rush, swallowing winter's last few bitter days whole. Snow disappeared and lakes opened as creeks and streams swelled in muddy turmoil and tumbled down out of the grey green hillsides to gnaw the darkening threadbare coats of ice into a chattering jumble. The landscape appeared trampled or to hang in tatters and the sky was in constant transition. From baleful dark clouds and sudden thunderstorms to bright clear blue to ethereal white eddies coursing overhead. Snow fell in big, soft flakes that turned to ice pellets that became a steady drizzle.

While the capricious weather churned through its inclement moods Simon and Joe Pete continued to look forward to the end of their banishment from each other. Joe Pete could hardly wait to usher her cousin into Poppa Sam's tar-papered shed where the rescued dog had been kept during his recovery.

The last thing Hank had done on that long night before collapsing next to his wife was to limp down the narrow upstairs hallway to stand over Simon who lay dazed but sleepless in his bed. For a quiet moment the boy stared up at the silhouette trying to make out his father's eyes. He had been waiting to hear him come in, wracked with terror that because of him his father might have met the same end as his uncle. He listened to the heavy footsteps as the man dragged himself through the house, the still night punctuated by involuntary grunts. It was an odd mix of relief and apprehension.

"Pa?" he said letting his father know he was awake.

"Stay away from Joe Pete and stay away from that dog till I get back..." another dark pause. "That miserable creature will be dead before morning."

It seemed he had more to say but only sighed and shuffled out the door. Simon twisted to bury his face in his pillow and sob. He didn't really understand this weeping and shook with the vain effort to suppress it, crying till sleep overcame him.

Out on the island Joe Pete slept under the vigilant watch of Poppa Sam who had rigged a makeshift shelter over the girl and the animal with what was left of the canvas tent. He kept watch by the fire, uneasy in that haunted place, certain there were spirits that did not welcome intrusions and unconvinced that the wolf hunters had simply left, deserting the dogs. He suspected something far more sinister and could not wait to quit the wretched place at the earliest opportunity. That night, seeing the dire condition of the dog he had been more inclined to agree with his son-in-law that it was a lost cause but could not bring himself to say so to his granddaughter. They were in a dangerous place and time seemed to stand still. Anxiously safeguarding the sleeping Joe Pete, he briefly contemplated surreptitiously throttling the frail dog. But that, he decided, would only be another betrayal for the heartbroken girl. He saw too much of her father in her passionate stand, that desire to nurture whatever small spark of life there was in the animal. He could not turn his back on that spirit of fierce compassion even though he felt it might be a mistake. He knew too much of death. Looking at the feeble dog and the grief-stricken girl lying side-by-side in the darkness, he couldn't douse the glimmer of hope flickering there.

He strapped the animal onto the sled before dawn, moving with a singular purpose as he listened to the ice muttering in grating whispers. The sleeping girl stirred and moaned and seemed to answer with her own anguish. He felt the wind change and knew that soon the swifts at the narrows would break free and begin to furrow an opening of dark impatient water. The strengthening sun would swell the flowing creeks and, channel by sinuous channel, the river would return. Against his better instincts, he woke his granddaughter at first light and together they dragged the emaciated mongrel home across the ice.

Hank returned after only two days, catching a ride with George Ronson on an Ontario Provincial Air Service flight from the District Office, gritting his teeth through the entire landing as the skis jounced along the rough runway. Surly and short-tempered and still walking with a limp, he had dropped his bag in the kitchen and immediately called his youngest son out to the woodshed. There, without a word, he meted out ten solid blows with his belt across the seat of Simon's pants. They were not dealt in anger but with a dispassionate reserve and Simon, for his part, flinched but managed not to cry. Afterwards, as they stood facing each other there was the feeling of a bargain having been completed, as if they might shake hands over a negotiated understanding. Then Hank led his son back into the kitchen where his mother was busy washing dishes and laid out his decree.

The prohibition against seeing his cousin, other than in class, or to go anywhere but school would continue for the next three weeks. After that he would be allowed to visit at the cabin or their grandfather's before supper, but he was not to go into the bush with her without explicit permission and he was to be home every day, on time, for supper. He was to keep the wood barrel full without fail and there was to be no more nonsense about spirits or Indian ghosts or messages from animals. He was adamant that even if the dog continued to recover it would prove vicious and untameable and have to be destroyed. His mother stood by the sink, drying the china through the entire proclamation, eyes on her busy hands, and Simon sensed that she was under her own terms and restrictions. She seemed distant and unhappy as she worked to quietly slip the clean dishes away in their proper cupboards. He was sure that an argument had been lost on his behalf and that there was cost in all of this to her and though he could not say what it was, he felt responsible for the lines of difference that were deepening around them all.

Joe Pete tended the dog with doting patience and he responded remarkably, growing stronger daily. Even Simon, who had not seen him since that dreadful night, but heard enthusiastic reports in the schoolyard at every recess, began to feel affection for the rescued mongrel and to look forward to finally setting eyes on the miracle of Casey Island. Still, he felt a deep apprehension as they made their way across Indian Arm and he saw how the swelling river had slithered well onto their grandfather's property. One sinuous coil undulated over the end of the peninsula, following a slight depression in the land, inching towards the dark shack, and there was something ominous in its languid power. There was a feeling that the river would never look the same to him. The saturated ground squelched under their feet as they walked, and here and there water-soaked logs languished, marooned by the high water. Clots of snow remained in the nearby bush and a speckled dark berm of it nestled against the north side of the house. They moved along a soggy fringe of seasons cleaving between the river and the land.

After the tragic winter, the black surge of water seemed ever more treacherous and hostile to him now unlike any other spring he'd known. A restless coil of fear that had somehow come between him and Joe Pete. Bits and pieces of other lives spirited away by the river bobbing by and underneath, hidden in the murk, mingled among the branches of drowned trees, the lost artifacts and bones of the dead.

Last Saturday morning as he waited for his turn in one of the chairs, he heard the men talking in the barbershop with his father about the high water and past misfortunes. The unpredictable nature of rivers and the suddenness with which life could end. The shop was run by two Italian brothers, Cesare and Nico, who most called Big Nick because of his lanky height. They nodded their heads as customers pontificated on how the water had crested higher than anyone could remember and each had a story from the past to add to the litany of misfortune. Children falling from docks, tangled fisherman tumbling from their boats, young swimmers caught in an undertow, canoes tipped in rapids. Disappearances and suicides. And Cesare who had heard all the stories chimed in with where the bodies were found. There was a particular undercurrent of sadness in the way they addressed his father, their heads shaking slowly as they glanced down to check the polish on their shoes. Cesare with nothing to say could only shrug and look towards heaven, scissors in one hand and a comb in the other.

As the scissors snipped and the men turned to their customary complaints about the Depression and speculations on the next day's weather, Simon contemplated on Joe Pete's grief and drifted into a morose vision. Rushing water sweeping over that part of the island where they had found Mohegan, claiming the mouldering carcasses and the scraps of canvas and remains of the camp. It was a relief to think of it all swept clean, the evidence of that awful day gone, but there was something menacing in the water's deception, in what it seized and dragged away to hide beneath its transitory surface. Drowsily sitting by the stove in the humid heat of the barber shop, where hot wet towels waited for the next shave, he drifted off a moment haunted by visions of the mauled dogs and his vanished uncle. He saw himself standing on the trestle watching a log, dappled and pitching in the current, suddenly become the bloated corpse of his father rolling its waxen face up to the sky. He started and gasped opening his eyes to see Nico looming close with a gleaming straight razor held in front of him. There was a moment of silence and then the men burst out laughing.

"You think is-a for you, little boy? I don't shave that baby face."

On the Friday the separation enforced by Hank ended, Joe Pete rushed to find Simon after class and drag him straight from school to Sam's place. She grabbed his arm, no explanation was necessary and soon they were racing down the path to Indian Arm. The old man was sitting on his front steps, smoking his pipe and contemplating the heaving river. He waved vigourously as they ran past.

"O-KI-MAH," shouted Joe Pete, her right hand raised high in salute then swinging down to retake Simon's hand and pull him towards the shack. She turned the rough piece of wood that held the plank door closed and opened it just enough to allow them to slip in, Simon swivelling his head around for one nervous look at the overflowing river only a stone's throw away.

She tugged him inside, pulling the door shut firmly before flipping the sturdy hook into its eye. "He sits there every day for hours and watches. Sometimes he's gone for a couple days searching along the banks, looking for...We worry about him."

Simon nodded. "I know. The river is dangerous."

She narrowed her eyes and took a big breath. "He's looking for him. But...I don't think he'll find him. I've been going out, too. Following the trails along the bank. Looking for signs." She turned away abruptly, calling into the shadowy interior. "Wachay, Mohegan. Wachay, wachay," she cooed. Over her shoulder, she said, without looking at him, "I want Poppa Sam to teach me Cree. I think Mohegan only heard cruel words and I want him to learn new ones. You should learn too and we could have secret talks."

Simon, knowing his father's aversions, only smirked at the suggestion. He had been surprised to find some relief in the prohibitions imposed by his father. Spending time with Joe Pete had become awkward, walking on eggshells, afraid to say something that might remind her of her loss or lead to an argument. He no longer knew how to respond to talk of receiving messages or signs or the fantasy of being with her father again. Mostly, to avoid betraying anyone, he tried to let these notions pass but, for reasons he could not precisely define, a slow burn would start inside his head. An agitation that stayed with him and grew into seething anger and then shameful guilt. She must have begun to sense this because lately during their brief encounters at school she only talked about the dog's healing and progress. Still, there were times when he saw her standing alone waiting for the bell, he would slip around a corner or hide amongst a crowd.

He blinked, his eyes adjusting to the gloom. There was something beguiling about the interior of the old windowless shed. It smelled of dirt and blood, creosote, cut pine, and the birthing of unknown generations of feral cats. Sunlight filtered in around the tilted door, through gaps and knotholes and tears in the tarpaper to lance down onto the sand floor. A long work bench made from three rough-milled planks ran along the right side and held a handmade wooden toolbox, several traps, a leather tumpline, a ball peen hammer, and a collection of lidless tobacco tins containing various nails and screws. Near the door, long-handled tools leaned into the corner: a scythe, a spade, a hoe, a rake, a pickaxe. A swede saw and a tapered hand saw hung on nails driven into the naked studs above the bench. On the opposite wall were some more wide shelves constructed of narrow spruce logs, where the dried whitefish were stored for winter and the heavy canvas that covered them was folded and placed neatly to one side, a double-bitted axe laying on top. Above, tied under the rafters, was a small cedar canvas canoe and across them were several hand-carved paddles, woven baskets, a collection of long wooden poles, and two hockey sticks. One was short and had been handmade for Joe Pete by her father.

It took Simon a few seconds to adjust to the shrouded soft interior and even before his vision cleared, he had the creeping sense of being carefully scrutinized. The dog came into focus in the far corner of the shed in an aura of floating dust motes and shadow pierced with pinholes of sunlight. It was sitting up, a much different looking dog than the gaunt, hostile apparition that had collapsed at their feet on Casey Island. Fuller and sleeker. Vigilant with a trembling energy. He caught his breath as Joe Pete ran to him and threw her arms around his neck. The dog accepted this attention calmly, without flinching, but watched over her shoulder with singular intensity. Simon tried to be reassured by the stout rope that ran from a leather harness on the dog to an iron ring screwed into the wall.

Joe Pete turned, one arm still around the dog, and asked, "What do you think? Surprised, eh?"

It was a relief to break from the animal's stare and meet his cousin's eyes. "He looks real fine, Joe Pete. Real...big!" He hoped the dog understood and took his words, or at least his tone as a gesture of good will. As if in response, the dog stretched out its front legs to lie down again, though still alert and tensed on all fours.

The girl stroked him from between his tall triangular ears to the base of his tail, her hand lifting so that her fingertips brushed ever so lightly over the scruff of his neck. Scarring from the desperate pulling at the chain was clearly visible, giving the appearance of a slight mane.

"Poppa Sam made up this harness from a dogsled rig so Mohegan's neck could heal. Everyone thought he would die." She watched her hand as it lovingly ran the length of the dog's back. "Your dad said I would never get him home."

"The others were all dead..." he said, shrugging over this weak defense of his father.

She stood suddenly and Mohegan rose as well, vigilant and ready to lunge. Simon took a step back, the shed shrinking around him.

She followed his brief retreat, came face to face with him, their noses almost touching. He heard a low rumble start deep in the dog's throat.

"I saw him." It was a whisper.

"Saw who?"

"That night, with Okimah, waiting for daylight. Hush Mohegan. I woke up and listened to hear if Mohegan was still breathing. I put my hand out to feel his heart. It beat strong. I felt it in my fingers. Up my arm. In my own heart." Her hand had traced the path of this shared pulse lightly along her sleeve to rest on her chest as though she were taking a vow. "The moon had come out, a half a moon low in the sky and there in the trees was the shape of a person. It startled me so bad that it woke Mohegan. The old witch. I had my back to the fire and couldn't see Poppa Sam and I couldn't speak. Mohegan lifted his head and looked and I know he saw it too. For a long time I thought it was a dream but we know don't we Mohegan," she said scratching under the dogs chin.

"Who was it?"

"Don't tell anyone. I'm only telling you. It was him." She grabbed his shoulders and the growl started again in the dog's throat.

He said nothing, only studied her face. She turned away and knelt to take the dog's face in her hands.

"Did you hear those frogs last night, Simon? They were so loud

I couldn't get to sleep. And the whip-poor-wills. There was one right outside my window somewhere. Calling and calling. Over and over and over. I was sure it was trying to tell me something and I had to sit up and look out the window. I didn't see anything but the whole night was sound. I don't know how to describe it. Like lifting. Like all that noise was holding the sky up." She sat cross-legged beside the dog and he licked her face and sat on his haunches. There was a long pause and Simon felt he should speak but didn't know what to say.

"And then," she glanced at him, but it was not casual, her eyes open and vulnerable, an act of trust. Then, looking back to the dog, she said, "I thought about my Daddy and I had never thought this way before, but I wondered, 'When was the last time he heard frogs like that?' Not much older than you, prob'ly. Do you think he remembered every spring how the night could be quiet and so full of noise at the same time?"

Simon had no answer and only stood watching the two of them perched together on the sand floor. A cloud passed in front of the sun, the streams of light faded out, girl and dog converging into a single shadowy shape. It sent a shiver through him and he wanted to reason with her, convince her that she had to let go, but he didn't know how to stand up to the conviction that flowed through her as strongly as the river spilling its banks outside. He wanted to remind her, impatience igniting inside of him again, that their grandfather was not the only one who searched. His father went out regularly, even on days he wasn't working. He took the freighter canoe with its kicker and patrolled up and down the river and when he came home at night Simon's mother would meet him at the back door with a sad expectant look and he would shake his head. He had even bribed George Ronson with a bottle of Canadian Club to fly low, long looping circuits over the river in his open cockpit Fairchild for more than a hundred miles north.

He watched as she stroked the dog, speaking to comfort it,

her voice low and soothing. He began to wonder if any of what she said was possible. Was there some remote chance his uncle still lived? He wanted for it to be real, for his uncle to come home and for his cousin to have her father back. He wanted to believe that against every shred of reason there existed some impossibly slim circumstance that could make it all be true. He remembered the story of Peter Chapise which he had heard often because it involved his father. It was the kind of story that belonged to the whole town.

Mohegan did come back but he would not be tied again, not even by Joe Pete. If he saw any kind of tether in her hand he simply stayed away and refused to come within arm's reach. At first he would only stay away a day or two and then he would show up curled in his corner of the shed. It seemed to Simon that all they did that spring and summer when they were together was search for the mongrel. She was constantly pestering him to go with her into the bush along the familiar trails looking for any sign or trace of him. She begged and pleaded with Poppa Sam but he was busy out in the canoe patrolling along the river banks. Occasionally she would catch a glimpse of him moving along the shoreline or standing with his nose raised to the wind and he might look and wag his tail when she called his name, but he would not come or wait for her. He just slipped away into the woods and was gone again. She convinced her grandfather once to return to Keesayskwao Island, though he considered it an evil place and it was against his better judgement. Simon had gone along, though he had not really wanted to return either and he knew his father would not approve. But he felt obligated because Joe Pete had recently stood up for him against Benny Naylor. Benny, who was a grade ahead of them, was steamed over Simon's father confiscating some his father's traps for some illegal trapping. Hank had waived the fine because times were lean, but Benny still felt this was some kind of persecution and took it as his duty to avenge the family name. He had walked purposefully up to the door and knocked and when Gina answered he had asked politely to talk to Simon. Simon came to the door doing his best to hide his reluctance. Threats had been made and a fist waved in his face right in the school hallway and he well knew why Benny was waiting on the stoop. Once his mother had left to go back to the kitchen, Benny had grabbed a hold of Simon's collar and jerked him out the door with the intention of giving him a sound beating in his own front yard.

Joe Pete, lurking in the hallway behind her cousin, saw this and came flying out in a mad blur. The screen door was flung so wide that it smacked against the house, stretching out the spring in a rising metallic note and slamming back into place like a gunshot. Even before the sharp crack of the door against the jam had resounded out over the street, Benny and she were vaulting together down the front steps, twisting in the air, one of his ears gripped in each of her hands. Simon watched open-mouthed from the porch.

Benny landed solidly on his back, his frayed cap tumbling off his head, and she came down on top of him, one skinny knee bouncing off his rib cage and knocking the wind out of him. She rained blows on his head in open-handed slaps as Benny covered up and squirmed onto his side to tip her off. He scrambled to his feet, vaulted the low picket fence, and stood looking at her confused over what had just taken place and what he should do about it. He couldn't hit her but he was loathe to tuck his tail and run.

He spied his rumpled hat lying in the dirt as Joe Pete got to her feet huffing heavily, eyes burning from under her dark bangs, her arms held rigidly at her sides, hands clenched into tight fists.

Benny puffed out his chest and strode back through the open

gate. "I ain't afraid of you crazy Indians." When he bent to pick up his hat, Joe Pete put her foot on it and dragged it back a step. He stood and looked into her pinched face, a shock of tangled blond hair standing up on his head.

"Give me back my cap." He bent again to retrieve it and she dragged it back further.

"Joe Pete..." Simon implored from the porch. He didn't like where things were going.

Benny bent again only this time Joe Pete left the cap where it was and brought her fist around in a windmilling uppercut that caught him full on the nose and stood him up straight. His head snapped back, blood starting from both nostrils and Joe Pete fell on him swinging her arms, elbows locked in wild blows that struck him all about the head and shoulders as she screamed like a banshee. He bent forward to keep from bleeding on his shirt and, leaving his hat where it lay, fled down the street holding onto his bloody nose. She continued to swing wildly even after he moved out of range, tipped off-balance and collapsed still wailing, beating the ground with her hands, tears streaming down her face. Gina ran to her and pulled her to her feet and helped her walk, sobbing, back into the house.

All they found on the island was the tattered remnants of the tent and a few scattered bones. Someone had claimed the few lengths of chain and the little stove. As Joe Pete wandered around the little glade, she kicked at the underbrush in the vain hope of uncovering some sort of clue. Poppa Sam had stood smoking his pipe, muttering and glancing from shadow to shadow. Simon could see his unease as he followed his cousin around not sure what they were looking for. There was no evidence of the dog's return as far as he could tell and looking about brought back unpleasant memories of that long night. Their grandfather, seeming to share his sentiments, went to stand at the shoreline and watch the river.

"Mah-hee-gun," shouted Joe Pete, and the long, exaggerated syllables faded away quickly among the thick trees and deepened the silence around them.

"Where do you think the stove was?"

"I dunno..." he answered, contemplating their surroundings which seemed so different with the snow gone. "...maybe about there." He pointed, measuring with his eyes from the maple tree where he could make out the scar worn by the dog's chain.

She went and stood on the spot he had indicated, nodding her head in approval when she noticed a pile of charcoal nearby. She squatted down on her haunches and tilted her head as she studied a small knoll to the north. "That's where I saw him." She seemed to be confirming it to herself, not really speaking to him.

"Saw who?"

She sighed but did not answer.

"Hey, Little McWatch."

They turned to see Poppa Sam knocking his upside-down pipe against the palm of his hand, the ash and smoldering tobacco dropping down into the water.

"Nothin' here but bad feelings. Let's go home and have some tea."

She was often late for school because she had chased after some fleeting glimpse of him on her way there. She caught fish and left them out for him and she hid meat from her own plate to tempt him.

The big dog came and went as he pleased. Sometimes, in the early morning, Joe Pete would look out her window and see him there, watching the house or sniffing around her grandfather's shed. They had left the opening under the wall and she often left an offering of food inside. Some mornings it was gone and sometimes the food was still there and occasionally Mohegan himself would be there curled in his usual corner, but he would not allow himself to be tied and if she reached for the rope he would slip out and be gone. Other children at school told of their own dog's food being stolen or claimed to have spotted him moving like a ghost through town in the evening. Once Joe Pete found a large bone, heavily gnawed at one end lying on the sand floor of the old shed. She had crept out that night after her mother was asleep, taking a length of rope she had prepared with a slip knot and crawled in to wait for him to return for his prize, determined that if she could make him stay for a day or two he would remember how much she cared for him. She fell asleep after a while and when she woke he was there beside her. She touched him lightly, not sure if it was a dream. She began to feel for the tether but found he was lying directly on it. She could feel the tension in his muscles and knew that if she tried to move him or to hold him in some way he would be gone.

"Don't leave me," she whispered, stroking the fur between his shoulder blades. "Stay."

The dog relaxed beside her and soon she fell back into sleep and dreamed of her father. In the morning there was only the gnawed bone and the impression of where Mohegan had rested next to her in the soft sand.

She did not see him for a long time after that, though she spoke of him often and always kept an eye out for him. She would watch long after she was supposed to be asleep, peering out through the thick distorted glass of her upstairs window, pressing her cheek against the cool pane to look as far towards her grandfather's and see as much of the tar-papered shed as she could. Every day after school was out, she ran home to check inside the shed, the fish she had left rotting on the dirt floor until Poppa Sam couldn't stand it anymore and used a pitchfork to carry out the remains to fertilize his garden.

"You're stinkin' up my shed you," he would say to her, and then when he saw the look on her face he would take her out in the canoe to catch more.

Whenever she could, she would walk along the riverbank and study the far shore and patrol the bush trails hoping to see him bounding towards her ready to give up his adventures and come back. She often tried to get Simon to come with her. She would plead that four eyes were better than two, but the truth was she was much braver with him along. She begged Okimah to take her out fishing only so that she could look for the errant dog. Every day she asked the other kids at school if they had seen any sign of him and she would spend any time outside standing on top of the low rocky knoll at the centre of the schoolyard to watch the treeline. If she was in class and saw a stray trotting past, she watched it hoping that Mohegan might come following behind or if it resembled him she would question if she truly remembered how he looked. She had been caught out by Mr. Duncan, her grade six teacher, several times and had been forced to take a note home to be signed by her mother reporting her distractedness. Once Simon found her weeping in the dusky confines of the shed after he had been sent by his mother to find her and bring her home for supper because Louisa was working. She had been late to school that day because, going out Okimah's door, she thought she had seen the tail end of Mohegan disappearing into the grove of cedars near the eastern end of the property and took off running after him despite her grandfather calling out that it was just a deer. She had pursued him for over two hours before giving up. When she finally arrived at school, the hem of her skirt was torn and clusters of seeds clung to her sweater and her fingernails were black with dirt from scrambling under fallen trees in her desperate attempt to follow Mohegan.

Vice Principal Leary, a portly man with wire rimmed glasses and slicked-down hair, who seldom smiled and was infamous for the licks he gave out with a heavy metal-edged ruler, caught her in the hallway before she could get to her grade six class.

"Well," he caught her by the elbow as she tried to casually slide past along the wall as if she was just coming back from the girl's washroom, "where have you been Miss McWatch? I have you marked as absent." He scrutinized her tousled hair and dirty appearance.

"And what happened to you? Did you sleep in a bush like a wild animal last night?" he asked sarcastically.

She could only look at the floor and shake her head.

"Come on, young lady. Down to the office for a talk."

They walked together, heels clicking loudly and echoing through the empty halls as they walked past the closed doors of the classrooms. Joe Pete kept her eyes averted staring at the polished tile, feeling Vice-Principal Leary's fingers clamped tightly around her arm.

"I've been made aware of your situation Miss McWatch. So many tardy appearances. Homework not done. Marks slipping. I've told Principal Mullen that I think you'd be better served by Residential School with your own kind. Out there alone on the point with no father, it's just an excuse to become another lazy Indian. We have quite enough of those in these parts."

The words bored into her and there was a scintillating flash of heat behind her face and the whirling rush of anger that had swept over her when she had attacked Benny Naylor. They were just crossing in front of the big double doors, about to swing left into the foyer that led to the reception area and the administrators offices. She wanted to express her outrage over what the man had said, she could feel it filling her lungs with the need to scream in defiance of his repugnant assertion. She wanted to speak in defense of her mother and her father and the struggle of their lives, but she had no words. She only sputtered and began to lean against the pulling on her arm. She did not want to be led anywhere by this bespectacled prig or be forced to listen to any of his callous reprimands. He looked back with raised eyebrows over her consternation but only strengthened his grip as if it had been expected all along. She twisted her arm and jerked it free and the portly man stumbled a little and let go as he adjusted to maintain his balance. She spun away and bolted for the doors, bursting through and out into the sunlight while Mr. Leary stood with his knees locked, his arms spread wide as if any second she might turn and leap into them, bellowing for her to stop with the face of a strangled frog.

Simon had expected to find her sitting on the hard wooden bench, awaiting another lecture about pulling her socks up, as he filed through the hall with everyone else for midday recess after lunch. He had been worried she missed her chance to eat but that would have been moot anyway because she had left her sandwiches under a jack pine for the errant dog.

Soon whispers reached him that Joe Pete had attacked Vice Principal Leary and fled from the school and that the sheriff and every available truant officer were on the hunt for her. As soon as school was out, Simon had run all the way out to Indian Point to find her house empty. He went to the shed and cautiously opened the plank door, half-afraid the big dog might be lurking inside.

She knelt, lower legs splayed out to the sides with her father's axe in her hands. She had cut the rope that once held the dog into several short pieces and Simon could see the deep gashes in the packed sand where she had driven the blade down in her fury.

"Joe Pete," he had whispered. "What happened?" Her head was hanging, her body limp, her long hair hiding her features as she held the blade up in front of her face.

"I just want him to come back to me, Simon. I just want to see him again."

She would not tell anyone, not even Simon who she was perturbed with over his reluctance to help her find Mohegan. He could not seem to grasp how very important it was to her. She felt certain the dog had something to reveal about her father but with each day that passed it became that much harder to hold on to that certainty. It was almost six months since her father had disappeared. She had watched the snow melt and the river open and the green leaves return to the trees but still her heart was frozen. She was frozen even though it seemed like life was moving on, the days progressing; she was still somewhere in the heart of that dark December night waiting for him to come home.

It could not be a mere coincidence that in the middle of that hard season she had found Mohegan. And now he too was like a ghost skirting the outer boundaries of her existence. Why would he not stay with her? What was she doing wrong? She did not want to capture him or hold him against his will. She only wanted to follow him, certain that the dog had something to reveal, convinced that they shared some mysterious connection; the trapped raven, the mysterious island, the dog, and her father.

Joe Pete received stern punishment for her act of rebellion, five crisp swats on each hand from Reverend Leary and a week of detention during which she was to redo any schoolwork that had "suffered from inadequate attention due to wild dog chases," as it was put in the note she was forced to deliver to her mother. It was also decided, mostly between the Vice Principal and Gordon, as the closest adult male relative, that during the weekdays for the remainder of the school year while Louisa was working at the Railroad it would be best for Alison to stay with her aunt and uncle. That way she would not have so far to walk, and Simon could be there to help keep her from straying. An official reminder was also sent to Rainy Bolduc, the town constable (his birth name was Rene but he had been called "Rainy" all his life), that dog-catching and the control of strays was a part of his responsibilities along with truancy.

Joe Pete had to bunk with the twins, but she did not mind this at all and in fact enjoyed helping to look after them and she felt strongly about pulling her own weight. Auntie Gina was always kind to her niece even if she found it hard to look into the little girl's dark, sorrowful eyes. She looked sad most of the time and playing with Simon or the twins she might smile and laugh for a while but then a stillness would come over her and the smile would droop away and you could tell she was somewhere else. For the most part she and her uncle avoided each other during the times they were in the house together.

Mohegan, if he was alive somewhere, stayed hidden, living by his own wits even though Joe Pete often claimed to have caught fleeting glimpses, though whenever she would elbow Simon or shush him and point there was never anything for him to see. "Manitou," he would offer until she came to hate the word.

No, she would say. No it wasn't, and she would want to say to him that it was not the same anymore because now most of what she loved was gone. How could so much of her life be nothing more than shadow? It was something she could not accept or put into words. And Simon would only shrug, confused by her anger. On her father's birthday she went to the place where Porter Creek flowed into the river with a round stone that when it glistened with water showed dark concentric rings like ripples in a pond stacked on each other and neatly spaced. When she pulled it out of her pocket and looked, it had faded to a dull grey and the lines were only faint shadows. She spit on it and rolled her thumb over it until it glistened and was once more beautiful. She held it up in front of her eye for a last look then tossed it into the dark water and it went under with a loud plop. She stood watching the ripples spreading as if the rings had come off the stone itself. She closed her eyes and dreamed that when she turned around he would be there right behind her with his head tilted to one side. He would stay and let her stroke between his big ears and ruffle the fur on his neck and they would be quietly together by the flowing water with the sun warm on her face. When she opened them there was only the smooth inscrutable surface of the water.

Somehow it became a game with her classmates, and every so often one or two of them would run up and tell her that they had seen the ghost dog on the way to school or after supper while they were playing in the yard. Sometimes they might claim that their dog's food had been stolen or that they heard another dog fighting with their own pet and when they ran to see they just caught a glimpse of Mohegan fleeing. At first she believed the stories and would hurry to wherever the sighting had taken place to look for herself. Sometimes a group of kids might come to find her if she was staying at Simon's house and report breathlessly that they had just seen the big dog and she would throw on her jacket or a sweater and they would all run off together. The children would lead her to a field or somewhere along one of the trails in the woods or maybe to a spot along the railroad tracks picking up odd bits of slag as they went. "It was right here," they would tell her, and together they would search around and maybe find an old piece of bone or a desiccated rabbits foot or clump of fur and hold it up as evidence. Soon the stories began to take on a supernatural aspect. Mohegan would appear then simply vanish, gone without a trace. One time Katie Lafleur, who lived on a small farm on the outskirts of town, claimed that as she headed to the outhouse on the evening before, she saw a pair of glowing eyes watching her out of the gloom and she just knew that it was Joe Pete's dog. Inevitably, because of the mystery around her father, more and more the stories became associated with the graveyard and sightings after dark and the sound of howling in the woods near where Sandy had gone through the ice. Sometimes when they described the dog it sounded more like Pinky and sometimes there were two dogs running together.

It even seemed to spread to the parents and late one night Monk Landry, stumbling home after a prolonged session of poker and moonshine in the back room of Downey's Barber Shop, saw a demon dog patrolling the overgrown back lane that ran behind the butchers. It did not growl and kept its distance but there was something in the confident manner which suggested this was not a dog who came to a whistle or wanted petting. When he bumped into Hank and his family the next day coming out of church, Monk said, "I seen it. I seen that dog the kids are always chasing after." Joe Pete, standing beside her uncle, could smell the tobacco smoke and bathtub gin on the man's breath but coming from an adult it was a story that carried some weight. Soon other people were repeating the story and adding their own embellishments and then others saw the strange animal lurking in their yard or loping across a misty field in the early light. They heard strange sounds in the woods and saw their own dogs cower and tremble and slink under the porch to hide. They would claim to have seen it through the window of the club car and that at first glimpse they took it to be wolf, but it was much bolder than any wolf and paused just at the edge of a clearing to watch the train as it passed.

Even Rainy Bolduc had a story of how he had watched Mohegan trot by under a gibbous moon as though he owned the town. He claimed that he had seen the dog while he was relaxing with warm milk and whisky on his front porch after his evening duty shift. "Always calms my nerves," he explained. Bull had stopped by to discuss a case of suspected poaching with Hank over a cup of coffee. Gina had noticed he always stopped by right around breakfast time, especially if she was cooking back bacon.

"He's a smug son-of-a-bitch that mongrel. Looked me right in the eye though I hadn't moved or made a sound. He's clever though, I'll give him that."

He'd come in through the back door calling out hello as he sauntered in through the small mud room, tipping his hat to Hank as he stepped into the kitchen. He pulled a mug out of the cupboard and filled it from the percolator off the stove. He didn't acknowledge Gina in any way and she sighed heavily and left the room. The constables general dislike towards Indians was well known.

He waved his mug in the general direction of Joe Pete but spoke directly to Hank. "I heard another tale about that wild dog again last week...Thursday morning I believe, I was getting ready to go into the office for some paperwork and Punk Johnstone told me how he saw him come bold as anything down Second Avenue to the corner there where he lives. Punk's old stubby-legged terrier Butch was laying by his little house chewing on a big hambone Punk had flung out the kitchen door for him after supper." The Constable sat down next to Simon and folded his arms on the table, one finger hooked through the handle of the white china mug. "You know Butch, right..." Simon nodded a spoon full of cream of wheat in his mouth. "...Butch is not what you'd call cuddly but he won't bother you if he's not provoked. Hardly even barks anymore." He paused for a sip of coffee. "Eaah, that could be hotter." He pushed the cup away dismissively. "So anyway, Punk says the mutt walks right up into the yard, I doubt the lazy Swede's ever gonna fix that gate, and tiptoes right over to where Butch is concentrating on ripping the last shreds of gristle off that bone. He stands there until Butch notices, which Punk says took longer than you think it might. Which Punk attributes to the dogs overall spooky nature but I'm pretty sure it's the bulldogs advanced years. At any rate the old dog finally rears up, snarlin' and slobberin' and takes after the cheeky mongrel. Punk was just watching out the back door 'cause he didn't have his boots on and he was sure Butch could handle the problem. But the other dog didn't fight, he just ran with Butch chasing after him right out through the gate, along the fence all the way to the back corner with Butch growling and snapping on the other dog's heels. Then wolf-dog," he refused to use the Indian name even though he knew it. "leapt over the fence and came down almost right on top of that juicy bone. When Butch sees this he turns on his sawed-off little legs and starts back towards the gate but the big dog just pops over the back fence and he's gone down towards the river. Punk said he had to laugh himself at old Butch just standing there, tongue hanging out, panting looking around like he was still trying to figure out where breakfast went."

It was a good story and Joe Pete had smiled when she heard it and felt heartened at first to hear of his cleverness and that he was doing well.

Constable Percy, seeing there was no bacon to be had, drained his mug and stood hitching up his pants, preparing to leave.

"Could have been some other mutt I suppose. Plenty of strays around this spring. Gonna have to get my rifle out one of these days." He pointed a crooked finger at Joe Pete. "This one getting' to school all right?"

Hank had only nodded

Little else was heard of Mohegan after that, right through to the end of school and the beginning of summer. The kids in town lost interest and found other things to occupy them. Her mother continued to work part time at the hotel making beds and cleaning or cooking meals in the café. Mrs. Taylor would take the train every two or weeks to spend a week helping with her father who was in miserable condition at home and too much for her mother alone. She had worked out a kind of rotation with her younger sister and a sister-in-law who lived in the Sault. This was an added expense for the Taylors, and in the slow weeks they augmented Louisa's pay with leftover food from the kitchen. There were a couple of deliveries and for a few weeks in June she was very busy.

Constable Percy did not put Mohegan or the other strays anywhere near the top of his priority list and Joe Pete enjoyed being in the busy household. She found herself beginning to feel like a little girl again and on Friday nights when she was usually back in the little cabin by the river it seemed too quiet and lonely. She would lie in her bed in the loft and look out the window to where the smooth shadow of the big river flowed ceaselessly, impenitent and aloof. Once or twice she thought she saw the figure of a man moving along the bank and she would start, her whole body tense as she stared intently. But it was always only a glimpse, maybe a tree swaying in the wind, or the way a cloud drifted over the face of the moon.

She thought less about Mohegan in her cousin's house and she stopped sneaking scraps out because it made her feel guilty and somehow beholding to her uncle. Her mother brought home the occasional leftover soup bone from the café but these were dry with every bit of marrow and meat boiled from them.

There were other distances in the house. Between the older boys and Simon, between the boys and the twin girls still in diapers, between Hank and his sons and a subtle gulf of obligation between Gina and her husband. Still, there was an ever-present warmth in the big house that went beyond the wood stove and the heaters. It was there even when the boys were feuding and glaring across the table and refusing to speak directly to each other. Despite the practised affection between her aunt and uncle and the open hostility that might flare between the brothers, there were strong bonds of warm regard emanating everywhere. It was something that had faded down to embers in the life of Joe Pete and her mother, as if one night the winter frost had crept up out of the frozen earth and cause something to wither. She was soothed by what she witnessed in her aunt's house, happy to be there and feel its tentative extension to her, though in many ways she was an observer and felt only a reflected glow.

It was the evening of the second-last day before the end of school and she had begun to surrender to it. To feel lighter in that house, lifted by the presence of those other people who all in their own way cared for her. For a long time there had been comfort in being alone. Even when her mother was there with her in the cabin they had been alone together. Silent and weary at the dinner table because she had been busy bringing new life into the world and caring for someone else's family. Or out in the shed stroking Mohegan before he too had left her, the dog asking nothing of her, only content to accept her affection while she took solace in memories of her ravaged family.

Clarence burst into the kitchen, just in time to eat as always, and the story began to spill out of him as he stood behind a chair at the table gripping the back. At first she had been caught up in the excitement. It was a very warm day near the end of June and Clarence had obviously run home to tell the story.

"What's all the hub-bub Clare?" Henry always called his brother this when he wanted to get under his skin.

Clarence waved his fist at him, his lips pinched tightly together, "Hey shut yer trap. This is good. It's about that crazy dog. He's back." He pointed at Joe Pete and she felt the bottom of her stomach drop out.

She could see it all unfolding in her mind as if she had heard it all before, as though it was one of the old tales that Poppa Sam might tell in the dark of his kitchen after she had stumbled in late one night.

Mohegan had gone after Bertie Swanson's chickens out on the Reserve. Bertie had noticed that over about a week or so five or six hens had gone missing. She had told her husband about it and he had gone out with his rifle to see what was skulking around. At first he had suspected a fox because the thief had been so sly and neither of their two dogs had been aroused. Then he found tracks that were much too large for a fox and he suspected one of the family dogs, but even their paws were not large enough. He surmised that perhaps it was one of the neighbor's dogs. Lots of them ran loose on the Reserve and sometimes even formed into hunting packs that became dangerous and began to wantonly kill deer and other dogs and had to be shot. He fixed up the coop which had become a little worn down and reinforced it. He took more care to secure the chickens at night as well, making sure the gate was closed tight and the dogs tied nearby. It had been a few years since they had any problems, the dogs had been good security and they had become a little complacent.

A couple of weeks went by and everything was quiet. The dogs had barked at night a few times but that was not unusual and every morning there was the same number of hens as had been there the night before.

Then one morning Thomas Swanson took the dogs who were good retrievers and went out to Keelow Bay after some ducks. Bertie opened up the coop and let the chickens into the yard where they could scratch and peck. It was a bright, warm morning; her boys had gone off to play and her daughter Helen, who would be four in the fall, was in the backyard pulling up blades of grass to feed to the chickens.

Bertie was happy in the kitchen, rolling out dough for pies and had the door propped open to keep an eye on her little girl. She did not see the big dog stalking out from around the corner of the coop intent on the hens. Helen did and she was afraid of the big dog. Mohegan was too intent on the chickens to notice the little girl. Everything seemed to come to a standstill outside except for the heads of the chickens jerking back and forth as they switched view from one eye to the other. A tremor rippled through Mohegan as he stood, one paw raised in mid-step, eyes locked on a big red hen. Then the chicken bolted heading straight for the kitchen and the other chickens squawked and scattered and little Helen, who only saw the big dog headed her way, followed the red hen straight through the open door with Mohegan, who was really only interested in the bird, hot on her heels. Bertie was sweeping the hall at that moment waiting for the stove to heat up and jumped at the sudden hoopla, hugging the broomstick and staring in amazement as the chicken ducked under the table followed by Helen, who leapt up onto a chair and then the table top as the dog lunged in through the door. The little girl kicked over a bowl and sent berries everywhere and the hungry dog was scrambling and sliding all over the linoleum and snapping after that chicken. The wily old hen was dodging in and out from under the table and chairs were knocked over and feathers were flying and Helen was screaming and finally Bertie waded in, winding up with the broom, trying to brain the slobbering beast that invaded her home. Helen leapt off the table on to her mother, wrapping her arms around her neck and catching her balance in mid-swing so that they both went down among the raspberries. The red hen flapped up onto the vacated table and then to a high shelf, upsetting two china mugs which crashed to the floor. Bertie was furious now and from her knees caught Mohegan on the side of the head with a rolling pin she'd found beside her among the squashed red berries. She lurched towards the cutting board where they kept the big butcher knife and when she turned the dog was gone, her kitchen all in shambles.

Chapter Eleven:

Hank II

Rebecca returned to him, the way she had in the trenches, on the second night of a long looping patrol meandering through the southeast corner of The Park. He had started out following the Big River in hopes of finding some trace of Sandy, trying not to contemplate what might remain of his brother-in-law after a winter under the ice. He wanted to put it all to rest and give his family some ease. He worried especially about Joe Pete despite being so impatient with her stubborn contrariness. All day he'd paddled north passing the place where he should have followed a narrow creek into Ravine Lake travelling well down river before reluctantly doubling back to find his intended route. Near dusk he made a rough camp where the stream widened out into Doyle's Arm and passed a fitful, dejected night before setting out at first light to battle wind and steady rain crossing Ravine. He discovered the carcass of a cow and calf moose near the shoreline where he stopped for lunch. Examining the skulls, he surmised the poachers had caught them swimming, overtaken them by canoe, and killed them with an axe. This only further soured his mood.

His progress had been much slower than he hoped; his fruitless searching and the illegal hunting had left him discouraged and listless. There was a refurbished trapper's cabin along a bend of the Ember River that had been appropriated for use by the wardens, but it was an arduous portage over the steep height of land between and a good five miles downstream. The constant ache in his spine and hip made paddling uncomfortable and his strength was fading with the early May light. Weary from a long night of struggling with memories, disheartened, chilled in his damp clothes, he capitulated to the wind and the past and veered towards a rocky island in the weedy bay at the very north end of the turbulent lake. He had often camped there with Sandy on their trips out together.

The pain that prodded him all day returned with fierce insistence as he tried to find a comfortable position for sleep and infiltrated along his hip to the middle of his spine. It pulsed its way up each vertebra and through his skull to throb behind his ersatz eye, a rhythmic echo of the long day spent propelling himself against the wind. It had been more than just the opposition to the elements or the choppy lake. It felt as though he was combating the inexorable flow of circumstance and loss that life had become, enmity spilling from him with every stroke. He stabbed the water as if it was something that could be wounded and railed against all that seemed to be conspiring to chip away his life. He cursed the unremitting goddamn wind and the cold water and the days that were slipping through his hands and every syllable of bile and invective was vehemently blown back into his face.

Then in the darkness, as distant thunder rumbled beyond the horizon, he began to think of her, a distraction from the gnawing ache. The physical pain tearing at him had been there every day since he had been catapulted off the earth and swatted down into that grim wagon full of havoc and ruin. He felt its teeth scraping against bones and pulling at his flesh, trying to tear him apart. He rocked and moaned and shifted his weight on the hard earth but it would not leave him be. He was not sure he had the strength to resist it much longer and endure these long trips. But he didn't know what else he could do and felt broken, beaten by the weight of the present and the past and all the days ahead he would face alone. It was out of this cloud of agony that he reached for her and she came to him as she had in the war, in those hypnagogic moments on the edge of exhaustion and terror. So vividly that for a second he smelled her perfume, felt the fleeting touch of her body there with him as she had been among the straw bales on that long ago hayride.

He lay fidgeting, shifting from one hip to the other, thinking of her and the choices he had made in life. He slept only fitfully, agitated by fragmentary dreams of the war and Rebecca and his lost friends until he woke that morning in grief as a gusting wind shook the canvas tent. He must have been dreaming about Sandy just then because he couldn't resist the impulse to throw open the flap half-expecting to see him, crouched over the fire, holding up a full pot of coffee. It was out in the bush, especially around camp, that the absence of his friend was most keenly felt.

The whole world was close and dull under the brooding sky. He longed to somehow awaken in the past, in those days when the two of them were unencumbered men and had travelled together living off the land. They subdued their memories of the war, burning them away together through long nights around a campfire under the ruminating stars. How many nights had they sat together watching the flames, hardly a word spoken or a gesture made? Sometimes he had muttered to himself, questions and angry declarations over things seen and done, and even though Sandy couldn't hear, it was enough knowing that he understood. There was something soothing in this silent communion. No weak condolences, nothing more reassuring then the presence of the other. A wavering image sometimes hardly visible in the darkness beyond the heat and smoke. They were like ghosts of each other in that territory of night and silence, the blurred comfort of trees and stars reflected in the still water.

He had thought that after the trenches and the hospitals there would be nothing better than returning home to the farm, getting back to family and days filled with honest labour. But too much had been altered for this to hold true. James, his oldest brother, was gone, buried somewhere in France, dead from gas gangrene after a minor in the foot. So was his cousin Garth, a year younger than he and one of his closest companions growing up whose end was a mystery, another among the tens of thousands missing, ground under at Ypres.

Walking the familiar landscape of home, memories of the dead haunted every step and being in the territory of their childhood without them, had made the old routines seem irreverent and false. Every morning, he rose to accompany his father in the pre-dawn darkness with the remnants of uneasy sleep trapped under his clothes, boot steps crisp in the chill of the beginning day. He took with him the dolour of his brother's absence, missing the drowsy way the two of them bumped shoulders as they followed the old man out to the barn. When he pulled open the big door, as he and James had always raced each other to do, and stood against it to let his father go past with the lantern, he could not bear to look into that haggard face because he knew it would make him weep. He struggled every day to conceal his despondency and to move on into the world and shake off the megrims, as his mother chided him to do.

At the end of a damp, drizzly week in early November they had undertaken the demolition of an ancient dirt-floor shed that sat out behind the big barn and had been built by his maternal grandfather. It had been a part of the original homestead, used for stabling animals before a proper barn was built and which in his father's day had been used for slaughtering and hanging meat. Hank had tried to avoid the place as a boy. It always smelled of spilt blood and damp rot and made his skin crawl. Kicking into the earthen floor often turned up an old, yellowed bone. In the past few years, leaning into decrepitude, it had become a place to store broken equipment and salvaged lumber and other things that held any meagre hope of someday being returned to usefulness. It had acquired a preposterous tilt and during the previous winter heavy snowfall had nudged it over onto the ground.

They dug a large pit close by and he'd tried to hide how going down into the ground had made him uneasy, struggling with every shovel full to maintain his composure. Whatever would burn was thrown in on top of a torn tractor tire coated with used oil and some kerosene. They had brought two of the horses to pull the heavy logs from the partially collapsed structure and after several hours of hard work a jumbled pile rose out of the cavity. His father wrapped a rag around the end of a broken scythe handle and nailed it in place. He soaked this in kerosene and lit it before thrusting the makeshift torch down through the debris onto the tire. Soon flames and black smoke were licking up through the old lumber and crates and other combustible trash. Lag bolts and wire and whatever else didn't burn would be buried and left to rot in the ground when they filled in the hole. Hank balanced on a worn-out ladderback chair pulled from the rubble. It was missing half of one leg and held together with baling wire and he planned to toss it on the conflagration when he was done with it. His father perched on the rusted metal seat of an ancient hay rake they had pulled out from under the collapsed building. Its iron tines jutted down clawing into the earth and the horses were loosely tied to it to prevent them wandering back to the barn.

Both men were sweat-soaked, enjoying the warmth of the growing bonfire and the pleasant weariness that comes after a day of hard labour. Hank had started to suggest they head to the house for coffee when the whole world erupted into flame and racket. A ball of smoke and fire blasting violently out of the pit sending chunks of wood and metal and molten rubber out over the sodden field. The main force, directed by the earthen walls, rocketed straight up into the air, flaming bits of debris flaring out to rain down around them. The horses whinnied in panic, shaking their traces and stamping their feet. Hank who had been closest was flung ass over teakettle backwards off the chair by the blast. His father had been jarred but not flattened and even in his befuddlement jumped down to snatch up the tethers to try and calm the terrified animals. He fought to keep them from bolting and injuring themselves against the old hay rake. Bits of lumber and trash burned all around and something smoldered in the bays tail. Hank on the ground could sense the hooves of the stricken animals reverberating through the earth, the concussion still echoing in his ears propelled him back to the war. The last thing to be thrown on had been a threadbare scarecrow that his mother used to set by the door every Halloween as long as Hank could remember. He watched it spin up through the air splayed and burning and coming apart as it fell. He thought of his dead brother and his cousin and their far away childhoods. He flashed to Priest and the others erased in front of him in that tattered second of heat and noise before the sky began to blink on and off. His father was hollering for him to get up, cursing as he struggled to be heard over the strident terror of the horses, demanding to know if he was hurt. He strained to get up onto his hands and knees but it felt like something was constricted around his ribcage, his heart pounding against his compressed chest under his damp clothes. He wanted to pull the clumsy work glove off his right hand so he could loosen the collar of his heavy coveralls but couldn't seem to do it. He looked down and was surprised to see a bent nail stuck through the cowhide into the back of his hand. He got to his feet dazed and disoriented, not quite real in that time and place, his nostrils full of familiar and terrifying smells.

His father hurried to loose the horses from the dilapidated implement and let them go, praying they would make straight for the safety of their stalls. In his haste he had wrapped the reins around his left hand, pulling to get slack and once he released the rig they bolted and he was pulled from his feet and dragged screaming for them to whoa, his arm nearly pulled from the socket before the strap uncoiled from around his wrist. Hank stood oblivious to this, clutching his hand and rocking on his heels. There was no other visible injury besides the square-headed nail piercing the glove. A distant voice was calling his name and he scanned the field, littered with bits of smouldering wreckage but his eyes refused to focus. The old terror of sudden death swallowed him again. The familiar world had become unreal, a mirage that might drop away at any second and the old horror was there just beyond a thin curtain. He could hear men howling, see the earth convulsing all around him, felt the weight of his own body rising up through the smoke, the salt taste of blood in his mouth.

A force gripped his arm, pulling at him and he fought against it afraid to be taken back, to again be thrown on top of all those mangled corpses. The broken and dead under him while the darkness pulsed in and out of his shattered body. One moment engulfed, gone with the lifeless who jostled like sacks of sodden earth beneath him, the next, restored into uncertain light and the smell of horses and corruption. The stench was with him now, seeping up out of the saturated ground, carried in the thick black smoke that clung to him like death.

Hank shook his head fighting off the memories and forced himself to stumble bent and groaning out through the tent flaps, right leg numb from the hip down. He sat by the cold fire pit brushing dry pine needles from his grey wool socks. The left big toe skillfully darned by Gina with blue yarn gave him a moment of homesickness. How could he feel sorry for himself when his wife had lost so much more? He pulled on his boots wincing over a spasm of pain that jolted across his lower back. A red squirrel scampered out from under the canoe where his packs were stored bounding for the nearest tree, chattering indignantly and Hank responded with a hoarse exclamation just to hear a human sound.

Deciding a hot breakfast was not worth the trouble he scrounged what he could out of the pack. Bannock left from supper and a few handfuls of raisins in the cloth bag the impertinent squirrel had chewed a hole in. He gazed across the sullen lake to the smudged treeline in the grey distance envying his niece who clung stubbornly to an implausible shred of hope that her father might still be out there somewhere. She didn't know Death with the intimacy he did, had not seen it in abundance as he had. Men stacked like cordwood in the mud, bodies sundered in grotesque pieces and scattered over the ruined earth. Had never seen the squalid certainty of a corpse emptied of blood and entity. He knew that it made no difference how young you were, how much you might cherish life, how strong or beautiful you were, how deeply you were loved. When Death came for you, nothing could delay it or deny it and the next moment the whole world advanced, even if only by a breath or a heartbeat, and you were, irrevocably, no more.

He worked the heel of his hand into his good eye then ran his fingers up through his thinning brown hair. He thought of spending the day right where he was but quickly put the notion aside. He was already a half-day behind schedule and was supposed to be home at the end of the week. He thought of his wife and their children with a mixture of guilt and regret.

The first time he had come looking for Sandy that summer back from overseas, fresh out of the hospital, back still bandaged from surgery, it had just seemed necessary to see his comrade alive and breathing. He and Sandy had spent a few days like vagabonds drifting through nearby lakes and rivers, then returning to Sam's to cook the day's catch and sleep. Sandy was just planning the cabin then. It had been an awkward time; he was self-conscious about his scarred face and patch-covered eye, Sandy was not so adept at lip-reading and communication was difficult. They were all still adjusting to the damage the war had wrought. He had enjoyed the simple straight-forward existence of his holiday but soon felt compelled to return to his family's farm. When he left, he felt he'd kept his promise and there was no need to ever come back.

It was a year later, a few months after the explosion in the pit, that he'd found himself standing on the platform of the train station unannounced, lost and looking for someone who would understand. Sandy and Louisa were already together then though not yet married. Sandy was trapping and guiding a bit when he could at that time, but he had dropped everything when Hank appeared. He had sensed the depth of pain in his old comrade and took him deep into the bush. They stayed out for two weeks, living off the land and what they could carry. Hank had poured out everything around the campfire, more than he thought he would ever share with another person.

Gina had been a complete surprise. She was so vivacious then, petite and pretty with long black hair and always ready for a good laugh. She was living with her father that summer in the house on Indian Arm and Louisa was staying with them as well. The girls were earning their keep by preparing supper for Georgina's father and, occasionally, Hank and Sandy. They were also employed part-time together at The Station Hotel. It was primarily a boarding house for railroad men where they worked making up beds, doing laundry and helping with meals in the small cafe. Hank moved in with Sandy who had taken up residence in the almost completed cabin and helped out with finishing touches, though it was still like a bare barracks inside. It was all undertaken in unspoken agreements without any kind of formal arrangement. It just seemed to happen and somewhere along the way he had decided to stay.

It seemed like something he'd read in one of Jack's books now. Whenever he and Sandy returned after one of their long sojourns in the woods, Gina and Louisa had been there to greet them. They were a happy foursome that first summer, fishing whenever they could and playing cards at night. She had flirted with him and whispered once into his ear at a dance, "I kinda like you, Hank," but he had kept his distance. In part because she was Sandy's little sister, out of school but still in her teens and partly, he was ashamed to admit, because of all the things he had heard about Indian girls when he was growing up. It had been easy, carefree living and he liked it that way.

Mid-September, Sandy had gone to help his father in guiding for some American hunters who came every season for moose. It was an arrangement made earlier the year before and he felt obligated to fulfill. They had discussed Hank staying over for the winter and the two of them working a trap-line together. Hank wanted some time alone to think this through and he spent the days cutting wood for the long cold nights and fishing and hunting small game on the Arm.

One warm afternoon, Gina had shown up out of the blue while reading *A Daughter of the Snows* on the front porch. She held up her handline and suggested they take the canoe out to try their luck and he had quickly agreed. He retrieved his bamboo rod from inside the cabin and they soon launched from the crude dock in front of her father's. Then mysteriously, for no apparent reason, a few yards from shore they had suddenly tipped and spilled into the water.

He came up sputtering and coughing, flailing as he tried to

latch onto the overturned canoe. He swivelled his head about, afraid Gina was still under and was astonished to see her already wading out of the water onto the bank and struggling with her saturated dress. She awkwardly threw her paddle up onto the grass, hampered by her thick wool sweater which was stretched by the weight of water it held and hung halfway down her back. She looked like a little girl, her hair slicked down, in clothes she had not grown into, giggling uncontrollably over something silly.

"Pull up the canoe," she shouted. She kicked out of her rubber boots which were full of the river and sent blossoming tendrils of water cartwheeling in the air. "Save that canoe, Hank."

"Hey?" he called back, slightly confused, his feet finding bottom, the sluggish current pulling at him. She was already waddling as fast as she could towards the house in her drenched garments, wrestling the sodden sweater off over her head.

He didn't remember how long he had struggled to get the canoe into shore and up safely on to the bank. His rod had been caught up in the thwarts and was safe but most of the tackle was on the bottom of the river. He was a little put out by her childish behaviour running off and leaving him to tend to everything. He passed her dark sweater flung off in a heap on the ground and saw her dress was hanging over the railing dripping onto the weathered boards. When he opened the door and went in she was crouched near the wood heater wrapped in a blanket.

"Hey." He was caught off-guard by the sweltering rush of heat that greeted him. "I don't think it's very nice you deserting me like that."

She turned and stood wrapped in a wool blanket.

"You better come warm up by the fire."

He took one or two steps and then stopped, unsure of what he should do. She let the blanket fall from her shoulders but shyly turned her eyes to the floor, her arms folded across her breasts. She still had on her wet chemise and bloomers and the thin material was transparent where it was pressed against her skin. He stared at the supple, brown hints of her curves. She did not seem the little girl now. Without looking up, she opened her arms to him. He hesitated a second and there was only the sound of his inhaled breath and then he went to her in a rush, clumsily pulling at his soggy shirt, the buttons popping and flying about the room, taking her in a rough embrace. She turned her face up to him and their lips were about to meet when suddenly she screamed and pushed forcefully against his chest.

He stepped back confused and stuttering. "I thought you..."

She twisted her body trying to see her right buttock. "Aii, you stupid, you pushed me against the stove."

There were tears in her eyes and he could see a hole burned through the rayon and a large white sinuous blister on her hip.

"I'm sorry. Shit, I'm so sorry." He quickly slipped off his soaked flannel shirt and pressed it against the wound. She batted the side of his face and folded her other arm across her breasts once more.

"I just want to help," he pleaded.

She took the cloth from him and squeezed it against her sore flesh.

"You better go," she said petulantly.

He complied, feeling defeated by his own clumsiness, filled with regret over the moment he had ruined. He stopped at the door, water dripping from his clothes, his heavy woollen socks halfway off and stretched out beside his feet like flat, eyeless fish. There was a trail of small puddles and wet smears where he had crossed the floor. When he turned, daring to glance up for only a second, he found she had retrieved the blanket from the floor and put it around herself. "I'm sorry," he said. "It's just you...well you looked so...so beautiful."

"Okay," she said.

He started to open the door.

"Hank."

"Yes?" he was expecting to be advised to leave town.

She held up the bunched wet shirt she was using to soothe the burn. "I'll sew them buttons back on for you."

"Thanks," he said, relieved that her anger had so quickly dissipated. He turned back to the door and pulled it open. His muddy boots were sitting on the porch and the cool air felt good. He only had to walk across the field to the small cabin.

"Hank?"

"Yes," the heat was leaving him in exhilarating waves.

"I heal quick."

The squirrel, high up in a red pine now, was scolding him with renewed vigour. "Shut up," he grumbled without even looking up. He started to stand and the old familiar pain ignited in his hip. He waited a second or two, most of his weight balanced on the good leg, then limped to the canoe. He kicked the toe of his boot into the gravely beach as if he might shake the hurt loose, like a small malicious creature with its teeth sunk into the meat of him. Still, it did not erase the persistent smile from recalling the odd beginning of his love affair with Gina. She had been very forgiving of his ineptitude and soon it was a private joke between them. A broken letter S and most of the U from Superior Stoves had been branded into her hip. "Well," he used to say, smacking her bare bottom with his open hand, the skin going crimson around the pale scar. "It certainly is a 'Superior rear.'" It had been a long time now since he'd used that line.

The portage to Ember was a long steep climb that crawled up along the face of the hill in a series of switchbacks. With each step the pain flared and with it more thoughts of Rebecca. It had been more than two years since he'd last seen her. His father had died that spring, dropped dead fighting a grass fire that had eventually consumed the barn. In the summer he'd gone back home to help his brother-in-law rebuild and to spend some time with his family. David, the youngest brother, had left at the beginning of the depression and rode the rails to the west coast where he was rumoured to be working on a fishing boat. They had not heard from him directly for years. His sister Elizabeth had married a boy from a neighbouring farm.

He had spotted her standing just around the corner of Gunnerson's Mercantile a few feet into the alley one afternoon when he had driven in on an errand to pick up more roofing nails. She was half-turned away, glancing furtively over her shoulder and he almost hadn't recognized her. When he slammed the door on his father's pickup, she swivelled her head around again giving him a look of annoyance as she pulled a stray strand of tobacco from her tongue.

"Rebecca?"

She threw her cigarette into the alley and pivoted quickly to face him, squinting to make out who he was.

"Hank, is that you? Damn it, I thought it was one of my nosy cousins. You know my mother thinks it's absolutely scandalous for a lady," she performed a kind of mocking half-curtsy, "to smoke in public."

He stood, hands in pockets, smiling, and unsure of what to say next. She walked to him, stepping up out of the alley onto the boardwalk and reached out to touch his shoulder.

"So sorry to hear about your dad. That was simply awful."

"Thanks. How's Danny?" He felt somewhat conflicted asking about her husband, using his first name as if they were old friends, especially since a part of him hoped she would answer that he was dead.

She looked away down the street and raised a hand to shield her eyes from the June sun. "Daniel's fine. Busy with bank business. I just needed to get out of the city for a while."

"Not working at the Hospital."

"No, Daniel asked that I give that up. He felt it was making me far too gloomy. I still do fundraising but of course that's not an easy task in these times. How about you?" she asked, pushing away the sadness that had begun to creep into her voice. "I heard you were some kind of mad hermit of the northern bush or something."

"I did do that for a while but the work wasn't very steady. Now I'm a warden in the big game preserve up there. So the government pays me to run around in the woods."

"Interesting. And how's the German scrap metal business?" she pointed to the jagged scar near his eye and it made him feel self-conscious.

"Haven't produced anything lately," he rubbed the side of his face reflexively and looked at his boots, suddenly aware of his grubby work clothes and the saw dust clinging to him under his shirt. There was an awkward silence.

"Do you have a family way up there in the North?"

"I do. How about you and Daniel? Any heirs to the kingdom?"

She frowned. "No. I'm afraid not. Something else the war took..." She turned her head away to pluck a strand of tobacco from her lip and her voice trailed off.

He understood the implication, shocked to find he was full of pity for rich Daniel Higgins and he did not pursue it any further.

"Here," he said pulling his billfold out of his jacket pocket. I have a picture."

He opened the folded leather and produced a photograph, folded lengthwise down the centre. Even though he knew it well he took a second to study it himself. Gina, wearing a dark shirtwaist dress, was seated and Henry in his Christening outfit with a huge flared bonnet was on her lap while Clarence in breeches and sailors tunic stood leaning against the chair. His wife had made all the clothing herself. There was a large-framed version hanging on the parlour wall at home. "It's a bit old and creased. It shows Georgina, my wife and our first two sons, Clarence and Henry."

She took the photograph and peered at it and for a second her smile faded and she blinked and shot him a quick look as if thinking perhaps he was playing a joke.

"These are your children?" She sounded slightly incredulous.

"Of course," he assured her.

"They look," she seemed to struggle for the right word, "... lovely." She returned it with a warm smile but there seemed to be a new distance in her voice and manner.

He stared down at the hand-tinted image. It seemed changed somehow and he paused a moment before folding it back into his wallet. He'd never really considered before how dark Henry's face was framed in the white lace or how sombre the unsmiling Gina seemed with her black hair pulled back so severely.

"Well. It was wonderful to see you, Hank." She brushed a golden strand from off her pale cheek, back over her ear. "Please offer my condolences to your mother. Perhaps I'll see you again."

She started off down the street and he called, a little too loudly after her. "I'll look in all the alleys every time I'm in town."

She stopped, turning to regard him and to see who else might be standing within earshot. He offered a sheepish wave which she answered with a subtle nod and a smirk then continued walking away from him. He swallowed hard, sure that he had embarrassed her and a little chagrined that he had felt the need to.

They had just finished the portage from Wabush Lake and the warm sun put everyone in a jovial mood. The two women were especially glad to be out of the house, away from their responsibilities and had been teasing each other, giggling like schoolgirls all morning. Louisa wore her husband's clothes, pant legs tucked into her boots and a belt with a sheathed knife cinched around the waist of a plaid flannel shirt. It was the first time since her husband's funeral that she had worn something other than her black widow's dress. Gina was dressed as practically in altered men's clothes.

There was still a small shallow cove to cross before they rounded a rocky spit and headed across the much larger Loon Bay to the sandy point where they expected Hank was camped. They were about halfway to the granite projection when movement on shore caught Joe Pete's attention. She pointed and they all looked to see a large black bear rooting noisily around a rotted log, digging out insects to lick up. Either he hadn't noticed them or he didn't care.

They had planned the outing over a goose dinner, a nice plump wavey that Sam had shot. With their bellies full, relaxing over a cup of tea, they had started to reminisce about old fishing trips.

"Why don't we all go out to meet my grumpy old husband?"

Louisa had hesitated not sure if she was ready to forgive Hank for the harsh things he had said to her.

"Mrs. Pigeau can look after the twins. We'll take Alison and Simon. Clarence and Henry don't really want to go along anymore. It'll be good for everyone. Like the old days. Get out in the bush before the blackflies get bad."

Louisa and Hank had continued pointedly avoiding each, though tensions had eased enough lately that Simon had slept over the previous weekend. Joe Pete held a grudge because her uncle still had nothing nice to say about Mohegan and would not allow the dog anywhere near his property claiming it was too dangerous for his baby daughters.

Louisa clung to her reluctance. "What about the boys?"

Gina smirked. "Clarence and Henry can help their grandfather in the garden."

She had caught them smoking behind the woodshed. The sin

had been compounded by the fact that they were rolling tobacco pilfered from Poppa Sam's in thin pages torn from a Pocket New Testament given to Clarence for his confirmation. Gina had all but given up on the wayward Clarence but he had been expressly warned against dragging his younger brother into the habit. They had agreed to their penance with the understanding that their father would not find out about the transgression.

Louisa, with some insistent cajoling from Gina, conceded it was best to smooth things over and finally agreed to go on the trip. At the very least, she thought, they could use the fish.

Gina was paddling in the bow and she turned to look over the children's heads at her sister-in-law in the stern.

"Louisa, you got that pistol?"

"Yes," she answered, eyeing the bear. "But he ain't botherin' us."

Louisa carried a captured German Luger that Sandy had brought back from overseas, tucked in a moose hide holster under her jacket. Gina laid her paddle across the gunnels.

"See how close you can come to him."

"He ain't botherin' us!"

"He's kinda rude ignoring us like that."

Louisa tilted her head and looked at her sister-in-law then turned to regard the bear again as it diligently pawed at the punky wood. Simon couldn't guess at the distance but it seemed awfully long for a pistol. He knew from stories he had heard that his Aunt had a reputation as a crack shot and Clarence claimed to have heard that once, on a dare, when she and their mother were in their teens, she had shot a coffee can from Gina's head.

"Gina, you know I could put one in his tail-end if I wanted to."

Gina sneered. "Ha! Maybe if you had your rifle and you weren't sittin' in a canoe."

Louisa set her dripping paddle down and Joe Pete and Simon looked at each other amused by this sisterly taunting. She opened her heavy shirt and eased the pistol from its soft pocket pointing it down over the side to pull back the slide and chamber a cartridge. She locked eyes with Gina, moving with cool, confidence and a mischievous energy that had not been seen in a long while.

"One shot, Louisa. Close enough to make him jump."

She crooked her left arm, laying the barrel of the Luger across her elbow and taking aim at the bear. "Oh, he'll jump."

The canoe drifted and rocked gently on a taut interval of mounting expectation as a slight breeze caused the few dry leaves clinging to the trees to quiver. They could hear rippling waves breaking against the point and the snuffling of the preoccupied beast as it tore open the rotten wood to lick up whatever crawled out into the warm sunshine. Gina looked down as the canoe pitched a little and saw a sunken deadhead on the sandy bottom and with sudden clarity realized how shallow the water was. The pistol barked and the canoe rolled back and in that same instant the bear roared, rearing up as it whirled to glare at them in black rage. The distance between them shrank. Bellowing its wrath, foam flying from dark lips, white teeth gleaming, the bear charged down the bank and into the water making straight for the canoe. Louisa fumbled to replace the pistol in its holster with one hand and reached with the other to take up her paddle, which had somehow slipped under Joe Pete's legs. Gina was already paddling like mad in the bow, switching sides every few strokes, trying to steer away from the enraged animal plunging furiously towards them.

"Paddle Louisa! Paddle! Paddle!" She was on the crumbling edge of hysteria.

"Move! Move! Get off."

Joe Pete and Simon, mesmerized by the terror cutting swiftly through the lake towards them, hadn't realized the paddle had become trapped. They shifted at the same time and the canoe tipped dangerously to one side almost taking in water and flipping. Gina screamed and clutched the gunnels. Louisa wrenched her paddle free and, leaning hard to the opposite side to right the boat, began to stroke with all her strength.

"Dig in, Gina. Dig in," she yelled, and Simon's mother began to use her paddle again. In a few seconds they had a rhythm going, pulling away into deep water and leaving the angry bear behind. When Joe Pete dared to look back the bruin had pulled himself on to the shore and was shaking the water out of his fur in a huge spray. He gave one last indignant look, swatted the shoreline in frustration, and then scrambled up the hillside to disappear among the trees.

Not a word was spoken and the two women kept up their strong pace. As they rounded the point into the bigger bay, Hank appeared in his government canoe, big rifle slung across his back. He reached out and grabbed the gunnel next to his wife.

"Gina! What the hell's going on?" He looked them over to make sure everyone was all right, his face pale and drawn.

"We come to meet you like we always do. There was a bear..." Gina said panting, trying to catch her breath after the fright and furious effort.

"I heard..." he looked at his son again and the relief was apparent in his face. Simon was surprised by how deeply it touched him. "I heard a shot and screaming and I didn't know what...What on earth happened?"

There was a long silence with only the sound of lake water splashing between the two hulls.

"I took a pot shot," Louisa said flatly, her eyes fixed on the bottom of the canoe.

"A shot," he said puzzled, and he looked for a rifle or at least the twelve gauge. Realization dawned on him. He fixed Louisa with a searching look. "Not the Luger, Louisa."

Gina put her hand tenderly on his gripping the gunwale. "It's my fault. I dared her, eh."

"You dared her to take a pot shot at a bear. I'm a Game Warden, Gina, for Christ's sake. What the..." he stopped himself. "What on earth were you thinking? What could have possessed you..." he sputtered, at a loss for words, or at least words his strong sense of propriety would allow him to use in front of women and children. He pushed off and began to sweep his paddle in an arc to turn the canoe around. "Head for the camp," he said without emotion, but his anger was there in deep powerful strokes.

By the time they landed at the beach he had already pulled the shotgun out and was loading it with a slug he pulled from an oil cloth bag in his pack. He thrust it at his wife. "Watch the kids and keep this close."

He pointed at Louisa. "You take the bow of my canoe. We'll look for your wounded bear and see if we can remedy this stupidity.

Louisa looked at him a minute and seemed about to offer some reply but instead she shifted her gaze to Joe Pete. "You be good and listen to Auntie."

They climbed into the canoe and set out back towards the small bay. The others stood watching for a while and the sound of Hank's scolding voice came to them all the way across the bay. Louisa said nothing, at least nothing that could be heard, and she did not turn around. She only looked ahead and kept paddling.

They were gone almost two hours and when they came back across the bay towards the camp there was absolute silence.

"We couldn't find a damn thing. A little blood by the log and I could see where he'd pulled out of the water and clawed up the bank. I don't think he's hurt too bad. Maybe grazed. What a stupid thing to do. Stupid, stupid. What could you have been thinking?"

They stood facing each other for a long, charged moment and

then Hank put his hands on his hips and shaking his head said, "You'd better give me that pistol."

Louisa took one step back and Joe Pete saw the way her face changed, her eyes piercing and her jaw set. "No."

"Louisa, don't be foolish." Hank extended his right hand, the palm open.

"No. It's Sandy's and you ain't taking it."

Hank took a step towards her and Louisa slid her hand inside her jacket.

"What? You're gonna shoot me?"

"You won't have it."

They stood, eyes locked on each other, not blinking.

"Fine!" Hank threw his hands up in the air, his face livid with anger. "Keep the thing you stubborn bitch but keep it in its holster!"

Gina began to sob.

Louisa said nothing. She picked up the small pack she'd brought, took her daughter by the hand and started for the canoe.

Hank stood with his hands on his hips his wounded leg trembling with tension. "Louisa, don't be childish. Don't make things worse. You'll never make town by dark and the winds coming up."

She only continued to ignore him.

"Louisa, I am a Game Warden. There are charges that could be brought."

She whirled to face him and looking him in the eye she said, "Arrest me then."

She waded out a bit and climbed in and took up her paddle. Hank ran out, almost stumbling face forward into the cold water, and grabbed the back of the boat. "That's not what I'm saying, I just want you to understand. Louisa, there's no way I can let you..."

She brought the shaft down across his knuckles forcing him to let go. She set the blade against the sand bottom and shoved off. Hank was bellowing, his rage echoing out across the brooding lake. "Don't be so damn stubborn, Woman! Think, for God's sake. Think about Alison. Louisa. Louisa!"

Louisa kept paddling, the indignation hot under her skin and Joe Pete paddled hard trying to keep pace, the canoe moving swiftly towards the darkness in the east with the sun very low. There was a pale lambent blue just above the treetops which had begun to melt together and the water was dark and rippled as the wind picked up.

Simon stayed by his father at the water's edge looking from the dark silhouette of the departing canoe to his mother who had retreated up the beach to where she was heating a stew over the fire. Her frowning face was brightly lit by the leaping flames and he could see her hand rising to periodically wipe tears from her cheeks. She did not look to see them go or even glance at her husband as he stood shaking his head in impotent frustration watching as the paddlers slipped around the point and were gone.

Chapter Twelve:

Mecowatchshish Underground

So many times he wanted to run. To drop whatever encumbrances duty had weighed him down with and flee. He could feel it coming even before it started. The terrible waiting emptiness when he hunkered down as deeply as he could into the shadows. The night gone and the stars hiding. Then streaks of light shrieking across the vacant sky, exploding into light and flame. The barrage plodding closer and closer, the earth shaking until it becomes like a great beast hovering over him, breathing its hot breath against his face. All the loneliness of his life, all the difference and solitude he had ever known was there with him, over him, upon him. It seeped out of the darkness around him, out of memory, out of places beyond simple memory, until all he could think of was escape. Up and out under the shattered firmament, over the torn earth, running till he came to a place where men were not killing each other and the world was whole. Instead, he forced himself into a kind of waking dream where he dashed headlong through a dark forest, like something hunted, weaving through the trees and deadfall with no clear path to follow. His heart pounding like a drum as he careened through the darkness, struggling up a steep hillside, feet slipping, hands clawing at the earth. Pulling with everything he has, pulling himself away from the terror behind him. The moon is high and full above him, lighting his way towards the sky. Up towards the stars, until the slope drops away in a sudden precipice and for a moment falling. Then with the stars and flying and he can see everything. Not just the earth or the moon, but all the people he has loved and who loved him. Their lives rising and falling and the full moon beating out a rhythm like a great drum.

Then the drumming ceases and now he is something else. A manitou materialized up out of the mud from under the duckboards, fully grown, formed out of the blood-soaked soil, a being with no past or future. Private Alexander McWatch. It still does not feel like a name yet, more like a designation. A place holder until he might be himself again. His beginnings back in Northern Ontario, those quiet years when he was Mecowatchshish, secluded away with his family in their little waskahekun, only a dream now. He had stumbled through some opening and fallen from that sweet land of trees and water, a green and blue existence, to plummet into a fetid open wound in the earth. An underground world of death and suffering. He knows, calmly bringing the cigarette to his dry lips and inhaling deeply, smoking to dull the stench that is all around him, that he can never truly find his way back. Something of the narrow, dank trench and its greasy stink of corruption has seeped into him. A stain under the skin that will be with him the rest of his life.

His family now was a six-man machine gun crew. This became his assignment because even though small, pound for pound, he could carry more and had more stamina than many, physically larger soldiers. The Vickers gun weighed thirty pounds and was mounted on a fifty-pound tripod. Each ammunition box weighed twenty-two pounds. Ammunition belts held two hundred and fifty rounds and a decent crew could fire ten thousand rounds in an hour. Every hour they changed out the smoking hot barrel and refilled the cooling jacket with seven and a half pints of water which boiled off continuously under intensive use. His skill as a marksman had further ensured his position. He could fire rapidly and with considerable accuracy; a proficiency that proved useful while the Vickers was being reloaded or when the barrel needed changing. It seemed that unknown to him, he had been in training for this all his life. All the portaging and canoeing and extensive hunting trips. He had been raised to haul what he needed to survive on his back, to live off the land and to do what was necessary without complaint. Survival depended on the ability to hit what was aimed at and to be ready to act on a moment's notice.

That old life was nothing more than a distant rumour of consolation to be savoured in quiet moments. It felt as if he had known the men who were now his comrades in the trenches all his life. That there had been no other existence before he was a soldier. He felt especially close to Preacher and Fox, who along with himself were the only survivors from the original crew of men he'd first trained with. Ahyamayweikeimahow and Mukayshoo he had named them, secretly in the beginning, as a kind of spiteful private joke when he'd been made to feel alone and isolated, as he had so much of the time in Indian school. It had started after he'd grown tired of Preacher's weak jest every time he introduced them to some other group of recruits.

"The wee quiet one there is Alexander though we call him Sandy." Mecowatchshish couldn't help liking his Scottish brogue. The way the r's rolled off his tongue. "I know he's a bit darker than that, but it no seemed right to call him Dirt."

It invariably got a good laugh and Fox always laughed the loudest. It was part of why Mecowatchshish had given him his particular *nom de guerre*. The way he threw his head back with its shock of red hair and yipped between nervous, darting looks.

Initially he'd harboured a strong antipathy towards Preacher because the big man reminded him of the Headmaster in Residential school. Another strutting Scot, Duncan Fleming, was tall and gangly with a nose like the beak of a bird. Aloof and unbending, he had been cruel and quick to mete out punishment and was especially intolerant of any evocation of traditional ways among the children. He was infamous for the narrow yardstick he always carried with him, slashing out with it over the slightest provocation. Once Mecowatchshish had seen him strike little Neisheem because she became excited upon spotting him in the hall, calling out to him, "Wachay, wachay, Mecowatchshish! Your hair!" She had started to giggle seeing his hair clipped so short for the first time.

The pious Minister standing like a sentry in the doorway of a classroom had struck her hard across the shoulders and she bent over whimpering and biting her lip. He immediately despised the man and done his best to avoid him. Despite attempts to not invite attention, Neistes and he and their little sister were called into the office one day to stand before his desk.

Hawkish face tilted to one side, the headmaster fixed Neistes with a hard stare through the round lenses of his wire-framed spectacles and ignored Mecowatchshish and the little girl who stood trembling between them. It was as though he could sense the enmity and defiance the older boy's impassive manner concealed.

"I have something to tell you," he said without any inflection which might betray the nature of what he was about to say, leaning forward a little as if to fully appreciate the boy's reaction.

"Your Uncle," he looked at the paper, "Franklin..." A brief pause while his lips curled in contempt around the syllables of their last name. "...Mah-cor-witch, has drowned in some kind of logging accident."

Neisheem threw her hands over her face and began to sob uncontrollably and Mecowatchshish put an arm around her shoulders as they heaved and shook. He fought to keep in his own tears. Uncle Franklin and Auntie Isabel had taken them in and provided for them as if they were their own children after their mother had died. They had lived there on the Killdeer Reserve and been lovingly cared for by their auntie when Nootahweh went with his brother to work for the CPR. They spent their summers there as well after being sent away with their cousins to Residential School. Neistes, who had often gone fishing with their uncle and cared for him deeply, stood unmoving. He had grown tall and strong and was in his last year. Mecowatchshish knew that his older brother would not show the man his broken heart or his tears. They knew that this man wanted to see them break down, that he took pleasure in the pain of others. He could sense, standing beside him, the tension in his brother's body and he knew a part of Neistes wanted to hurl himself across the desk and seize the old rooster by the throat but was well aware of the ways of Duncan Fleming. He knew his siblings would suffer as much as he for any such an action.

Mecowatchshish too was determined that his sorrow for his uncle and his love for his family were his to bear in his heart. He would not take any comfort offered by this man or give him the opportunity to insinuate himself any further into their lives. He had seen how so many others had been turned away from their families and their people. If he gave in now, even a little, and allowed himself to accept consolation from this enemy he might not be able regain his resistance and that part of him that still lived hidden away with the memory of their home in the forest would crumble and turn to dust.

The blow surprised him even so, the sudden slap of the wooden yardstick across his brother's right cheek.

"You little savage! I've just told you your uncle is passed on. Have you not got an ounce of Christian decency? Not one tear for your uncle then?" Duncan Fleming was standing now, his long lean frame stretched out over the desk, the knuckles of his right hand white with anger as they clutched the incremented stick.

Neistes told Mecowatchshish later that he was thankful for the pain. It hardened his resolve and dulled the sharp agony slicing through his heart. His silence was his retaliation and he would not surrender. "Hit me with your stick again, Waymeisteikoshoow, I thought to myself," he told his brother. That night they had crept from their separate beds down to the pantry to take turns licking molasses off a wooden spoon dipped into the half-gallon can. A small act of insubordination. "I said in my mind, 'Make me hate you more. I accept your gift. Hit me. Hit me.'"

The Minister had seemed about to raise his hand once more. He studied the boy's face, his eyes narrowing at the sight of the dark welt rising on his cheek, then sat back heavily in his chair, suddenly weary, forcefully exhaling his disgust.

"Out! Take your sister and get out!"

It was not until late into the night, when he was sure all the others in the long rows of beds were asleep that he held the pillow over his head and cried. He wept for his uncle and for the courage of his brother.

But he'd been wrong about Fox, and wrong about Preacher too. He'd been wrong to fear him. It was just a shadow from his childhood, one bad dream leaking into another. At first he ignored them, followed orders, spoke only when spoken to, lived within himself as school had taught him and tried to be grateful for each day, each step closer to getting back to his life. Then the war forced them to depend on each other, become comrades and they had no choice but to trust each other or die.

The first real push from the enemy had been more horrifying than he ever could have imagined. They emerged up out of the ground like creatures in one of Nootahweh's stories. An army of Witikos made of mud and steel, their blood and hearts turned to ice, they wanted only to kill. They came forward through the smoke and erupting earth, heedless of death, unaffected it seemed by the hot steady stream of bullets pouring from the Vickers. Men fell as if swallowed by the ground and more surged forward to fill the gap, unstoppable. Desmond, who was loading in a fresh belt took a shot to the face and fell against the hot barrel knocking the gun to one side. Bullets strafed the churned earth in front of them until Priest's hand was pulled from the trigger. There was the sound and smell of Desmond's skin and leather jerkin sizzling on the hot metal before Fox could yank the corpse away, a patch of the dead man's cheek cooked to the barrel and smoking. The other's rushed to right the gun so it could fire effectively but the sandbags that held the feet of the tripod had been knocked out of place and had to be set right. A bullet pinged off Priest's helmet in a glancing blow that left a dent and sent him reeling backwards off-balance. A gap had now opened in their suppressing fire. Mecowatchshish stepped forward and began to shoot, firing as fast as he could and the dark grim things crumpled and fell as bullets cut the air like angry hornets. His Ross jammed and in one motion it seemed Fox took it and another was in his hands and he kept shooting into the line of men. Priest regained his composure, the gun back in its proper position and the Vickers was barking again peppering the horde as Fox fed in the belt. Mecowatchshish's rifle clicked on an empty chamber as he sank back to reload. It seemed it would never end, the steady roar of the gun, the thud and spray of dirt as grenades went off in front of their redoubt, bullets cracking the air all around them. They had to keep replenishing the water in the cooling jacket as it boiled away. The flexible hose running to the condenser had been blown in half and the steam hissed into the air so the water could not be re-used. They fought on, reloading and reloading the 250 round belts. So it went firing and reloading until they were down to pouring the piss cans in for coolant. Then they heard the whistles and the awful host turned, repelled and slouching back under the smoke and mist to their places in the earth. Mecowatchshish and what remained of the crew sank back as well, exhausted. Preacher and Fox, working on the Vickers to change out the hot barrel and repair the condenser hose, looked at him and shook their heads. It was sometime before they remembered Desmond with his ruined face lying dead on the far side.

There were more skirmishes in the next little while and then they were on relief in the rear, huddled together in a bunker. Priest squatted brewing up some of the strong tea he called Gunfire and Mecowatchshish reclined his feet up in a coveted location formed from several well-placed sandbags. They were taking a break from hand-loading ammunition belts. A fresh young recruit named Hank Baer had been sent to them as a replacement for Desmond and they were a little subdued by his presence, not as boisterous as they often were at such times, waiting to see how the new man would fit in, trying to judge just how green he was. Mecowatchshish had seen the surprise in the youth's eyes when Priest had introduced him using the standard Dirt joke. He hadn't laughed but neither had he extended his hand. The gunner in his usual provocative manner, noticing Hank's reticence had said, "Do they not have wild Indians where you're from? Don't worry, we've tamed him. Well almost."

Hank had shrugged and looked away. "I've seen Indians before..." It seemed like there was more to say but held back as though still assessing the situation.

A squat sturdy man from another crew ducked in perhaps having smelled the tea brewing. He stood a second, stroking his prodigious mustache, looking down at the snoozing soldier in front of him then kicked his legs from their resting place and declared loudly, "That's a place for a white man to sit."

Priest came up off his heels uncoiling his full length and

delivered a single powerful punch that sent the man reeling backwards to land unconscious in the rough doorway, his upper body laying out in the parados. Fox began to drag him back inside to prevent anyone of rank seeing him lying there. He looked up at Hank quizzically then cocked his head. The new man caught the signal and helped pull the groaning soldier inside. Blood ran out of his nose into the thick wiry hair that adorned his upper lip and a piece of broken tooth could be seen stuck to his collar. Mecowatchshish and Priest stood looking at each other while everyone else watched them. The fallen soldier came to and began to sit up. Priest leaned over him pointing a finger, "No one disrespects a soldier in my crew, understand?" The man could only grunt and nod, one hand over his mouth as he got shakily to his feet and without looking back stumbled out of the dugout.

The lanky corporal looked down at his feet, "Aw, Christ. I've spilt the tea."

Others died around them but somehow the four of them survived together. Priest, Fox, Hank, and Mecowatchshish along with their dependable Vickers. Priest started calling Hank Little Bear because he was short and wiry and although he was two years older than Mecowatchshish, he was a new recruit and green. If he used this name in front of an audience of other soldiers, he would wink at Mecowatchshish and say loudly, "Aye, we've got our own little tribe of Redskins going here. Before you know it, there'll be filthy Hun scalps a-hanging from our belts."

Sometimes it seemed to him there would be no escape from this world of metal and death and blood, that it would spread like disease, a rampant, festering infection sweeping over the earth. Trenches snaking through the land sucking the trees and the plants and the blue rivers down into the churned earth, filling with corpses and rats and the stink of death. Till everywhere you went there was only ruin, the green earth drowned in blood and the flesh of men, crushed under the weight of bullets and shells and bones. At the height of the bombardments there was only smoke and clamour and the ground thrown up over them till it seemed to him the sky itself would be buried. And then it happened, they had moved forward under their own shelling and sporadic sniper fire to take up a flanking position in a shell crater, struggling to move the gun and its tripod and boxes of ammunition into place to cover the coming advance. While they lay waiting, Fox had turned to him and asked, "Sandy, when the heavy guns are going, I can hear you always saying the same thing. Again and again. Like you're prayin'. What is that anyway?"

He looked a moment at Fox. The shock of red hair, the big ears that seemed as if they were about to twitch and swivel around. He lowered his face down near the breach of his rifle; for some reason that had to do with trust and uncertainty he had to look away when he spoke the words. He had to speak them to the earth. "Wahpahkay."

"Wahpahkay. What's that mean?"

"It just means tomorrow. I just think about tomorrow. You know, about being home."

"Wahpahkay. I like that. Wahpahkay."

There was a pause in the shelling and he could hear Fox swallow hard.

"I never told you Sandy. I never told anyone, but my mother is part Indian—Ojibway. My Gramma came from north of Thunder Bay, up in the bush there somewhere. I..."

"Jesus Christ." Priest and a new man spilled into the deep hole behind them. "Is the whole tribe here then? Fox. Yer no gonna tell me you're an Indian too you red-headed bastard?"

"No. No. Well kind...just part. My Gramma..."

Priest had turned away not really caring to hear any answer. "Where the hell is Hank? I thought he was right behind us with the ammo? It's just the five of us today boys and I practically kidnapped Vincent here or we'd be really short-handed."

Vincent nodded to them and shook hands with Fox. He turned to Mecowatchshish smiling broadly and extended his arm. They heard it at the same time, saw it in each other's eyes and they knew by the sound what was coming. The whole world went black and disappeared and a great pressure surrounded him like a giant snake had coiled around his body, dragging him down into a deep tight hole.

Chapter Thirteen:

Muckwa and Mogehan

Louisa studied the expression of her sleeping daughter from the other side of the campfire, her face shifting in the flickering light like their inconstant days. The past months had been so difficult and their time together like quicksilver. Always either colliding or pulling away, unable to find a balance. A log shifted, rolling over on the collapsing coals so that the shadows deepened and the girl's features became distorted. The makeshift shelter took on the aspect of an open malevolent maw and brought a catch in her throat. She wanted to throw herself bodily across the fire and clasp her daughter tight. A bright tendril of flame leaped up swaying and dancing, and the girl's features became distinct and vital with unambiguous virtue and Louisa's heart swelled and beat again.

She could not reconcile the self-reproach swirling inside of her, the nagging regret that she had been too selfish in coping with her own grief. She could easily have missed that bear, but when she sighted down the barrel something gripped her, a wicked brutal need to cause the animal some pain. As though it were somehow responsible for all her tribulations. Some long held vexation had boiled to the surface and filled her with a scalding, turbulent hatred.

She looked west into the darkness. From where she sat now, hugging her knees, crossing in that direction would lead to the long winding trail over to Little Mossy Lake. Then, after that, into Loontail. It was the very first place she and Gina had gone fishing with Sandy after his return home from the war.

He had been known to her since she paddled into the bay with her father and brothers, full of fear for what lay ahead, and he'd had the audacity to point and call them Indians. He had looked so confident, standing there shirtless and barefoot, pant legs rolled up over his knees, one arm stretched out towards them. As if he was somehow different. She had held a smoldering grudge against him all through their time together at Indian School over this rudeness. From the first day in that terrible place she was best friends with Gina and the two of them soon found they were bound together by similar tragedies and bereavements. Still, she refused to speak a word to him. He was a few years ahead and boys and girls were kept separated so their paths did not cross all that often. Whenever she did see him with Gina she only offered a sharp sideways look or two as emphasis that she was pointedly ignoring him. He seemed oblivious to these slights and that only made her resolve to hold the grudge against him that much stronger. Eventually he left to follow Daniel, his older brother, into the army and was gone overseas.

He had returned after three years away while Louisa and Gina were down south together with Louisa's older cousin working that summer on a table gang for the tobacco harvest. Their job had been to sew the ends of the broad green leaves together so that they could be draped over laths that were then hung in the drying kilns.

Things had rapidly spiralled down after Sandy's exuberant shout echoed out to her across the river and he had become the focus of her disappointment in the world. The changes had started some time before going all the way back to the death of the woman she knew as her mother, but somehow that boisterous exclamation seemed to accelerate the decline. Her father had grown weary of the hard scrabble of life in the bush and made the decision to live closer to town. She was to go to the Indian School because, he had told her, it would mean a better life for her. That first summer he'd met an Ojibwa woman named Ramona who lived on the Beattie House Reserve. Drinking had been their lives from the beginning and they never had time for their children. Her older brothers had soon gone back north to make their own way and she had been sent to the Indian School. By the time she was twelve she started going home with Gina and staying in the house with Poppa Sam. No questions were asked. It was just the way things were. Daniel was already gone overseas and Sandy had left for training camp. The hard feelings she had for him were softened by her affection for Gina and the kindness Poppa Sam showed taking her in like a stray. The last of it was washed away by the grief that came with the news of Daniel's death in France. She felt Gina's sorrow as if it were her own.

Even though the fishing trip had been her idea, a chance to get reacquainted with her brother, they still had to wait in awkward silence under the soft dawn light for the dawdling Gina. She came bolting out of the house, fifteen minutes late, tying a kerchief over her buster brown haircut and leaping down the porch steps. A trio of mergansers squawked in complaint, motor boating out across the river, their webbed feet kicking furiously at the racket of the screen door slamming. She was wearing a dark pair of wide-legged light cotton pants she called beach pyjamas that she'd seen in a magazine and made for herself. The voluminous legs flopped back and forth around her ankles as she ran up to them oblivious of the strained silence they had endured or the sharp look from Louisa.

"You look just like Gloria Swanson in Photoplay," she said it as a sarcastic dig, but Gina took no notice.

"God it's early," she said, yawning.

They started out paddling through mist on the river, the water as dark as if the entire span of the previous night had spilled into it, flowing over the drowned stars to some other mystery. The sun rose behind a veil and began to burn away the clouds. She and Sandy paddled while Gina curled up in the centre and dozed. There was more to the quiet of that morning than shyness and the silence of his unhearing. She sensed a strained but shared reverence. He was becoming fairly adept at reading lips but it was difficult for him. It was an intimate act, after all, this close observance of mouths and tongues. She had always thought of talking as only sounds before, had never considered how words travel on breath through the ear and into another person's understanding. Or how lips and tongue and teeth worked together to make this happen. It made her self-conscious to have him watching her face so intently and she could not bear it for long without turning away or holding her hand in front of her lips. It was easier to let Gina do the talking.

By the time the sky went blue they were on the first portage into Loontail Lake. Louisa walked ahead with a small pack that held the hand lines and a lunch she and Gina had made that morning. His sister walked in between them carrying the paddles. He followed, with the canoe, the centre thwart resting on his shoulders. She turned every so often just enough to look back and say a word or two to Gina but each time glanced at him, his head half-hidden under the canoe. She wore a pair of trousers that had been her father's, a green plaid shirt, and a canvas hunting jacket with a light wool sweater rolled and tucked into the game pocket so that it showed a pronounced bulge where it draped over her rear-end. An old fedora with the crown pushed out and a brim that had gone floppy protected her head and worn railroad boots were on her feet. Her hair was pulled into a single tight braid and hung to the small of her back. She was suddenly very aware of the way the weighted coattail bounced with each step she took.

They fished using handlines over the side of the canoe, jigging with bacon rinds for bait while Gina lay napping on the beach, curled under her brother's jacket. It took no time at all for them to pull in ten nice-sized perch. They cooked them on sticks propped in the sand over the fire, keeping half on a stringer to take home to Poppa Sam. They enjoyed them along with a small bannock Gina had roused herself to bake. After, they made more tea and he re-filled his pipe offering her some tobacco which she took and rolled and shared with Gina. After a leisurely hour or so they doused the fire and started for home.

At the next portage she jumped lightly from the canoe and pulled the bow up onto the muddy shore. The pack was still on her back so she reached in to grab the stringer of perch. Gina sprang from the middle of the canoe in one leap, her foot sliding on the slick earth, her arms wind milling as she teetered on the edge of balance but did not go down. Instead, she grabbed Louisa's hand and set off running up the trail towing her friend behind. Louisa resisted for a half-second then gave into the adolescent impulse, the pleasant tension of the long day impelling her to run with her friend. They ran giggling, the fish swinging like a pendulum at her side, held out at an angle so as not to bang against her knee. It seemed immature, this playful feeling as they moved swiftly along the ascending trail, almost tripping over big, exposed roots, screaming as they vaulted hand-in-hand over a fallen log. The incline grew steeper and steeper and they had to dig in with their toes, panting and gasping, until Gina collapsed just before the crest and laid on her side, her arm thrown up over her face gasping and it was hard to tell if she was laughing or sobbing.

Louisa sat heavily beside her fighting for breath, the muscles in her legs burning.

"You're crazy. What are you running for?"

"I...was...afraid...youse two...would start...would start kissing or something."

"There's not gonna be no kissing," Louisa said, smacking her on the shoulder.

They laughed a bit over this and then Louisa stood and began to brush dirt from her pants.

"Jesus!"

Gina sat up, "What is it?"

At first she thought it was some other fisherman's dog loping along the path, coming to greet them as some dogs liked to do, happy to meet other humans where ever they can. It moved with such heedless purpose, a black silhouette flickering among the trees where the trail zig-zagged in quick switchbacks up the steepest parts, that at first it seemed it could not be dangerous. She started to laugh, imagining Sandy's shock when the dog arrived to romp about his feet. Then the breath caught in her throat as she realized the truth.

All her life there had been stories of bears attacking people but usually the bear was the loser. Everyone had a story of some encounter; maybe once or twice she had heard of a hunter caught by surprise and killed, but mostly they were stories of bears running away. The animals in those stories were nothing more than persistent, often comical pests.

This bear was different. It moved with single-minded intent, loping swiftly, a grim, ominous shadow closing on Mecowatchshish trudging unawares beneath the canoe. There was something in the determined, purposeful way it moved that stiffened her spine with fear.

"Sandy!" screamed Louisa. "Sandy! A bear," her voice rising in desperation.

"He can't hear you, Louisa. He can't hear."

Louisa heard her inhale as deeply as she could, felt the tight knot in her own stomach that made her want to shriek another useless warning before the cold realization clutched her throat and left her mute. Gina careened off back down the incline, desperate to warn her brother, the flared bottoms of her pants whipping back and forth around her ankles. She did not get far before she became entangled and fell hard on the trail, one knee glancing off an exposed rock.

Louisa stood on the verge of tears as the animal closed the distance, stunned over their helplessness, the moment stretching out before her in terrible detail. The animal's paws throwing up clots of dirt and pine needles, the black shimmer of rippling fur, the menace of the power she saw there closing on the oblivious man. Sandy with one hand holding the gunnel of the canoe, the other hanging casually at his side, his head and face hidden, his legs working in steady, heedless rhythm. She saw the ragged ends of his laces the way his pant legs folded around the boot tops, a curled leaf clinging to the sleeve of his chequered shirt, his belt cinched tight, the tasselled sheath that held his knife. She was held transfixed as the beast became a dark smudge of momentum half-hidden behind him. He stopped as though sensing her eyes burning through the hull and began to lift the front of the canoe, the back tilting down, trying to see where she was. Then suddenly the animal collided with the lowered stern, swatting it aside without breaking from its run, sending man and vessel pirouetting wildly off the trail and tumbling down the tangled slope.

She was surprised to find herself running towards the beast which was now barrelling steadily up the trail towards her. She could see that the canoe had become wedged between a small cedar and the hollowed-out hardwood wreck of some giant harvested decades before. Sandy was still in motion, tumbling out from beneath it and cartwheeling farther down the bank among some mossy boulders. The animal had not paused in its mission, had barely noticed the man it had sent ass over teakettle into the undergrowth and this puzzled her. She ruminated over it even as she pounded down the slope towards it. She abruptly became aware of the string of perch as they flopped and bounced against her leg. The fish. Muckwa must want the fish, she thought and without breaking stride she swung them in one long loop over her head full circle. The string was only an old piece of rawhide salvaged from a discarded snowshoe and it snapped sending the striped catch arcing out through the overhanging branches flipping and pitching through the air. One smacked down wetly on the path in front of the bear. It didn't slow down, didn't even sniff the dead fish. She saw one hairy forepaw crush the head of one then the surging back feet scattered the remains into the underbrush. She wondered if she would be trampled like the fish when a sudden weight hit her from behind and she was knocked off the trail through the branches of a spruce, somersaulting down the slope arms flung up over her head. She flipped over the yielding carcass of a spongy log, the pack on her back adding an extra bounce that tossed her up on her knees against a spindly birch. For a cold, elongated second she tensed to feel the bulk of the bear come down on her, its hot breath against the nape of her neck, the long yellow claws tearing into her flesh. There was nothing. She swivelled her head and peering out from under the brim of her hat which was now crammed down over the upper part of her face she looked for Muckwa.

It was gone, as if it had never been there. She heard a groan and there was Gina directly behind her in a heap, one bleeding knee sticking out through a rip in her Gloria Swanson beach pyjama pants.

"Mecowatchshish," she called out, part exclamation, part inquiry.

Louisa helped her to her feet and they scrambled up the bank and stood on the trail swiping the mud and leaf litter off their clothes and examining each other for injuries. They started back down the portage and saw that Sandy was struggling to right the canoe and pull it back up out of the brush where he could inspect it.

He looked at them in astonishment, a few leaves decorating his hair and a trickle of blood running down his cheek from a cut above his left eyebrow. A look of relief flickered across his face when he saw they were both unharmed.

"Muckwa? Was that...," he started. He looked past her up the hill the way the bear had gone and then looked around, down into the churned slope where he 'd tumbled and at the ground at his feet. Louisa thought at first he was looking for his cap, then his gaze turned up into the trees and higher still into what was visible of the sky over their heads. He looked around in all directions as though confirming where he was.

"That was one crazy bear," Gina said to no one in particular. She looked dazed.

Sandy looked from his sister to her as though he had something to confess. Their eyes met and then she looked into Gina's and knew they were all bound now by the incident. They turned as one to stare up at the hilltop over which the animal had disappeared.

In the half-light of dawn Louisa and Joe Pete packed quickly, loaded the canoe, and set off under the few fading stars. Yawning in turns, their empty stomachs growling, they paddled steadily and made good time aided by a favorable wind, pulling up at Sam's dock hungry and tired by mid-morning. As they gathered up their hastily stowed things, Louisa thought of how Sandy would have disapproved of their slipshod ways and the whole sordid affair with wounding the bear. It filled her with chagrin and a deep melancholy. She thought Muckwa was a messenger, a protector. Why had he turned his back on them? Struggling with her guilt and the clumsy load, she began to trudge up the worn path to the cabin. She noticed smoke rising from the firepit near the river and looking more closely saw fish bones and an old bleach bottle she knew was popular for use by bootleggers. Poppa Sam's whitefish net lay strewn on the wet earth in a way he would never have abided.

"I think we have some company," her voice absent of any real emotion.

When she pulled the door open, despite the overcast morning, enough illumination spilled in for them to make out a shape huddled on the floor near the heater. She had some suspicions about who was inside but it was possible she was mistaken and she was ready to slam the door and bolt for her father-in laws if it proved to be one of the tramps from the hobo jungle. The figure threw back a corner of the blanket and revealed himself and she sensed Joe Pete slipping in behind her at the sight.

"What are you doing here, Uncle Jimmy?" she asked only partially relieved.

The man did not answer but began to slowly pull himself up off the floor, pulling the blanket around his thin frame.

He dropped into the old armchair saved from the house fire that still smelled of smoke when the air was damp and heavy. She could not blame Joe Pete for feeling uneasy, even her skin crawled a little looking at her stepbrother sprawled in the chair. His back and face had been burned and his left hand scorched so severely that they had been forced to amputate the fingers and thumb down to the second joint, leaving stubby, scarred tapers.

"Hey, how about a hug for ol' Uncle Jimmy."

Louisa took her daughter's hand holding her in place. "What are you doing here?" she asked again.

"I come to see ya, Sister. See how yer doin' in this bad time. Hopped the train into town yesterday but nobody was home. So I thought I'd wait, eh," he said in a hushed voice. "Where were you anyways?" He lifted his chin and pulled at the dishevelled tuft of hair on top of his head.

"We went fishing but Mom..."

"Alison!" Louisa cut in. "You better go check on Mohegan."

"Wolf? You can make good money off of wolf." He smiled at the girl, a gruesome gap-toothed expression.

"Go now, Alison."

She noticed an empty bottle of vanilla extract, Perkins Double Strength, on the floor near the chair and Sandy's good pipe and tobacco were there beside it as well. He followed her gaze.

"Didn't have no tobacco so I borrowed some, eh."

She turned back to close the still open door and put a hand up to the shelf behind it, lightly stroking the vacancy where the pipe and tobacco usually sat, lingering over the emptiness. A scream started up in her chest threatening to explode out of her. Get out, Slyboots, that was his nickname in school, started by one of the teachers, Get out. She wanted to snatch up the broom and chase him from the house like a dirty little mouse, but she thought better of antagonizing him with Alison there. She turned back to see Jimmy boldly holding the pipe in his stubby fingers and filling the bowl with what was left of the tobacco. He was shirtless, Alison's rabbit blanket thrown over his shoulders, a pair of wool socks heavily darned at the heels on his feet. He smiled up at her, a half-smile that his drooping lower lip made seem all the more mocking and struck a match.

"Just enough for one good smoke. Hey, where'd you get that dog."

Joe Pete bounded up on to the porch and burst through the door. "Mama! Quick! Come to the shed. Mohegan's hurt."

She turned to her daughter, a sick feeling starting in her stomach. "What do you mean hurt? Is he sick again?"

"No," Alison was tugging on her arm. "Hurt. He's bleeding."

"Bleeding?"

"He's got a big scrape on his nose!"

Jimmy stood and threw the blanket aside. He retrieved his shirt from the back of the couch and began to put it on the pipe hanging from his mouth. Joe Pete's eyes grew wide as she saw the scars on his arms and upper body. His skin seemed pulled too tightly over his bones and bunched even more tautly around the scars on his side. The man took note of her reaction, pausing a second before shrugging the garment up over his shoulders.

"You're a lot bigger than last time I saw you. Growin' up nice. Pretty like your Mama was."

Louisa pushed her daughter towards the door, "Go get Poppa and I'll be there in a minute."

Joe Pete went out but did not wait, she ran to the closed shed anxious over the dog.

"You should go, Jimmy."

"I don't think that old man is there. Didn't see him all day. No lanterns last night." He took a long drag on his cigarette. "That's a mean dog, that one."

She moved past into the cabin and put the couch between them before slipping the small pack off her back and squatting down to open it. She pulled out the Luger in its holster and stood holding it casually in her hand.

"Go, Jimmy."

He nonchalantly buttoned his faded shirt, squinting against the smoke rising up from the smoldering butt held loosely in his lips.

"Dogs turn on you." He snapped his teeth together. There was a large breach on the right side and one front tooth was broken off. She had never liked him much but after the fire he had become something else entirely.

She remembered her second year in Residential School walking alone through a damp mist, an old shawl wrapped around her shoulders. It was pleasant to be outside sauntering idly along a trail that led beside a small grumbling creek as it swelled with melting snow. The thick fog hung in the damp air like morning turned inside out among the stark and silent trees and it was if she had walked into a dream. She could be superstitious about such things, vaguely remembered cautions and stories she had been told as a child about malicious spirits and shapeshifting creatures. At the same time, concealed in the shifting shroud, she felt alone for the first time in a long while and able to forget where she was. There were no watching eyes. She was not just a small part of a whole, a class or body of students. She was herself and she revelled in isolated parts of the world around her as they came into focus. A frost-tinged blade of grass. A large brown leaf twirling in an eddy. The sharply outlined tracks of a raccoon, like small handprints in the mud along the bank. She had tried to find comfort in the church faith that was constantly pressed upon her, but when she was alone her expressions of faith encompassed a vision of God that was open to influences and interpretations unrecognized by the ministers and teachers.

Jimmy appeared suddenly out of the fog, a sinister apparition, standing on the trail as if he had been waiting for her. He carried a long pole cut from a maple sapling that he'd casually whittled to a sharpened point on one end with a small pen knife. There was an air of menace in his demeanour. She turned and started back down the trail wishing the day would clear and the stolid angular shape of the three-story school assert itself in the distance.

Jimmy followed, limping after her. He had been burned only a year before and his scars were much more prominent then. Raised and discoloured, lighter in the centre with purplish edges, it reminded her of features on a topographic globe in her classroom. She had seen how people turned away from him in disgust. He shoved her with the blunt end of the pole.

"You ain't really my sister you know."

She ignored him and kept walking, praying they might meet someone else coming the other way.

"I could marry you even." A tap on the shoulder with the stick.

The fog deepened as they approached the river and hung in a dense shroud over the swamplands. The rain had fallen through the night and everything still dripped around them in a steady tangible echo of the downpour. A ghost rain that soaked them and chilled their bones as they moved within the small bubble of what was visible. Ahead and behind was obscured by the fog, the known world appearing and vanishing as they moved through it. She wanted to put more distance between herself and her stepbrother who periodically swung his stick in a wide arc so that it hummed a fraction of an inch over her head.

Jimmy abruptly stopped pursuing her and she turned to see him fixed now on something below on the edge of the woods. He was barely visible through wisps and tatters of mist as he slowly pulled his arm back, high over his head, the pole poised as a spear. At that point the road ran along the slope of a small hill and at the bottom was a marsh, with tall reeds along the edge and ancient dead spruce brooding naked and grey in the fog. She was captivated by the intensity in him, the quivering energy coiled in his muscles and she flinched at its sudden, brutal release.

The day expanded then collapsed around a dreadful screeching. High pitched, strident, it pierced through her like steel. She told herself it must be a rabbit, she had heard their cries before, caught in the jaws of a weasel or some other predator. But this was different somehow. An anguish that ripped the fog-shrouded morning with a palpable terror causing her to step back in revulsion. It did not seem of the world and at the same time sounded much too close and real. As if it had become an animal itself, maimed and dying, flailing in wild circles on the slope, out over the murky swamp, always concealed behind the thick curtain of fog, everywhere at once. All around her things came sharply into focus; the stunted grey limbs of the trees, the stink of the black muck, the long yellow grass collapsed. The rattle of rushes as something other than the wind twisted among them.

She was afraid to see it, terrified over what apparition might come convulsing and howling up onto the road. Terrible and wounded, flesh torn open, mouth agape in pain. It seemed to go on forever, Jimmy hesitating, wavering in repulsion before springing down the bank out of sight. It was done, the silence after almost as appalling.

He came back up to the path sticking the sharp end into the ground to clean away the blood.

"Damn, you hear wabush scream! Scream like a damn woman. Had to crush his head just to shut him up." He checked the heel of his boot and laughed.

She turned and hurried towards the school looking up to the sun, a dull orb now like a clouded eye behind the mist. She could not believe it was something as small and mute as a rabbit. Something had worked its way down into a deep dark reservoir in her blood and she knew it would never leave.

Now she faced him, unflinching, and pointed to the door.

"Mama, come quick." Joe Pete was calling from the shed in distress.

She moved past him to the door and paused as she stepped through to meet his eyes. "We don't want you here, Jimmy. Get yourself gone."

"I was goin' anyway. Gotta see friends in town."

It was dark inside the shed. A heavy cloud was crossing the sun and no beams of light angled down into the soft sand. It took a second before she made him out, alert and watching the door as it swung open. A tensed, brooding shadow, head held low and menacing with her daughter crouched beside, arms around the big dog's scarred neck. It was unnerving.

"Mohegan," she said, trying to remain calm and put her own fear aside even as she adjusted her grip on the holstered pistol. "Mohegan, what's wrong."

She could see the open cut across the top of his snout, the fur around it lightly stained with blood. She walked to them slowly, stepping over a broken paddle strewn in the sand. The dog growled a bit and then turned to lick the girl's face. She could see the right front fang had been broken.

Louisa turned, surprised at the anger welling up inside of her and stepped out looking for Jimmy but he was not on the porch. She just glimpsed the top of his shaggy head as he hustled down the slope on the other side of the tracks heading for town.

"Jimmy left in a hurry."

Joe Pete sprang up and ran to embrace her mother.

"He hurt Mohegan didn't he?"

Louisa looked over the top of her daughter's head and saw the dried blood in the dog's fur.

"People can be cruel."

"Mohegan hates cruel people."

Mohegan woke them several times that night barking loudly and growling which he had never done before. When she let him out of the shed in the morning he bolted, jerking the leash from her hands and ran to patrol along the edge of the thick woods ignoring her calls for him to come back. She found him a little ways in near the remains of a campfire, his nose to the ground. It gave her an eerie feeling and she wanted to leave and get back out into the open. She took up the leash and tugged but he resisted and would not follow her back until he had sniffed around thoroughly. When she told her mother what she had found Louisa took the sixteen gauge out of the closet and kept it loaded by her bed.

From that day on the dog stubbornly refused to be led and he was too powerful to hold back with the leash on the harness. Poppa Sam tied a loop with a slip knot to go around his throat that would choke him if he resisted but Joe Pete could not bring herself to use it. After a few more nights of barking and growling, with Poppa Sam yelling once at someone he saw moving along the treeline, they decided to bring Mohegan in when they went to bed and he slept pressed tightly against the door.

Then one day, not long after, when she got home from school and went to the shed full of anticipation to feed Mohegan and groom him with an old curry brush Poppa Sam had given her, he was gone. He had dug out under the log wall to escape. She stood for a second stunned by the profound emptiness, then ran to her grandfather's but he wasn't home and from the top step she could see his canoe was gone. She hurried home calling out to her mother all the way, but she was not there to answer either. She slammed the door in frustration cursing her mother for her frequent absences and immediately felt guilty because she knew she worked hard to provide for them. For a moment anger flared at her father for leaving them, but she bit her lip and quickly put it aside and ran out to search all over Indian Arm. She sprinted from place to place, along the shoreline then into the trees then back to Poppa Sam's but found no sign of the dog. The sudden fear gripped her that he had headed up the road towards town and had maybe gotten into some trouble.

She set out running back up the road but before she got very far she ran into her mother who was headed home.

"He's gone," she shouted out the moment she saw her mother coming towards her.

Louisa hurried to meet her daughter sensing she was upset but not fully comprehending what had taken place.

"What's wrong, Alison? What is it?" she asked gripping her daughter by the shoulders.

"It's Mohegan..." she wanted to say that he escaped but didn't like how that sounded in her head." He's just gone! I think maybe he's in town. Maybe he's hurt." She began to cry.

Louisa had to hold her in place. "Why? Why do you think that?"

"I don't know. I'm afraid. Maybe he's looking for his old owner."

"No. He wouldn't do that. Dogs get away. They do it all the time. Remember Pinky? Pinky was gone for days sometimes."

They stood for a few moments in front of each other while Joe Pete stared down at the flattened tufts of last summer's grass on the mound of earth running down the centre of the road. She felt her heart pounding in her chest her back damp with sweat and her legs suddenly weak with the need for the dog to come back to her.

"Listen," her mother spoke softly, her arm circling her daughter's waist to support her, "Let's go home and have some tea. I'll tell you about my new job and then we'll start cooking supper and I bet he comes home. He's smart. He knows where the good life is."

Chapter Fourteen:

Mecowatchshish II

Mecowatchshish no longer feared the strangeness he felt in graveyards. He was on familiar terms with Death, had seen many lives end in the war, their corpses scattered like fallow seeds across a torn and furrowed landscape half a world away. He had seen the work of bayonets and bullets and artillery shells that turned living flesh into clods of ruined meat. In the fervour and confusion of battle he had trod upon the dead and dying. He had taken enemy soldiers lives with a hot determined intent and even been swallowed by the sundered earth to lie side by side for a brief time with the freshly killed.

As a boy growing up, he'd felt a potent unease the first time he had been brought to walk over the neat hallowed grounds that covered the deceased. It had intensified in Europe where he had seen huge cemeteries, and massive monuments commemorating the dead. Centuries of death laid out in neat rows. In France they had sometimes been forced to march through them, trampling the graves, and once a nearby graveyard had been hit by shelling and the graves torn open with bones and remains scattered about and the body of a young girl in a white dress propelled out onto a wrought iron fence. Now there was something even more unsettling about the solemn stones because he had seen such a place torn asunder and knew what lay beneath the neat green plots and the respectful silence among the sparse trees. He could never say why exactly and certainly he could never explain the peculiar feeling that rippled under his feet and arced up through the marrow of his bones in such places. As if a kind of subterranean energy was being drawn up through him, emanating out of the decaying bodies, releasing their squalid essence out under the manicured grounds. Not the decay of decomposition but something more vital. It was more than morbid imagination, not the stuff of ghost stories or mythical spirits. A real palpable sensation that emanated up through the soles of his feet to writhe along his bones and under his skin. It had something to do with all those lives put in the ground, all those endings funnelled into one plot of ground and hidden. He had seen dowsers at work with a y-shaped willow branch and he imagined it like that. That some part of him was like a divining rod witching all those stories buried underground. It felt to him as though he were walking over a tenuous pulsating layer. That at any time he might plunge through into the strange dynamism pulsing below.

Between Wapistanoshish and his own birth, while his family lived their quiet life alone in the woods, Neikahweh had delivered a stillborn girl. His parents had buried her in a quiet grove not far from their home and from time to time in the years after they had taken their sons there. It was a quiet place, marked only by the trees and by the time Mecowatchshish saw it there was no sign the earth had been disturbed. She had been returned to Kitchimanitou having never drawn a mortal breath. He preferred this to the fenced gardens of stone with their wrought-iron barriers and pathetic weathered wooden crosses.

The cemetery he visited now was a mostly forgotten place that had once served the people of Killdeer. The reserve land had been appropriated and all the people moved after the Park had been formed in the mid-twenties but the dead, of course, had been left behind. It was the last resting place of his mother. The grave marked by a simple wooden cross painted white with her name carved into the cross piece. Mecowatchshish recognized the marker. He remembered when his father had carved it and put it together from two pieces of white cedar that Nootahweh had made a pilgrimage back to their waskehegun to retrieve. He had done this alone while Mecowatchshish and Neistes were still in school and pulled the wood from their deserted home. He had carved the wood in his shed over the summer, flaring the ends of the crosspiece and setting it in a notch in the upright, held in place by wooden dowels. Mecowatchshish had helped to sand it and had stroked the smooth surface lightly with his hand again and again in a ritual of remembering. After it had been painted white and the letters of her name burned into it with a hot metal rod they had all made the trip out to Killdeer to place it together. Nootahweh, Neistes, Mecowatchshish, and Neisheem just before the war when he was still a boy. It had seemed like a very long journey and the sensation was never stronger as when he stood before his mother's grave trembling as his mind filled with the stories of the life they had together.

He had not been back since then and it had not been his destination when he had set out from the small cabin he had built near his father's house. He had told Nootahweh he was going fishing for a few days but that was a shallow ruse and when his father only nodded his head without looking up at him it was obvious that it had not worked. They both knew he had to shake the oppressive new dread that went with him now when he travelled alone in the bush. The only way to accomplish this was he would have to spend time alone in the woods. He had been living with it for over two years now, avoiding being by himself in the bush, staying close to town. It would have to change before he could truly put the war behind him and reclaim his full life. Since Hank had come to town this had been made easier because he was a good and constant companion, but now it was time to face the fear.

Even though there was much that was tacitly understood between him and his comrade he doubted that it was something Hank could fully appreciate. There were times when he felt that the world had swallowed him again. That the existence he had known as naturally as an old friend had for some inexplicable reason become estranged from him. The first time he had gone out alone after returning from the war, carrying with him the extra burden of silence, a cold undeniable fear had overcome him. Since the day he had left for the war he had been surrounded by people. More people than he could have imagined inhabiting the world. Once again, after a long absence, traveling alone along the ancient trails through the woods, paddling the canoe routes and portages that had been there for centuries, he could not shake the feeling of something closing in. He had been able to manage to stay out for one night but could not sleep or stop himself from peering out through the tent flap every few minutes. He perceived a hostility in the darkness around him that he had never known before. A malicious secrecy that closed around his campsite and seeped into his thoughts. He had been forced to give up on rest and sit up by the fire clutching his rifle, his head swivelling around unceasingly to peer into the darkness.

It was more than just the sounds of the world that he missed. Somehow the world was not complete. Pausing somewhere for a rest, dropping his pack and reaching for a smoke, he found it hard to fully relax. He looked about constantly, his attention swinging around from shadow to shadow, forced to rely almost solely on his eyes. It left him somehow displaced and tentative in a world that did not seem complete. Everything was familiar, and yet altered and strange to him. A bird or squirrel or trees swaying in the wind were not fully animate or realized without sound. Even the lakes and hillsides seemed incomplete and ominous in the unnatural silence.

Seeing tatters of birch bark caught like hair ribbons in the yellow limbs of a tamarack, he could recall the faint echo of the rustle that belonged to them. When winter came he would look at the snow and feel day to day its different textures and know the particular sound that should go with each variation. They were all there still, trapped in his head, but muffled and insubstantial, fading reverberations slipping away from him. He would watch a big woodpecker and try to remember the rattling drum it made on a dead tree trunk or the song of a sparrow flitting tree to tree or the crackle a robin makes bounding among fallen leaves. They were all dead and flat, nothing like hearing, there was no resonance and if he closed his eyes tightly most of the world was gone from him.

Or maybe he was vanished from the world the way he had disappeared when the shell landed and out of the corner of his eye he saw the silhouette of Preacher and Fox together brutally transformed into another thing. Melting into each other and then subsumed in a fleeting image of a dark and twisted presence, like the lurking maymayquaesiwuk he had glimpsed when he and his father had paddled past the high painted cliffs with his dying mother. Then everything came apart in bolts of fierce light that were quickly extinguished by a wave of utter darkness. And in the second after there was only noise. Before it left him completely, a terrible cacophony that vibrated in his skull and swept all other senses away in noise that rolled over him and shook his bones the way a wolf breaks a rabbit's back. As if everything he had ever heard, every cry or whisper or distant echo of a loon carried on the wind became liquid and rushed out through the broken dams in his head. A torrent of clamour and tumult that raked the channels of his hearing clean and then nothing. Forever after only the faint hiss of what had once been the sound of the world.

It was a chance meeting with Nanny, the old medicine woman who still defiantly lived within the borders of The Park, that inspired him to seek out his mother's grave. Mecowatchshish had paddled to the CPR bridge and flagged down a train, then loaded his canoe and pack on to an empty flat car and rode it north west about twenty miles to where a portage crossed the tracks from Atim Lake over the height of land. He was determined to stay out for a week working his way south through a chain of small lakes until he could make his way back to the tracks and catch a south bound freight. He had not had any definite destination in mind, other than being far enough from home that he could not easily return and he knew this route was not well-travelled.

He had endured three fretful nights in the bush and was making his way along the long rocky portage into Little Shiner when he ran into them. He was moving steadfastly through his own silent world, canoe on his shoulders, eyes down, drowsy with lack of sleep. He had been lost in thought, deeply depressed over his condition and mulling whether he should stick it out or push out to the railway before dark. He was frustrated that he could not seem to regain his place in the world and was contemplating the option of just heading for home to finish work on his hermit's cabin when the front of the canoe bumped into something and brought him to an abrupt halt. Some force drove the bow of the canoe downwards and at first all that was visible were a pair of large bare feet and thick shins coated in black muck. He raised the front of the canoe, like a man slowly tipping back a broad-brimmed hat, to allow the rest of the apparition to come gradually into view. It was a young Indian man with pants rolled up over his knees, his torso bare and muscular and then, unexpectedly, two heads appeared. One belonged to the young man with long black hair and the other to an old woman riding piggyback and glaring over his shoulder. She was scowling, upset by the intrusion and shaking her fist at Mecowatchshish.

He retreated a step, startled, and slipped the canoe off his shoulders on to its side on the trail, propping it between his leg and the trunk of a Norway pine. The man stood, head tilted down slightly, looking up through his eyebrows, straining against the tumpline that ran across his forehead. He was using the long leather strap, doubled up, to support the white-haired crone on his back and she was still vehemently scolding Mecowatchshish. He could see there were only three teeth left in her mouth as she shouted and shook her fist and periodically in her passionate tirade sent spit flying in his direction. Her carrier stood as impassively as any beast of burden, one hand on either side of his head gripping tightly on the tump. The muscles in his neck strained with effort and his head moved side to side in slight jerks as the old woman shifted around throughout the animated harangue. Aside from these mild adjustments he remained in an attitude of bored indifference, as if he had been through it all many times before. Then, without making any kind of gesture or other attempt at communication, the man started forward to pass while the woman, one arm tight across his powerful shoulders, pointed a wrinkled finger and offered some parting abuse.

Mecowatchshish could only shrug and point to his ears and shake his head. The woman seemed then to understand and said something to her porter to get him to stop. She peered boldly into his face, they were only inches apart, and seemed to suddenly realize who he was. She reached up and touched Mecowatchshish's ear, her wrath dissipating as she shook her head sympathetically and let her small, calloused hand linger on his cheek. She seemed to be speaking the whole time but her lower lip was turned out slightly and protruded past the upper and it was hard to read them. He was fairly sure she was not speaking English at any rate.

Her hand dropped away and she turned to speak to her companion who nodded but would not look up. The moment her fingertips touched his cheek Mecowatchshish realized who they must be and remembered how they had looked that day. Then there were only streaks of grey in Nanny's hair and he recalled with a sharp pang their long journey down the river and how Nootahweh had carried the dying Neikahweh over the portages, supported by the tumpline, piggyback the way Bush Nanny travelled now.

Daniel boosted the old lady a little higher up on his back and adjusted his grip on the tumpline to re-establish his hold. It caught her by surprise and she squawked and slapped him on the top of the head. He glanced towards Mecowatchshish and it almost appeared as though a half-smile flickered across his lips. Mecowatchshish waited unsure if there was something that Nanny wanted or that he himself wanted from her. Their eyes met again but she only nodded as though affirming something and then like someone swatting at a fly waved her hand above her head. He wasn't sure if she was dismissing him or it was a signal to Daniel that he could carry on. At any rate they were on their way.

"Wachay. Wachay," he shouted after them but there was no response. He watched them depart for a few seconds and as he gazed at the odd pair, memories of his boyhood flooded over him and he thought of his mother's final days and her lonely grave and he knew where he needed to go. He hoisted the canoe back into place and resumed walking. When he got to the end of the portage he found their small birch bark canoe waiting there. He dropped his pack and dug out some flour and tea and folded all the tobacco he had into a red handkerchief and left it there in the bottom of the boat.

It has changed a lot since the last time he visited. The woods have grown denser around its perimeter and in places trees have begun to creep in among the worn wooden crosses and simple headstones. He had followed Black Creek back west under the small trestle and crossed into The Park and it had taken him all the way to Little Killdeer. In places the creek became very narrow and the trees tangled their branches overhead and formed a tunnel he had to force his way through while dragging his canoe behind him. The first night he had been forced to sleep in the canoe with the bow tied off against the sluggish current. He had pushed on into the dark of night before crawling over the gunnel to lie half on his pack, his pants wet above the knees. He'd felt somewhat protected under the interlaced branches like a bird in a nest and slept less fitfully till dawn despite the occasional spider that lowered itself on to him in the darkness.

He travelled the whole next day without eating, putting in at the southeast tip of Little Killdeer before noon, much relieved to be paddling again and out from under the bulwark of brush that guarded Black Creek. The lake was a series of long twisted arms like the body of a squashed spider and a section of the Chachakayloo River meandered between them. It was a half hour after sunset before he camped at the foot of the steep portage that led over to Killdeer Lake. This time he slept, exhausted and hungry under the canoe, though he woke once from a dream about being in a coffin and beat at the ribs of the canoe for a few terrified moments before realizing where he was.

In the morning, knowing he did not have far to go, he took the time to fry up some bacon he had wrapped in a vinegar-soaked cheesecloth and then cooked a small bannock in the grease to eat for breakfast. Then he made the difficult carry around Atikameg Falls and launched out onto Killdeer Lake. As soon as he paddled out of the small bay and headed south he could see Maymayqauesiwuk Point and memories of the desperate trip they had made with the dying Neikahweh filled his mind. This time though it was a sunny summer morning and the waters stayed calm as he rounded the point and swung in close to study the reddish figures painted on the rocks. He looked up at high stone face and studied the cracks and deep crevices but he saw no moving shadows. No ghosts peering out of the dark hidden places. He landed at the beach and stepped out into the water as he had as a young boy but this time there was no one to greet him. There was no sense of urgency or fear. Only the open beach and a few grey lengths of driftwood and the deep silence that he always carried with him now. He pulled his canoe up onto the sand and lifted his packs out and turned the canoe over. Then he stood for a few minutes to study the cliff face of the point across the lake and the still water and the far green hills. He turned and walked slowly towards the village, that small cluster of homes that had been the wide world for him a decade or so before. He found where his uncle's house had once stood but it had apparently burned to the ground some years before; the house next to it was also gone. Perhaps a fire started by a lightning strike. Many of the dwellings had collapsed in on themselves with no regular maintenance; they leaked and rotted and buckled under the weight of snow. One had been crushed by a large aspen that had been felled by an ambitious beaver. The forest was steadily reclaiming the land.

He walked carefully and cautiously among the graves, feeling that mysterious connection rippling through the ground underneath. This time though it was almost welcome and he felt somehow connected to it. He found her plot.

He stood looking at the place that was hers among the tidy collection of neglected graves then closed his eyes and tried to conjure the mother he had known.

"I've come here to tell you, all these years later that now I understand and appreciate what you taught me. I want you to know I still carry the stories of you and my brothers with me."

At that moment, as he stood before her name burned into the wood, a dark shadow passed over the ground and he looked up shielding his eyes against the brilliant sun. It was a raven drifting lazily across the sky. It landed on the crown of a skinny pine and he could see it open its beak wide and throw its head back with such vigour that the spindly treetop swayed back and forth. He had memories of such insistent squawking but he could not quite conjure them. All there was for him was the pantomime of the enormous raven and its gleaming gaping beak trying to swallow the naked sky. He threw his hands up in the air and filled his lungs to scream out his own hoarse caw with such effort that it made his throat hurt. The bird tilted its head to regard him more intently across the distance.

"I can't hear you Kah Kah Ge Ow," he shouted.

He saw the ebony head bob three times as the bird croaked out an answer, its shiny black beak opening and closing as it called out.

"No use, my friend," he said pointing to his ears with both hands.

He spent the rest of the afternoon fishing and cooked his catch over a driftwood fire on the beach. Five of the old dwellings had been maintained and were obviously used for seasonal camping, though no one was there now. Most likely they came in the fall to catch fish for the winter and possibly hunt, though this was of course illegal now. Several of the other places, though dilapidated and windowless, would have provided adequate shelter for the night. This, he decided, would have defeated his purpose in coming and instead he cut poles and set up his small pup tent made from two pieces of canvas he'd sewn together.

He returned to the graveyard to sit beside the simple marker with a blanket over his shoulders against the evening chill and watch the setting sun drop behind the distant hillside. It was eerie peering out over the half-forgotten graves towards the deserted settlement. He could just make out one or two dilapidated houses through the brush and saplings that had sprung up everywhere. Yet it was somehow comforting to watch twilight settle over the ghost town. After a while, clouds began to gather, and a steady breeze came up and in the open space it kept the mosquitoes down. Flashes of lightning began to light up the dusk over the eastern horizon but without the sound of thunder he could not judge the distance. In his head there was the long-ago echo of the big guns. He thought about retiring to his tent but there was a certain comfort lying there close to the small mound of earth that marked Neikahweh's final resting place. Surrounded by the buried lives of those who, like him, had carried their stories out of the north in common blood. Weariness began to overcome him, the strange force seemed to hold him in place and he rolled himself in his blanket to lie on his back, his cap pulled over his face to fend off the few persistent insects that were out despite the wind.

The wind was like a caress as he thought of his growing up, drifting calmly into sleep in that place where his childhood had ended and he had been swept into the world and he reached out a hand to blindly stroke the weathered wood carved by Nootahweh. He mused dreamily over where the salvaged timbers had come from. Perhaps from a place on the wall near where he had slept? Had Wapistanoshish rested against it or had there been nicks where Neistes had thrown his knife into the logs as he liked to do when their parents weren't around? What was there that was left of his brothers whose own graves were so far from this place? How had his little family become so widely scattered?

The light came back in fragments and his eyes stung and filled with tears but he could not move at first to wipe them away. Faces appeared hovering over him and one or two turned and put an ear to his lips as if he was meant to say something. He saw the grim faces and the uniforms and the smoke-tattered sky and he knew he was dreaming of that day in France and he surrendered too it. There was a rushing, receding echo in his ears that reminded him of the long dark nights on the troop ship on his way to England, though now there was not the sound of men sighing or weeping quietly as he sometimes heard. Only a whooshing that seemed to fill his entire head. He was being pulled, dragged over the broken earth and the horizon tilted wildly all around him. A wave of nausea washed up out of him and he choked and sputtered and could taste bitter bile and wet earth but could not hear his own retching. His head bobbed and swung wildly and it was like someone had grabbed him by the ankles and was spinning him around and around and at any second he would fly off into space. He struggled to put a hand up to his ear and pull at the lobe to clear out the grit and his fingers came away bloody. Someone picked him up bodily and tossed him over their shoulder and ran while he bounced and swayed like a bag of potatoes and all he saw were boot heels kicking up clods of mud and a rifle butt dragging along the ground. Then he was sent tumbling into the trench. He managed to twist to one side and vomit, then he was pushed onto his back while someone cut the field dressing from his jacket and used it to wrap his head. He was thrown onto a stretcher and carried off with the world still swirling nauseatingly around him.

At the aid station they sat him in a chair and wiped his face and cleaned the blood from his ears. Someone pulled his identity discs out from under his uniform by its rawhide thong and took down the information. People were running everywhere and he saw wounded men writhing on stretchers, their mouths gaping as if screaming but he could hear nothing. He rolled onto his back and closed his eyes and he must have slept for a while because when he woke the sky was different and different men lay about him. After a while he tried to stand but his head was still spinning and he was not very steady. A corpsman came and took his head in his hand and looked into his eyes, then he led him back to where a few of the walking wounded had been gathered. The corpsman took him to sit near another, a soldier who had his left arm heavily bandaged and was missing his hand. He pointed at him and said something to the other man who looked at Sandy and nodded. After a while as dusk began to settle in, his comrade stood and pulled him up and held onto his sleeve with his remaining hand as they were moved farther back to a hillside amongst a stand of trees that overlooked the rail line. Everyone sat down at an order that he did not hear and his companion pulled him down beside him and pointed at the tracks to indicate that they were waiting for a train. The wounded man held onto his sleeve for a few minutes before releasing it and rolling away onto his side. Sandy lay back and began to clutch at the ground, his hands opening and closing compulsively as though there might be something buried in the soil, something left amongst the leaf litter and pine needles that might help him. Finally, a calm settled over him and after a few seconds he became aware of the sky, of the first few stars appearing in the growing gloom. Of how tall the trees seemed reaching up into the silent dark. He listens and the whole world is silent. Not any sound. No whisper of wind. Nothing calling or squawking or singing to the moon. No moans or snoring or breathing from the men around him. He hears nothing other than a high-pitched buzzing deep inside his head. The noise of his own living that is not really sound at all. He closes his eyes and the world is gone. A terrible wake of terror and pain has been cut through the universe, like something on fire, like a meteor flaming across the atmosphere, igniting the air, the horrible force of its arrival consuming it and searing everything around. Striking the entire living world deaf and dumb with its passage.

The rain pelted down and soaked through his hat and he woke with his face wet, lightning flaring across the sky. He stood and as he pulled the blanket up over his head a sheet of stark light burst across the sky and he flinched away and lost his balance and in that glaring second he waited for the earth to rise up in a wave and crash over him. He flung out his hand to brace himself and it landed on the cross and as another ribbon of lightning seared through the night he saw his wet shimmering hand splayed against his mother's name etched into the smooth wood. The memories and the loneliness were alive in his mind now. All the things he would have told his mother if she was not gone from the world. He had fought so hard to remember her through it all. His time in the Residential School he had begun to feel that connectedness slipping from him. There had been a vague, persistent premonition of it from the moment the train had begun to pull away from the station beginning the journey that would take him to the war in Europe. It had grown throughout his journey, in training camp, on the ship for England. Mecowatchshish often found himself looking at the men around him with a feeling of bewilderment. He was already Alexander McWatch and he did not fully understand how he came to be among them in their world. He had memories that didn't seem to belong to him. Long train trips and the ocean, the world growing more and more immense before his eyes every day and the constant press of others all around him. So many people. Day after day learning to march and kill other men, kill the memory of the boy he had been. Then terrible storms that flung the earth into the sky and rained metal and blood. Things he never could have imagined in his own mind and part of him feared that perhaps, for all he knew, it had always been this way there. Perhaps he had been tricked into leaving his green and quiet world to come into the land of Death. Sometimes huddled in the dark narrow trench, wet and shivering, the smell of corruption and cigarettes hanging over everything, he would recall the tales of Nootahweh. As a boy, in the spring when the snow had just melted away from the ground he would see the raised tracing on the ground. Narrow sinuous patterns on the earth, sometimes almost like the syllabics his mother was teaching him. As if messages were being left and he asked his father one night who made these marks and Nootahweh had told of Nahspatiniskaysoo who one day had fallen through the earth, deep down into the ground, lost to his family and friends and forced to battle the blind and hateful creatures that lived in the bowels of the earth. He had been cursed and told never to be seen again in the world of light and air, alone, constantly hunted and forced to hide. But he lived, burrowing just under the skin of the earth. Still breathing the air and feeling the warmth of the sun. He lived in that narrow band of the world that was left to him.

When he had watched the enemy rise up out of the ground and charged towards them and the guns had roared and cut them down and especially when he had used his rifle and fired at the grey shapes shambling towards them. They were not men but shifting shadowy creatures with the earth erupting and smoke roiling around them and he had recalled these stories and told himself as they fell that they were only clots off earth. Made from the soil, spirits clothed in dirt, things that had been banished from the daylight. he fired his bullets into them, turned them back into mud. Sent them howling back down under the ground where they belonged

He stumbled away from the graves through the storm with the wind pulling at his blanket, blowing hard into his face and the memories of the war peeling away from him with each step. He made his way among the deserted houses with the sky above him a great murky swirling of clouds, turning as if the earth itself had accelerated in its rotation. He fell into his tent and into sleep drenched and dreamless and did not wake for hours.

He woke mid-morning with the sun high and the day warm. His clothes were dry and the day was calm and the night before was like a dream. Or several dreams folded into one. He slipped from the tent and the world was green and bright. He took a few minutes to pull himself together and scoop water from the lake then went out onto the lake to fish. He had good luck and before long he reeled in a good size pike.

He gathered what he needed in his small pack and strolled through the shambolic remains of the village back up to the cemetery. He left his pack and took his axe to one of the dilapidated houses and found some dry lumber which he chopped into serviceable pieces and carried back to a spot by his mother's grave and built a small fire. He cooked the fish and some bannock and divided it into two portions. One he ate and the other he folded carefully into a thick piece of birchbark. "I know now that you can be very strong when you are young. Stronger than your own heart. But your heart never forgets. I told myself that what I was doing was right and good. That I was a warrior and I never missed an opportunity to kill an enemy. I remembered the things that Nootahweh and you had taught me and my heart didn't want to do these things but I had the strength of young men and I put it in my eye and in my finger and I pulled the trigger. In a war with so much going on, you can forget the men you've killed and the friends you've seen die. But after, when the war is over and you're alone at night, your heart will open its wound and show you these things."

He leaned forward and placed the birchbark with the meal inside onto the flames and offered it to the spirit of his mother.

In the afternoon he gathered his things and began the journey back except now he felt at home in the world once again.

Epilogue:

Blood and Singing

Blood and singing.

All four directions pulled at her at the same time and she felt a rising, as if picked up by the wind, like a leaf swirling in a dust devil and everywhere around was light and the song of Okimah.

How did she get to be there? She remembered night, wind and snow coming at her out of the dark, pushing and tugging as if trying to spin her off into the unknown. Like Matchi-manitou wanting to take her and the wild-eyed moose was there. Was she chasing it? Was it chasing her? Then that terrible hot pain had torn through her body.

Her eyes blinked open and there was Okimah above her, looking down. She could see tears and the deep sadness in his face. His lips were moving but the sound that came out of them was not the singing she had heard. It was a hoarse, choked muttering, the way he prayed at night in his bed when all the lights were extinguished and he recited the names of the dead. Was he adding her to that list? She wanted to speak but could not utter a sound. She looked up into his eyes in her mind pleading for an explanation. She wanted to understand what was happening.

Poppa Sam slid out of his coat and let it fall to the ground.

"Don't worry," he said as he slid his suspenders off his shoulders and tore his shirt open, the buttons flying off into the snow.

"You won't be alone." She could see the tears in his eyes and he was muttering again as he sat down and began to untie the laces of his moccasins.

She tried to raise her head but the world spun around her and shrank to a single pinpoint of light. An eerie wailing started and there was the salt taste of living in her mouth. All around her, as if it were the ground and the sky, there was the broken voice in its lament. She felt enveloped, cushioned from the world like a mouse in a pocket and she might have surrendered to it but the pressure was becoming oppressive, making it hard to breathe and squeezing her heart, slowing the blood in her arteries and veins. She felt the need to move, to somehow shift the terrible weight off her but could not. It was like that time she and Simon had dug out a snow cave and when she crawled inside it collapsed, the thin blue light around her going black and for the first few moments she felt shut away from the world, then in the next second hungry for light and air. The difference now was that it felt as though she had no body to fight with.

"Okimah..." It was only a whisper.

"Don't say that now. Don't..."

She felt his hand take hers and squeeze.

"Poppa," it took several quick shallow breaths before she could speak again. "Help me."

Another squeeze and she could hear him singing but it was a low rhythmic chanting. Not the wailing that had pulled her from the darkness. She turned her head and watched as he cast aside his undershirt so that he was naked from the waist up.

"I'll go with you, Alison. Don't be afraid." He settled down in the snow next to her.

A silence settled over them and she drifted into shadow again.

She blinked her eyes open and the trees seemed strange, like spectators watching over them. A raven drifted through the treetops tilting its head to look down upon them. She smiled watching the dark shape slide across the pale sky remembering another time. The raven squawked loudly and her eyes popped open.

Kah...Kah...Ge...She could only mouth the words, the last syllable a wet gurgle deep in her throat.

Large white flakes drifted down, she felt Poppa tremble beside her, his own sighing barely audible, not meant to be heard by the living. They would whisper out of the world like the snow landing on her face, melting on her lips. She licked at the moisture, held her tongue out for more the way she had as a little girl in the schoolyard with the other children pirouetting as they tried to catch the elusive flakes in their open mouths. A kind of dancing, arms outstretched, bouncing off one another, giggling over the cold phantom kisses on their cheeks.

Sam could feel the chill creeping into him and he welcomed it. He was ready to die with his granddaughter. He could not face any more loss in his life. He'd had enough. He would go. Something clamped on his wrist and jerked him hard to the left.

"Wah!" He shouted in surprise and twisted to look at what was tormenting him. That damn dog. He thought it was dead. Had it come back now just to mock him? He was the one who saved its life.

"Hah! Get out of here, Devil! Let us die in peace." He folded his arms across his chest and threw himself back in the snow."

The dog grabbed his pant leg, snarling and yanked hard enough to tear the fabric. Sam kicked at it and growled in anger himself. "Git. Leave us alone."

Mahegon jumped back then sprang in again to latch on to the other cuff. He snarled and shook his head violently from side to side pulling the old man a few feet through the snow.

"Devil! Wicked, wicked Devil!" He snatched up a snowshoe

and rising up to his knees flung it at the animal but it deftly dodged to one side then moved in and worked its snout under Joe Pete's head, nudging it up off the ground, then licking her face.

"Leave her alone stupid dog. I killed her! I did it! Attack me then." He stood up on his numb feet and lunged towards Mohegan who bit into the collar of the girl's jacket and began to drag her away. Joe Pete moaned and her eyes flicked open.

"Damn you, you goddamn dog! Goddamn you!"

The girl had never heard such anger come out of him before. He had never used bad language in front of her. She felt a need to protect the dog. She could see her grandfather on his hands and knees flailing about in the snow then suddenly come up with his rifle, swiping it clean with his bare hands which were red and raw from the cold as he knelt beside her.

He swung the gun around, nestling the stock into his naked shoulder, and sighted along the barrel pointed at the dog's head. The animal did not run or turn away but walked a few steps as if getting clear of the girl and met his gaze.

"I'll fix you good now, SonavabitchDevil."

He worked the bolt and his finger moved to the trigger. A chill gripped him and he shook so violently that he had to steady himself. He took a deep breath and squeezed his arms hard against his naked torso before levelling the rifle again. Narrowing his eyes as he took aim, staring down the barrel into the dog's unflinching eyes, he hesitated a moment. There was the same defiance as the first time he'd had this mongrel in the sights of his gun. Something flopped against his ankle and he heard Joe Pete mutter. He turned to see her hand, pale and small, reaching to try and grasp his pant leg. He remembered how she had fought for this dog when everyone else had given up. How fiercely the dog had clung to life and then once it had recovered had lived on its own terms. He turned back and the dog remained, waiting as if it knew that if the bullet came and it died then they all would walk the three-day road. Poppa

Sam raised the gun, his finger found the trigger and he fired up into the sky. Worked the bolt and fired twice more.

He had rigged a simple harness with rope and the dog had accepted it all with patience. Covering Joe Pete with his coat first he had bound her to the sled with the tump line. When he had examined her wound he found it was through and through and had pulled material from the over-sized undershirt, actually one of her father's, right through the wound. This had slowed the bleeding. He had tied his scarf around her to keep pressure.

He went as quickly as he could breaking trail, the dog following closely, sometimes tripping him up by stepping on the tails of his snowshoes. He persevered for as long as he could and then stopped to rest, his heart pounding in his chest. The impatient Mohegan would not wait and jerked the lead out of his hand as he surged past.

"Wait! Damn you, dog. Wait." He yelled but the animal bound on through the snow. After a few leaps the sled veered to one side and tipped. It jerked forward as Mohegan struggled to pull and Joe Pete moaned as her face plunged into the cold snow and her weight settled against the leather straps holding her in place.

Sam stumbled to the sled and pulled hard on the ropes to make the dog back up and provide some slack. Then righted the sled and wiped his granddaughter's face.

"Hold on Joe Pete. We'll get you there. Don't worry."

He whispered into her ear, "Never give up." She had turned onto her back and looked into his face, chagrined by the fear she had shown. She tried with her eyes to let him know she was sorry and that she understood the extraordinary meaning his words carried.

Never give up.

Acknowledgements

My community not only helped save me, but this manuscript, during a very trying time of loss and trial, 2019-21. You know who you are...but I would not be able to present *Joe Pete* to the world, were it not for the loving reader's eye of Tim Robertson and the editorial expertise of (Dr.) Louise Ells. Also thanks to Denis Stokes, who was persuaded to add his personal Introduction to the novel.

Migwetch to Maurice Switzer, for his input, support and for connecting me with Cree artist Jack Smallboy.

Much appreciation to Mithcell Gauvin for his editorial acumen.

And of course, thanks to Heather Campbell and Latitude 46, for keeping the faith.

Laurie Kruk-McCulloch
North Bay
September 2023

About the Author

Ian McCulloch (April 18, 1957 – September 23, 2019) was born in Comox, B.C. and raised in Northern Ontario. He was the author of three books of poetry: *The Moon of Hunger* (Penumbra, 1982), *The Efficiency of Killers* (Penumbra, 1988) and *Parables and Rain* (Penumbra, 1993), and three chapbooks, *Balsam To Ease All Pains* (Alburnum Press, 1998), *A Box of Light* (above/ ground press, 2019), and *Certain Humans* (above/ ground press, 2020). He was also the author of the novel *Childforever* (Mercury, 1996). A founding member of Northern Ontario's longest-running international reading series, "The Conspiracy of 3," he read twice at Toronto's prestigious Harbourfront series. Two of his poems were included in the anthology *Tamaracks: Canadian Poetry for the 21st Century* (LUMMOX Press, 2018). His writing was deeply influenced by family and his Indigenous heritage. Ian was the father of three and married to poet and professor, Laurie Kruk.